Also by Joanne Greenberg

The King's Persons

I Never Promised You a Rose Garden
(as Hannah Green)

The Monday Voices

Summering: A Book of Short Stories

In This Sign

Rites of Passage (stories)

Founder's Paradise

High Crimes and Misdemeanors (stories)

A Season of Delight

The Far Side of Victory

Simple Gifts

Age of Consent

Of Such Small Differences

With the Snow Queen and Other Stories

To Laura,
Caroline's Doctor should read this!
I hope you like it.

Joanne Greenberg

No
Reck'ning
Made

Joanne
Greenberg

Henry Holt and Company
New York

Henry Holt and Company, Inc.
Publishers since 1866
115 West 18th Street
New York, New York 10011

Henry Holt® is a registered trademark
of Henry Holt and Company, Inc.

Published in Canada by Fitzhenry & Whiteside Ltd.,
195 Allstate Parkway, Markham, Ontario L3R 4T8.

Library of Congress Cataloging-in-Publication Data
Greenberg, Joanne.
No reck'ning made/Joanne Greenberg.—1st ed.
    p.   cm.
I. Title.   II. Title: No reckoning made.
PS3557.R3784N6   1993
813'.54—dc20   93-10198
                                CIP

ISBN 0-8050-02579-0
ISBN 0-8050-3849-3 (An Owl Book: pbk.)

Henry Holt books are available for special promotions
and premiums. For details contact: Director, Special Markets.

First published in hardcover in 1994 by
Henry Holt and Company, Inc.

First Owl Book Edition—1995

Designed by Paula Szafranski

Printed in the United States of America
All first editions are printed on acid-free paper.∞

1 3 5 7 9 10 8 6 4 2
1 3 5 7 9 10 8 6 4 2
              (pbk.)

TO THE TEACHERS IN MY FAMILY:
SAUL AND MARY GREENBERG

*Special thanks to
Marta Palos, Ann Miller, John Martin, and
Sarah Moench.*

No
Reck'ning
Made

1

*D*uring the First World War, wagons had run daily between the Ute River towns, and children could ride to Callan, where there was still a school. The Callan School could be seen for miles. In the morning, the sun caught the building square on its east face; in the afternoon, its windows were fire-gold in the westering light. There was dignity and solidity in the height and squareness of its structure, and it had been built of local stone, a warm red in color, cut and dressed by men who worked their days in mines with no shoring. They knew the value of solidity.

Callan School's students came from Gold Flume and Blue-bank, and from high and isolated mine works in the gulches along the Ute—Weasel Gulch, Placer Gulch, Chinaman's Creek, Jackass Creek, Luxor. At the bottoms of these gulches, wagons and sledges would pick them up and take them to and from school.

But as the years went on, there was a slow, long leaching away of people, an abandoning of houses and stores, and of the mines to their desolation on the sides of the mountains.

Clara Coleman's Moment of Knowing came on a day in September when she was nine and in fourth grade. Her brothers had left Callan School, and every year more of the gulch's prospectors abandoned their claims and took their families to hope and starve in other places. Katy Rubano, her classmate, was sick that day, and Bobby, the bully, was absent.

The wagon had let Clara off at the bottom of the gulch, and she had begun the three-mile walk up the narrow trail. The Coleman cabin was three-fourths of the way up. Beside her, the creek ran with the tailings from the mines that had once been high on the mountain's hip. It was an opaque, yellowish water and would burn the mouth like bile.

Without the noise of the other children there was no distraction from the sweep and lift of the mountains as Clara looked out from her stopping places. There were no longer any breaker noises. With so many works abandoned, the spaces had been left to birdsong.

She had to move quickly; there was need at home, but halfway up the gulch, the hill curved wide and there was a stopping place where the trail hung in the sky, sending her glance outward into the full, blue dome. Had she been told that some Knowing was to come to her, she would have imagined it coming there as she stood unattached, looking away over slope on slope ending in the white snow-reaches above timberline. But today there was only time to catch a breath and hurry on.

The Knowing came as she was struggling up the dustiest, most difficult part of the trail, the way strewn with fallen rocks

2

and the washouts of last spring's runoff. She knew, suddenly and in words, something that hadn't been there before: Father is wrong about me. Mama is wrong, too. I'm afraid of Father, but—the school stands against him. The building and its height and its windows stand against him. All the roads that lead to it say he's wrong. The school is mine and bigger than the churches or the firehouse or the cemetery. People have built it for something I will know and will someday possess.

She said it aloud as she labored up the road: "My father is wrong." Then came another thought, a quieter one. I can obey Father and love Mama, but I don't want to be like either of them. I will not be like either of them. And the thought stopped. She said it over again, as much as there was, aloud. The feeling in the words comforted and was of a dry wisdom. The power of the books, pencils, the teachers, the school building, was the power of order, regularity, fact and its mastery. There was a strength in those things that she would learn to use and then to possess.

Nothing had been done in the cabin. There was no wood in the box and the beds were unmade. Mama hadn't opened the shutters and the air was heavy with the smell of dishcloths, mice, and old grease. When Clara came up to the bed in which she lay, Mama groaned and rolled over. "Oh, hell, you're home and he'll be coming soon."

She was a large woman, even larger with the bulk of her pregnancy. Clara could remember the winter before, when they had all seemed happier, and when Seth and Oliver were still in school. They had all gone to the top of the gulch to a Christmas party. There, Mama had worn her bolt of dark red hair coiled smooth and shining around her head. Her bigness gave her presence and she danced and danced and her eyes snapped with fun. She was large-grace, like a statue in a schoolbook coming alive.

But Mama wasn't a tidy person and now in her hard month, her body was doughy and sleepy and gave out a strange odor. Father hated smells, mess, and disorder of any kind, and together the mother and daughter tried with a familiar desperation to bring order into being. They cut the potatoes small to cook faster; they split stovewood so frantically Clara was afraid one of them would get hurt; they cut, swept, smoothed, dragging the rooms into place like pulling in balky cows. Winston Coleman's hand was quick, but the punishment they feared more was constant and left no mark. His scorn showed them to themselves as ugly and stupid. "Ah"—coming into the crowded house— "here are *the ladies*." He could poison with that term. His wit burned, his anger had claws that could tear at the will.

They spread the cloth and set the dishes out—he liked to come home to a ready table. There were four places now that Seth was away, working for the doctor in Aureole. Father liked what he called "graciousness." It meant they had to boil and scrub tablecloths and napkins along with the sheets and his white shirts. The job loomed over their Mondays. Clara didn't go to school on Mondays.

Was it ready? They looked around. What was missing? What would he notice undone? Did they have five minutes to polish the stove-chrome or pull clothes out of the closet where littering mice had given off an oily smell? No, the hand of the clock was pinching the minutes up to the twelve. Seven o'clock.

But something had changed in Clara. Her father's homecoming didn't bear in on her as it had done before. She dreaded but no longer feared it. Now it was unpleasant but impersonal, like cracking the ice in a water-bucket. For a moment she marveled at this change, standing at the table and letting her eyes circle the room for the last thing out of place. Apron. She took it off quickly and put it over the towel stand. Then she remembered the Knowing and the words she had

4

heard and those she had said aloud. Because of the words, a barrier had been removed. Later there would be time to think about what she had learned. She heard Mama in the bedroom trying to struggle into a dress. He couldn't stand anyone—no matter how tired or ill—sluttish, as he said. Through the side window the westering sun threw its last finger down the far wall and lit a cloud of cobwebs in the clock-corner. She ran for the long broomstick just as the clock closed on the moment. The stick was in her hand as she heard them coming, Father and Brother. Winston Coleman's short laugh sounded through the window, then their steps were on the warning porch. Mama's struggles in the bedroom increased. A hairbrush had fallen. There was the sound of glass breaking.

"Good evening, Father."

His eye ran over her. "Can't you do anything about that haystack your hair is imitating? Don't they provide combs in your part of the world?" She guessed he wanted her to stay and take the criticism rather than go and fix the problem. "Where's Helen of Troy?"

Clara didn't know who Helen of Troy was, but she sensed the barb. "Mother's in the bedroom."

Something in his daughter's tone alerted the father, and he stared at her, but she turned quickly and moved to the stove to start serving.

Mama came out and her eyes went from one to the other of them, husband, son, daughter, in a desperate wonder. "I can't fit into my shoes. . . ."

Clara brought out biscuits and the venison stew some miner had paid for an assay with. Mama had gone to her chair and sat, shoeless. The hand that lay on the table was swollen, the finger overwhelming its ring. The cabin was cool enough for a fire, but there was a sheen of sweat on her face. Clara had seen other Gulch women in pregnancy, and some as new mothers, but

5

Mama looked different, and that smell—it was almost like the mouse smell. It hadn't been about those women.

Father was in a talkative mood. He cursed two miners who had come in with ore samples, lying about where they had gotten them. It was an old story, but he told it often because it showed the greed and stupidity of his clients. "They were afraid I would try to do them out of their claim, and that for silver barely worth refining!" Beside him Oliver laughed loudly, trying too hard for Father's approval. With her Knowing to make her watchful, Clara wondered if Oliver might be trying to lead Father into the talk where his good mood would continue to flow: silver, wealth, then Virginia, where Winston Coleman had been raised. Father had begun on a childhood story. She and the boys knew his people were wealthy and had been used to settings of three forks and three spoons at dinner, and gleaming silver kept polished by black servants. Clara looked over at the side table at the placer-nuggets of that past life, a set of candlesticks, six nutcups, and—since Grandmother Coleman's death last year—a woman's silver-backed brush and comb set and three perfume bottles mounted on a small silver stand. She and Mama were supposed to polish all of it every week. Clara cleared the dinner plates to the familiar words that always followed a childhood memory: he had run away from the formality, the artificiality of that life, and ended here in a howling wilderness, the inhabitants of which were insane with greed, syphilitic with lust, and so moronic they couldn't complete a three-word thought. "We've had the stew course and the biscuit course. Where's the sweet?"

He had often lectured about dessert. Savages feed; the civilized dine, and dining concludes with a gateau, "before the coffee, brandy, and cigars, when the female element retires." There hadn't been time to set risen-dough or beat up a cake. Mama had discovered that dried fruit could be soaked and then baked, and if cinnamon-sugar was sprinkled over it and a half-pat of butter added in tiny bits, the sugar formed a crust like frosting. They had put a pan of this into the oven along with the biscuits. Clara served it, watching Mama, who hadn't eaten yet and lay exhausted, as though at the end of a banquet.

Then Mama got up, put on some felt slippers, and went out to the privy. She was gone a long time and when she came back, she seemed better. Clara had cleared the table and begun to wash the dishes. Mama came to where she was standing and began to dry the plates and glasses. After a while she spoke softly. "It's gone wrong. I don't know if I'll pull through this one."

A clutch of fear shut Clara's breath in her nostrils and stopped her motion. Was there someone who could help? "Let me go for Mrs. Rubano," she said.

"Later. I want you to know some things. Your father's not a bad man, but he's unhappy. That wears on other people, even if they're kin. If you have to leave, you can go to my brother in Denver. I've got the address in my little diary. You know where that is."

"Yes'm. Mama—"

"Just listen. You remember the cave we found, the small one up near the low berry vines?"

"Yes'm."

"There's a dark gravel in the back of that cave and in that gravel, maybe a foot down, there's a tea-box I buried, a flat box. There's some jewelry and money there." Mama was having trouble breathing. She paused after each word. Clara had begun to cry and the release and need for it grew in her until it was almost a burst of sobbing. Mama stepped up and onto Clara's toes, leaning hard and whispering in barely controlled impatience, "He'll see. You know how he hates sniveling. There's no time for that, or my having to explain. I've got to go to bed now, I'm so dizzy I can barely stand up. When I know how it's going to be, I'll let you go for Tessie Rubano." She took a step back and wobbled as though she had misjudged the location of the floor. "Oliver—" He and Father were cleaning rifles, getting ready for fall hunting. The boy looked up, annoyed. "Help me to bed." Oliver got up unwillingly and Clara watched, her Knowing slipping away in the rat-scrabble of fear.

2

*T*essie Rubano, up at dawn to light her stove, saw the dimming lantern wave down the path and knew who was holding it
long before she could see. It would be the girl. She sighed. Marlena Coleman's time had come and it wasn't going to be an easy
birth. Tessie didn't want to go. Her own Katy had been sick these
three days and there might be a fever carried up on the mid-
wife's clothes to that friendless woman up there. A nice woman,
Marlena, if a bit of a hoyden. You had to feel sorry, the way it was
for her. Winston Coleman was disliked up and down the gulch.
Tessie woke her daughters. "You, Doris, get dressed and ready to

come with me. Miz Coleman's time is here. Jean, you see to things till we get back." The girls began to stir and stretch.

The knock at the door was soft, a polite tap. When Tessie opened it, she saw Clara standing, shivering. "Come in here and stand over by the stove." She sniffed. Marlena must be far gone to send her girl down shoeless and without a jacket in this cold. Clara stood unmoving and Tessie started to say something, but she stopped and was pulled into the vacuum of the stare, into the wordlessness behind Clara's eyes.

"Oh, my Jesus!" Tessie's hand reached behind her to fan down the sounds of Jean and Doris coming with questions. "And the baby? Did the baby come?" Only a shake of the head. Tessie spoke slowly to the tall girl who was still shivering and holding the lighted lantern in what was now full day. "Get in here. I'm going to wake my mister. Do you hear me?" A nod. "Do what I say, then."

Clara stepped as though unseeing over the threshold and walked where Tessie led her, relinquishing the lantern to Jean to be blown out. Her stiffness had alerted the others in the house and everyone had gone quiet, even Katy, her classmate, who had come out of bed to see.

They heard Rubano's grunts of waking in the back room as his wife explained the thing. They'd need help with a coffin and all. With Waltham and Sedges gone, there were only three men left this high on the gulch. There was a mumble, then her voice, low but passionate. "Think of the kids, then. There's times to close the door on what was said and whose pride was hurt. Lord, Charlie, a girl our Katy's age is sittin' out there like a ghost—" More mumbled words and the sound of his rising. If Clara heard any of it, she gave no sign.

Tessie came out of the back room and walked to Clara, now sitting in a chair drawn up to the stove. The shivering had slowed but not stopped. "When did your mama go?"

"I don't know, ma'am; when she got sick, Father moved her up to the loft. I was sleeping on the floor near the fire. I went up to see her and she was all stopped. She wasn't—"

"Were your father and Oliver awake?"

"No, ma'am, but they are now, and I left them a note on the table."

"You did right. Now, let me tell you what's going to happen. We're going to eat breakfast here, and you're having mush and eggs and bread with us, and then we'll go along up the gulch."

Clara ate as much as she could, though Tessie urged more on her, and afterward, tried to fit her with something warm for the walk up the gulch.

There was no one in the cabin when they got there. Clara thought Oliver might have gone to Aureole for Seth, and Father might be up in the assay office, knowing she would come with help.

The Rubanos took care of the body and Clara folded up the bedsheets, all stained and filthy, feeling ashamed that Mama had lost control of herself and made the bed her toilet. She and Jean pulled the shuck mattress out into the backyard and took the covering off. Then they rinsed the dirty sheets and Mama's nightclothes in the creek. When other neighbors came, they set up washtubs in the golden iridescent blue of the September day and got water and started the fires going to do a load of wash. The sight of the women working and the smell of the wood fire comforted Clara. Mrs. Rubano had come out with Doris, and although the women murmured low and didn't laugh, out of respect, their companionable talk was such a pleasure that Clara forgot the reason they were there and, once, opened her mouth to say, "Wait till I go get Mama . . ."

Winston Coleman came back at noon, but Oliver wasn't with him. With no particular grace he allowed the neighbors to do for

11

him, and only grudgingly offered the men who made the coffin and dug the hole some of his hoarded store of whiskey.

When three days passed and neither of the boys had returned, Winston Coleman burned their clothes and declared them dead. His disinheritance was vivid and theatrical, but for Clara, their leaving was a betrayal as chilling as Mama's death. They had left her alone in Father's house, under the whip of his sarcasm. Grief and fear began to nibble away at the Knowing.

Four days after Marlena Coleman's burial, Tessie Rubano heard another soft knock at her door and opened it to Clara, who was standing before her with a bundle. Something in Clara's manner made Tessie speak to her as to a woman. "Come in, Clara."

"I want to thank you for doing for Mama," Clara said. Tessie nodded. "I have this," Clara said, and she opened her bundle, took out the cloth Mama had planned for aprons and held it out to Tessie. "I need to ask you for a favor," she said. "I need to go to school. Father says they won't have me because I'm dirty. If you'll help me with the washing, I'll work here with you before school and when I come back with Katy."

"You want to go to school that much?"

"I have to go, ma'am."

"Doesn't your father want you home to do for him?"

"I found a way."

Tessie looked at the girl in wonder. Tall as she was and old for her age, she was still a child. What could she have used against that bitter, soured man? "What way?" she asked, curiosity overcoming tact.

"I told him if he wouldn't let me go to school I'd go and stay with his people in Virginia."

Tessie put her head back and laughed.

The Callan School was three stories high, its gable rooms higher than the steeple of the church. At the time Clara was in the fourth grade, fewer than half the rooms were still in use, and the size of the assembly room made the remaining students self-conscious as they clustered near the side door for their programs and high school graduations. Because of the shrinking of the classes, instruction had become less formal and teachers spoke of things not in the official curriculum. They discussed silver prices back east, and why the towns were dying and mines were closing. Sometimes they were optimistic about a new process being developed. A mine or two would reopen and a gulch would echo with work for a while, but then the price would fall or the process change and the mines would close and the new people would disappear as the former ones had.

At home Father had few calls on his skill as an assayer. In December Oliver came back, ghost-thin and starving, and was struck very hard, twice, and then let back because Father needed him. Oliver never spoke of where he had gone. He and Father began to scrounge for the leavings of abandoned claims. They labored over mountains of tailings to get, at great peril, the shoring wood and old ore carts, the unstable explosives and rat-chewed fuses, old rope and lengths of chain out of the derelict mines. The Coleman yard became a way station for trading and the cabin like the wheelhouse of a scow.

The Callan School closed when Clara was in the seventh grade. She had managed to keep attending regularly, stopping at the Rubanos' on Mondays and Tuesdays to help Tessie wash and iron the clothes that included her own. On Mondays, she had a bath behind the house in the tepid rinsewater. Tessie was philosophical about the school's closing: "Don't you girls worry," she said to Clara and Katy. "No good man's going to look down on your education. Our Doris never went past sixth grade and now she's doing fine with her man and a baby on the way."

Clara shivered and whispered, "I won't ever marry."

A teaching couple, the Prillers, were taking students at their house. They lived at the bottom of Callan Gulch and a mile closer than the school had been. "Come with me, and let's go down," Clara said to Katy. Katy had grown stronger in the past year, but she had never liked school or felt she needed it. She shook her head and went back to stirring the clothes in the boiler.

Sophie Priller opened the door to Clara and looked at her with distaste. Once high school teachers, she and her husband, Anton, harbored Town's prejudice against Gulch children, a scabby, nit-ridden, ragged and barefoot bunch from the places of poisoned water and no wells to give them the means for keeping clean. Some of the Gulch children spoke in home languages of grunts, whistles, or gestures. Some had the wild fears of moonstruck parents living in the solitary confinement of isolated gold claims. The couple had come from the East and before that from some European place that hardened the ends of its words and blurred the sounds into *d*'s. When Clara asked if she could become a student, Sophie waved the question, "From dere?" pointing up to no particular place, to any of the gulches and canyons where there was mining. "Filthy," she said, "they smell."

"I'm not filthy," Clara said. "I wash every day and my hair is clean."

"What can you pay?"

"I can bring you chain and wire. Father says it's worth three cents a foot."

"Very well. Whenever you come you bring so much and we'll measure, but if you stink or have bugs, you cannot come."

A year passed before Father found out the Callan School was closed. By then Clara had walked the gulch to the Prillers' every day, often necklaced with coils of wire or heavy chain. Because she took carefully and judiciously from his supply, he didn't miss it although he continued to ridicule her intention to complete

14

her schooling. "Do you imagine you will attract a better husband with your brilliance? I think not. Whom will you charm with your recitation of world capitals, I wonder. The parroting of facts from one fool to another is not education. Education comes in a rearing, a culture which pervades one's life and isn't force-fed."

Over time, a year, then two, Anton Priller, then his wife, began to change toward Clara. Their active discomfort grew to a guarded acceptance and then into a frank delight. She continued bringing them scrap in winter and wild greens in summer. They taught her poetry and literature, and later, Latin, mathematics, science, and history. They began to praise her capacity and love of learning. Something in this praise made Clara feel like an impostor. Perhaps what Father said was true and she was only parroting words. She wasn't sure whether she was striving for knowledge of the world, for the truths of science and the beauties of literature, or for mastery over the stench and bugs and filth the Prillers hated. Did she love learning or was it only hunger for a passport to distant buildings as grand as the now relic school standing at the empty crossroads of Callan? Sometimes Mrs. Priller's smile of approval gave Clara a feeling far from what it intended.

Oliver left home again, disappearing from a bed disarranged as though it were an ordinary day. The betrayal almost broke Clara's resolve. Oliver had said nothing, had given her nothing, but had left her alone with Father to be his only servant and the sole object of his bitterness and rage. "I suppose you're next," he growled, "with whoever has the train fare. Do you think the world is waiting for the wit and charm you keep so well hidden here?"

At night she lay under the roof and cursed Seth and Oliver, dreaming up a hundred humiliating punishments through which she put them, finally saving or not saving them as her mood rose and fell. Father's anger at her still attending school reached beyond scorn when he discovered the loss of almost all his chain.

Then the truth about school and the Prillers came out. "I will have to whip you," he said.

"Then I will have to leave," she answered, and she did, sleeping in the cave for three days and blessing her luck that it was summer and warm enough for her to leave. After the third day, she returned and he said no more, forcing himself to overlook her studies with the Prillers and the continuing dwindling of his hoardings. Another winter came and went.

Then one April day when she went down the gulch, Clara found the other students gone and the Prillers packing. "Relatives from home," Sophie Priller said. "They have moved to California and we will live with them—" She was weeping tears of joy and relief. "A chance to get away from this . . . this *place*."

Clara went cold and her words came out by themselves, surprising both of them. "Take me with you." Mrs. Priller looked at her blankly. For a moment Clara stood dizzy with the blow and tried to formulate plans, reasons, talents, offers—what she might do to help or serve in exchange for . . . Mrs. Priller blinked her eyes and her lips pulled into a false smile. No room, a small house. They were from the Old Country and used to finer ways.

Clara turned and went away. For the past two years she had been able to wear Mama's shoes when she went to her lessons. They were still too large and if she wasn't careful, she stepped out of them. Except in winter she came barefoot down the gulch and put the shoes on in sight of the Prillers' house. She was so caught up in her trouble that she was halfway up the gulch before realizing she had lost the shoes somewhere between their door and the place where she now stood. Now, there was only Mama's jewelry and the money buried in the cave. She had the address of Mama's brother, but she didn't want to appear at his door like an unordered parcel come with postage due. Ahead of her was the place on the trail where she had gotten the Knowing.

She climbed to it and stood where she had walked that day, and waited. The answer came like a friend moving toward her, clearer and closer until it was there. She turned and bolted down the hill back to the house of her tutors. Mrs. Priller wrote:

To the Dean
San Pablo State Teachers College
San Pablo, Colorado

Dear Sir:

The bearer of this letter, Clara Evangeline Coleman, was a student at the Callan School until its closing in the spring of 1931. Thereafter, she has been tutored by us for three hours daily, five days a week, summer and winter. She has studied mathematics, English, Latin, history, and literature. She has also studied whatever science could be learned without a chemical laboratory or microscope. My wife and I are both certified teachers. In the almost four years we have known this exemplary student, she has shown a perseverance far beyond average. She is bright, truthful, and able as well. We believe she would make a fine teacher.

Anton Priller
Sophie Priller

Clara found one shoe at the bottom of Placer Gulch, the other almost at the Prillers' door.

3

*T*he dean stared at the girl across his desk. She was wearing a hat with three ostrich plumes and a coat that was too loose, obviously tailored for a large-busted woman. She was pale, her pallor gave her the powder-whitened look of a whore. In the ruin that had visited all the southern counties, child and girl prostitutes could be seen on any of the poorer streets of Denver and Pueblo and they filled the cribs outside San Pablo, dozens of girls from the county's ruined farms. A pinched face, a long-starved body. What did she want? "Well?"

She handed him the letter, its envelope worn and smudged. He took it gingerly, opened and read it. Then he peered at her again over the edge of it. Out of what closet had those awful clothes come? "Where is this . . . uh . . . Callan School?"

"Callan is one of the towns on the Ute River, sir. I'm from Placer Gulch, north of here in the mountains."

Then he smiled slightly and seemed to relax in his swivel chair. "The day is warm. Perhaps you might remove your coat and the, uh, hat."

Her own clothes were homemade, a cotton blouse, blue, a gathered skirt. When the hat came off he realized she had used it and the pulled-back hair to try to look older than she was. This girl wasn't eighteen, and she wouldn't have any money.

"Because times are hard," he began, "classes are crowded. People who would in better times be going to private colleges are coming here."

"Yes, sir." He looked at her closely to see if she had made her way to his idea. "I can pay, sir, and if classes are crowded, I can stand at the back."

"Do you know what our tuition is?"

"Yes, sir, and I've been making my way here in San Pablo for over a year. I have two jobs. I work for Mrs. Sanders, reading and housework, and I read to the ironers at the laundry. I've saved enough."

"I thought those laundry women were all Spanish."

He let her explain. She had begun reading to them as though Spanish were Latin. Each ironer paid her five cents a day, and they had helped her with the pronunciation. She had actually begun to learn the language from the newspapers and romantic novels they liked. With two jobs, he asked, how would she be able to go to school as well?

There was a plan for that, too, as courageous and as ludicrous as the ostrich-plumed hat. He sighed. "Telling you the difficulties would be a waste of time," he said, and signed the application she put before him.

19

"The beautiful and the wealthy marry." The instructor was saying the first words of their college years. "The bright and talented go east and make names for themselves. You are none of these things. What will help those of you who have no wealth, beauty, talent, or charm? Work. The schools into which you will go will have no use for talent and less for charm. The poet spoke of children as trailing clouds of glory. One wonders what children he knew. The children we teach are stubborn, awkward, and nasty. They bully one another and they blind cats to laugh at their antics. Wit is lost on them because their minds are a chaos. Work brings order into that chaos. Perseverance is your prime virtue."

Clara stood in the crowded hall and listened, and the word *order* flew out of all the other words and hung in her mind like a winter hawk over its hillside. She accepted the instructor's words as true—the class was poor, plain, and dull, but order evoked Callan School, cool rooms, desks in neat rows, someone's modulated voice reading. The random, accidental, sudden evils could be kept at bay by perseverance and work. The words meant to strip the class of wonder had inspired and exalted her.

Work loomed like a wall at which she chipped day by day. Mrs. Sanders was giving her room and board for the reading she did and the housework. School ran from eight to three. In the afternoons Clara went to Mr. Macheris's laundry and read to the ironers. She also read to them for four hours every Saturday. By the second half of her first year she had lost fifteen pounds and was beginning to starve.

Mrs. Sanders had once been a generous woman, but she was old and she had an old woman's fear of being taken advantage of and an old woman's tiny and peckish appetite. She looked with resentment at the casseroles Clara cooked when all she wanted herself was a clear soup and a piece or two of toast for supper. At the laundry, Clara watched the women take their Saturday lunches of tamales, burritos, posole, and hearty soup. One afternoon, she asked if she might eat with them. From then on they shared their food with her, refusing pay. That summer Clara moved down to the San Pablo riverside and Spanish Town.

San Pablo's river lay flat and greasy like oil spilled on a gray-yellow floor. In the long drought that had eaten the land to a dry rind and sent the substance of a thousand farms miles into the air to hang in choking curtains of dust, the river had exhausted itself and retreated. Even in flood it lay flat in its bed, fallen in on itself, long in tooth and high in bone, smooth with wearing.

Spanish Town was a collection of shacks with tin can–covered roofs, but a family of *adoberos* had come and their well-made clay houses were slowly replacing the poorer ones. Clara moved into a closet-close space in the Apodaca-Cisneros compound and, for her room and board there, taught the children of the settlement, little and big, who came to Mrs. Apodaca's dawn kitchen.

Around their studies domestic life went on, hushed in the still gray lit with two kerosene lamps, the frying and chopping, the rich smells and whispers of the five women who cooked for husbands and brothers, sons and daughters. There were no books, no dictionaries. She and the students hounded the words from English to Spanish and back again with slate and chalk. "Teach them to talk right," Mrs. Cisneros said. "It's the only way out of the fields. Teach them counting or they'll be cheated."

"The kitten sleeps," Clara chanted, "the black kitten *that* sleeps *in the basket*. Wake up the black kitten that sleeps in the basket near the fire." *Ay, hermanos,* can you not understand that *todas las madrugadas, la señorita* is struggling also *contra la confusión y la ignorancia?* "Ramon has a field. The field is sixty feet long and thirty feet wide. He wishes to grow delicious lettuce but the deer are always eating it so he must fence the field. How long a fence must . . ."

21

Grandpa Luis, on his way out to the privy, snorted: "Get a dog, not a fence. Deer will jump fences five feet high and leave nothing but mounds of deer-grapes to mark their dinner."

Summer came. She took two classes and tutored more and read longer to the ironers, at the summer rate of seven cents a day from each woman. She didn't realize how well she had done to support herself until autumn came again, school resumed, and she looked around and saw that half her class had disappeared, overwhelmed by work, by poverty, or by subtler kinds of need. There had never been time to talk or form friendships with the other students. Everyone raced away after classes to study or clean houses or to cook or nurse in San Pablo. But they all worked in white San Pablo; few people even knew there was a Spanish Town.

The stilted, flowery quality of her spoken Spanish charmed and amused the women. Tales of her comments went through the settlement—"Will the serviette be procured?" "Is the difficulty of my presence adequately surmounted?"—and they would put their hands before mouths of missing teeth, laughing, but someone always added, "Spanish is a beautiful language. Maybe we should talk better."

The men of the settlement did field work or were ranch hands. Some worked at the sugar beet factory. Some worked for Villareal, one of the few Mexican farm owners in the county. He raised broomcorn.

In the spring of Clara's second year at San Pablo, the drought deepened. The fields withered and cracked. People walked through the days sleepless and despairing, coughing up gray globs, their teeth gritted with the floury dust. It was in the food they ate and the words they spoke. The dust filtered through closed windows and lay stifling them in its breathing heat. July came with no change except that huge thunderclouds hung unmoving in the south. Every day the clouds grew greater without releasing their saving rain. Tempers flared. Men drank and fought and slapped their women. The settlement lay panting with fear and helplessness. Two grain farmers and Villareal had had enough money to afford irrigation systems from deep wells. Everyone else had been driven out. The town survived only because of the school and its business as county seat. It was survival bitter as an unloved wife. It took no care of itself but weathered and went old.

On a July afternoon of buzzing heat, Villareal himself rode into the compound. "I need you all. The broom's half-cut and the clouds have bottomed and will break any minute."

"Tell your machines to do it!" someone yelled.

Villareal yelled back, "My irrigation pipes didn't put you out of work. If I didn't have them, the fields would be blown to Kansas by now. My mowers are down with the dust. Will you come?"

So they all went, and Clara with them. Someone slipped a sickle into her hand, rind-thin with years of sharpening, and a truck took them to the fields. They jumped off and started to cut. Immediately she began to run with sweat in the afternoon's stare, which was like facing into a furnace. Everywhere heat rose, carrying little bits of cut straw into their noses, throats, and eyes, burning.

Broom has a delicate look. Its thin golden stalks are headed with miniature tassels and tiny kernels the size of pinheads, but when the stalks are cut, they whip back against the slow hand. A dozen, a hundred, a thousand, of these little stings and the sickle hand swells and the bent knuckles bleed.

In an hour, Clara was exhausted and cutting stupidly, raggedly. A Cisneros cousin showed her how to bend so as to save her arm and back. Ahead of her the others were moving in an inexorable rhythm. Thoop. "Bend your arm." Thoop. At the ends of the field, Clara saw the carts lumbering behind huge horses, getting ready to come down the field for stacking and loading. Only half the huge area had been cut. People had started gathering the fallen stalks into sheaves and binding them. The wagons began to roll.

They were in the middle of the field, Clara bending to gather, others binding and tossing, when the sky was shattered by a paroxysm of thunder-lightning. The horses screamed wildly, but the drivers were ready with blankets to throw over their heads to keep them from bolting. The men got the wagons covered with tarpaulins when the first hail, the size of peas, flung itself on them. Everyone went under the wagons or dove in and burrowed under the piled broom. The hail stopped and Villareal lashed the tarpaulins down over the broom and covered the horses with old burlap sacks when the hail broke on them again, this time the size of grapes. Clara had buried herself as deep under the broom as she could go. The air inside the pile was heavy with dust and the broken fibers of the broom. Choking, Clara began to push and paw at the broom for a cave in which she might breathe. If she could reach to the surface with her arm, there might be a way of parting the broom for enough fresh air. Then, there came a movement beside her, a stirring in the darkness, a body pulling close, and then, suddenly, the body was on her. Hands found her and began to pull and knead and stroke. Her eyes were closed against the sharp ends of the straw, but she pulled her arm down and wrenched the hands away. They came again, harder. No one would hear a cry in the pounding of the hail. The two of them, eyes shut, began to fight, wrestling in the stifling place. Clara tried to get to the attacker's face.

She felt herself losing force even as he gained it in knowledge of her position. Then she remembered having brought the sickle with her. She had used it to clear her space in the broom. Where was it? Here. She kicked against the attacker, grunting with the effort, while she found the point of the sickle, cutting her hand as she did. His hand was on her thigh. With all her strength, she pushed down on the back of the curve, driving the point of the sickle down through his hand and impaling it in her thigh.

There was a scream and a desperate scrambling to pull away. She pulled up on the handle of the sickle. It didn't move but pain shot through her leg. Now they were both in a panic. Clara pulled back and up and the sickle pulled free. He was gone.

The hail stopped and she crawled out. Her dress had been pulled high so it wasn't torn or bloody, but there was a deep cut in her thigh that bled copiously. Later, she said she had been cut by a piece of metal on the wagon. At first she thought to wait and see who in the settlement had an injured hand, but she realized she couldn't afford to do this. In so close a group, a look would matter. To see would be to know, to know would be to accuse, and accusation would provoke defense. She might be forced to leave and she had come to realize that Spanish Town was essential to her now. It made her school life possible when brighter, wealthier students had been forced to drop out, and it was giving her a picture of family life she deeply craved.

So she continued to tell her lie and she let Mrs. Apodaca treat the wound with carbolic. After it healed, there was a ropy scar about two inches long. She remained in the busy, noisy communality of the Apodaca-Cisneros compound, but after the day in Villareal's broom field, the occasional stiff distinctions people had made began to disappear from the settlement. Teaching became easier. If any of the children was loud or inattentive, a glare from any passing adult would humble him. There were three other Claras in Spanish Town, and on their saint's name day she and the other Claras sewed holiday dresses on Mrs. Cisneros's machine.

Clara began tutoring Mr. Macheris's son in arithmetic and made her third-year tuition.

She was free in a way she had never been before, and for the first time in all her schooling, she was at leisure to think about what her professors were saying, and to weigh their ideas. Walking to the college from the river and back, there was time to frame in words her vague suspicion that there had been two opposing ideas current in the school and given without explanation. The classroom lectures presented the child as a stubborn savage, frightened of change and inherently lazy. The child had a savage's need for justice and accepted discipline from those in authority if it was fairly applied. The other idea had no representative at school but was in all the texts they read. It presented the child as an innocent, a naturally loving, creative, and eager spirit. Restrictions corrupted this spirit and destroyed creativity. Clara remembered the cruelties and bullying of her childhood and wondered whether those bullies had been born or made.

Both ideas had been given the students, but no one spoke of their incompatibility. Clara puzzled over the problem, trying to reconcile the opposing ideas. Her grades were good. Her teachers told her that she was understanding the material correctly, but whenever she raised the issue of the opposed ideas she felt puzzlement in her classmates and annoyance in her teachers. After reading a book called *The Growing Child*, Clara copied a few passages and referred to them during question time. "We talk about controlling the class, and I feel like a lion tamer, but this book wants me to feel like an orchard grower. Which is correct?"

The professor gave her a long, cool stare, and then his face relaxed. "There must be absolute certainty of the teacher's authority," he said. "Then, that teacher asserts that absolute authority to good purpose—to the purpose of teaching."

The mothers in Spanish Town had their own opinions. Mrs. Apodaca shrugged her thin shoulders. "There are loving hearts and wicked hearts. My Gabriel—a good heart. I couldn't whip such a boy. My Luisa, the same. She would die of shame to be bad. My Hernan, and this I say between us only, a cross for my sins. I could whip him every day or kiss him, and neither would make a fleabite of difference."

"You must make them know with a slap that they cannot have what they want," Mrs. Ortiz said, and slapped the air in demonstration, "or the world will use its heavy fists later."

"Children are mankind," Mrs. Cisneros said, sucking an aching tooth, "and fallen creatures like the rest of us."

Clara wanted to establish the warm and happy classroom the books spoke of, but she didn't know how. Her own memories of favorite classes were that they had been orderly. But they hadn't been gentle. The best were quiet and their teachers just and evenhanded. For children whose lives and experiences were chaos, the very lines on a sheet of paper were a symbol and a relief.

After the Thanksgiving holiday the dean called her to his office. She thought fleetingly of her questions about order versus love and wondered if a professor had construed her questions as impertinence. She hadn't been to the dean's office since he had signed her application. The room seemed less daunting.

He leaned back in his swivel chair. "Miss, uh, Coleman . . ."

"Yes, sir."

"Please don't be anxious. I look over your records and but for a dip last year, I see the grades are very good. Attendance is perfect. You plan to graduate this June. . . ."

"Yes, sir."

"I understand that you've been teaching, too, instructing those . . . children down there near the river."

She thought she understood, then. "I only teach what I'm qualified to teach, what I've passed here, and it's only tutoring. The ethics sheet said that was all right, even if I wasn't certified yet."

He waved at the words with the slight gesture of dismissal. "There's nothing wrong with your teaching them down there. The problem is your *living* down there."

Silence. The room seemed suddenly small. She tried to think of what to say, how she could show him the ricketiness of the structure on which she had balanced her years of training. Who had reported her?

"I'm living in an adobe house," Clara said after a silence, "and it's got a well very close, so we all keep clean."

"You are listed as staying with Mrs. Sanders."

"Yes, sir, but when I was there, I didn't have enough to eat. She's an older lady and she couldn't . . ."

Clara had begun to breathe harder. Her face was hot and her throat felt constricted. She knew that her criticism would sound like ingratitude to him.

The dean sighed and sat up, the chair shifting him forward. "Wherever you live, if you want to stay in this school and to graduate from it, you'll have to reside somewhere other than Spanish Town." And he dismissed her with a wave of his hand. "You'll have one week to find new lodgings."

4

All the student lodgings charged money. She went to two of her teachers and asked if she might board with them for work. Both were already boarding students, and neither knew any place available. She walked San Pablo from end to end, looking for places, trying to think. She cursed the dean in her mind and raged at him, a sanctimonious gatekeeper barring her way because of meaningless prejudice. She saw his hand come up in that gesture of dismissal, of wiping her words away. She had been in Spanish Town for almost two years, acceptably healthy and clean.

And it dawned on Clara suddenly that the dean hadn't wanted to be bothered with the problem, that his gesture of annoyance might have been as much for the problem her lodging had created as for the act itself. Someone had brought her arrangement to his official notice and he had been forced to act. With a dummy address, she could stay in Spanish Town if no one made an issue of it and if she traveled discreetly. She went to her afternoon class in relative calm.

"Greek mythology," the professor said, and handed out a list of names for memorization. The gods and heroes listed were mostly familiar to Clara from her reading, but near the bottom was a name she had never thought to see in print. She had always thought Father had made it up: Helen of Troy. Clara's face went hot with remembered humiliation. "Ah, look, it's Helen of Troy," as Mama stood shivering and burdened with the corpselike shirts and trousers of frozen laundry. "Behold, Helen of Troy!" as he peered down at her scrubbing. The name evoked ugliness, winter, cold hands, chilblains—

Clara's memory of Mama suddenly blended with the picture of a migrant woman scrubbing. Mr. Macheris had a shack at the back of the laundry, and migrant couples sometimes stayed there for a day or two. That afternoon she went to Mr. Macheris and told him about her problem. The laundry was off Garfield Street and the shack faced a deserted railroad siding at the eastern edge of town. Neither had an address. Mr. Macheris's Greek-accented English was still a problem. He said, "For black, for car, is call *strit*. Is dirt, is for mule maybe, is call what?"

"Alley?" Clara said. "Lane?"

"Lane," he said. "The feed store there. When I come is number 330. So. I am here, maybe 331. My place there is 332. The strit, front is *Garfill*, there," and he pointed.

Clara reregistered her address, changing the one listed in the school's records to 332 Garfield Lane, and she continued to live with the Apodacas. In the spring she would be graduating and then taking the state certifying boards, and she would be a certified teacher like Mr. and Mrs. Priller. Few of the teachers in the rural areas were certified. She would have protection and not be forced to depend on the friendship of a particular school board. It was time to tell Father these things.

She hadn't written to him since she had left the note on the cabin's heavy table almost four years before: "I am going away to be a teacher. I will write to you when I am one."

This letter took two days to write:

Father: I am a senior in San Pablo Teachers College and I plan to be graduated in the spring. Then I plan to be certified. If you wish, I will return for a visit after I get my diploma. I will see the Rubanos and other neighbors, and learn about Oliver and Seth. If you wish this visit, you may write to me at the school.

Christmas came and went, and in January there was a reply:

Dear Clara,

Your letter got to me from Ma Rubano, Tessie Rubano, who is now my mother-in-law. Katy and I are married now. Father died the winter you left. He mixed the wrong chemicals for an assay and there was an explosion. I heard about it in Aureole where I was working and went back to get him buried. There I saw Katy again, still quiet and sweet, and she's a good wife to me. [Clara read "good wife to me" and shivered.] Katy will have a baby in the spring and sends her love. She wants you to come in the spring. I work for the Ute County Engineer's Office in Aureole.

Seth is still missing and no word has come.

When Father died I wrote to his people in Virginia. They answered that they didn't have money to spend on shipping him

31

back there for burial. I'm real proud of you and what you have done. Ma Rubano sends her best, too.

Your Brother, Oliver

Clara sat in the unaccustomed silence of the Apodacas' dinnertime and reread the letter. Letters were rare enough in the settlement to give them the importance of life-and-death news, so the family was silent as she read, waiting for what would probably be the tragic news. Her first feeling was simple surprise. Oliver back, grown, married. They were changes as great as hers had been. Then there was a wash of resentment. Deserter. He had run away and left her without a word, to carry it alone. Then, He had it harder than she did—he had Father all day— So she sat, lost in the news, weighing, eyes gone blank, until Mrs. Apodaca said gently, "Is it good news or bad, then?" Clara was startled and said slowly, "I forgot that other people grow up, too, and change." *Katy Rubano?* Clara remembered her as small and sickly, her long, straight black hair in two tight braids, making her look more birdlike than she was. Now she was grown and Oliver had come back, grown also, and they were soon to be a family.

If Clara thought carefully, consciously, allowing stories and plays and her school reading to influence her, she could think about the idea of family without trembling. She could see the Prillers looking gently at each other over the heads of their students, setting out their careful teacups and their single un-iced vanilla cupcake on the little table at the shady side of the house. If she could think of the Apodacas' matter-of-fact division of labor, an honoring of the work the women did in the hot kitchen and of their power there, then the word *family* didn't seem fearful or hateful to her. She wrote a letter to Katy Rubano, now Katy Coleman:

32

Dear Katy,

Do you remember our mama, Marlena Coleman? I think how
happy she would have been with a daughter-in-law to come and
laugh with her. I never had a sister and I missed having one, so
you are a happy addition to my life, too. I just realized that I'll
soon be an aunt! All this at once!

Your sister-in-law,

Clara Coleman

That evening, with the world suddenly peopled and a geography suddenly awakened, Clara confided about her brother and
his new wife to the women at the pump drawing water for the
evening dishes. "Look at her smile!" Celia Cisneros said. "She's
gone to girl on us!" It was true. A tightness that Clara had not
realized was part of her had been loosened. She felt light-headed.
Breathing was easier and the easy breath came out in a laugh.

That spring, after her certification exams, Clara traveled up
to Aureole to visit Oliver and Katy and the new niece, Mary
Louise. They seemed like a loving family with none of the scorn
Oliver might have learned from Father. Still, her brother was
cautious and a little afraid. Clara saw it in him now and then,
echoes of fearing and hating family life. It made him serious and
unsmiling.

She tried to get work in Aureole, but there were no jobs to be
had. The Ute River towns were dying, Callan all but a ghost
town, Bluebank left to a few old squatters too poor to move,
Granite and Gold Flume spent. Oliver said he would keep his
ears open for teaching jobs in Aureole. Clara went to Denver.

She was a certified teacher and an independent woman. Now
she could visit Mama's brother, but when she went to the
address on the carefully folded paper, no one had ever heard of

Everett Springer. Perhaps Mama had mistaken the address. Everett Springer might have moved away years ago, or died. Perhaps Mama had given Clara the address as a talisman, a charm against fear. Clara didn't tear the paper but put it carefully, whole, into a trash bin in City Park.

For a year Clara taught as a substitute teacher in and around Denver, now in one school, now in another. She lived in a rooming house and had acquaintances there but no close friendships. Her life was spartan simple. Now and then other women teachers would suggest double dates. Clara refused these invitations. She preferred loneliness to fear.

Sometimes at lunch or after school, the teachers talked about their plans. Some spoke about the possibility that America would be drawn in as the war spread through Europe. Clara argued that there couldn't be a war; the country was too poor to fight. Where would the money come from to buy the battleships and airplanes when the wealthy couldn't even open their factories for work or mines to mine even when there was still silver and gold to be gotten?

That spring the drought broke. The torrents ran high, the farmlands waved under a covering of purple and yellow blossoms. Clara read that San Pablo was back to farming wheat and broom and sugar beets, but there had been a reduction of the population by three-fourths. The county had miles of abandoned farms and dust-choked wells. That summer she got work at the office of a plant that shipped scrap iron, war iron, abroad. If war continued in Europe it would clear all the metal from derelict holdings in America's ghost places. All the chain, wire, ore carts, riffles, stopes, and chisels would go to distant wars. The land would be left to itself.

Back at school she talked about this now and then. It would take the gulches years to recover and the mines, decades. Winter came. On a mild Sunday in December when the boarders had just finished dinner and Clara was planning to lay out a dress pattern on the dining room table, the radio news from Pearl Harbor shattered the peace and changed everything that was real, possible, accepted, ordinary, and believed in.

From sudden shock and fear, possibilities blossomed. Clara found herself working in a defense plant in Pueblo. Because of her comfort with Mexicans, she gravitated toward the Mexican areas of town. Her experience at San Pablo had made her careful and discreet and kept her in a passive double life. Her job was in the paint shop, a mixed Anglo-Mexican shop, but she took the trolley every day to the barrio at the end of the line. At the plant, she let it be thought that she was married and had a husband overseas. Where she lived, she let it be thought that her mother's people had been Mexicans. Someone suggested that her husband's name, Coleman, was a name the Tewa used. She didn't correct the impression. She told few outright lies, but she did begin the deception of a narrow gold band on her left fourth finger.

This meant that she wasn't asked for dates, and the urgent, hectic lovemaking that went on between the factory women and the men at the nearby army bases was only a rill of talk at the edge of her day, coming on or going off shift. She let the days and nights melt into one another, working double shifts when she could, eating, sleeping, and up to work again. Katy had another daughter, Donna. Months passed, a year, then another. The paint shop workers wore heavy masks and special outfits and in a reaction to the drabness of their environment, they, along with the other plant women, went color-mad, wearing hard red lipstick and wildly patterned cottons. Clara didn't realize how much she had changed until she went up to Aureole again.

It was in the middle of her second year in Pueblo that the plant got its E for effort and the workers were given a bonus week off. Clara's week came in mid-August and the height of the berry season. She escaped north, hitchhiking all day and all night up to Aureole. There she took off the heavy makeup and shook her hair free of its colored turban. Katy left the children with neighbors and she and Clara climbed the draws and gulches around Aureole gathering the berries whose abundance that year hazed the wet places with dark red and blue. After four years of drought in San Pablo, a city year in Denver, and the windowless paint shop in Pueblo, the watercourses of the Ute seemed as lush as Eden to Clara, an enchantment. Her awe made her sister-in-law smile.

Every afternoon with the sun still high, they caught rides back home and boiled the jelly of the day's gathering. Everyone Katy knew traded gasoline for sugar, or eggs and butter for coffee. Shortages that galled in cities were passing inconveniences here. "It's paradise," Clara said, and let Katy laugh.

"Whatever happened to that Gulch girl with the stone-bruises and the hair smelling of kerosene smoke?"

"I want to live here someday, Katy, to live here and teach school, and make jelly in the summer, and—"

There was a knock at the door, which was open for the breeze, and when Clara went to see, the man standing in the bright light looked nonplussed. "Is Mrs. Coleman here?"

"Yes. I'm her sister-in-law." Then they stared at each other.

Katy came up behind Clara, drying her hands. "It's Percival!" she said with a smile. "The wild man!" She laughed, and Clara heard the liking, the fun in her voice. "Have coffee with us."

Clara didn't know if Percival was his first name or his last. He was very tall and bony, big-footed, big-handed, and with a mop of unruly dark red hair, a homely man, but, she decided, not an ugly one. He limped as he came in, as though the commands to walk came more slowly all that long way to his left foot. The foot wasn't turned or misshapen. She wondered what had caused the limp. He reminded her of someone, but who could it be? Katy

36

had begun to explain what "wild man" meant and Clara cleared a chair by the kitchen table so the man could sit down.

Percival opened the cloth bag he had been carrying and shook its contents onto the table. Morels, a pound or more of them. She had eaten this rare, gridded mushroom in Spanish Town. "I've got good, brown eggs," Katy said, "and a stewing rabbit, but we're making jelly now. Why not stay for supper? Clara, get this man some coffee."

As Clara poured it, Percival smiled up at her. It was a smile of great charm. His teeth were white and strong, but they didn't seem to grow in any order. "Call me Andy," he said. Clara had to bite her lip to keep from laughing. The name had triggered the memory: Raggedy Andy.

The kitchen was hot as a foundry with cooking, but they were comfortably talking, the women getting up to stir or pour the hot jelly and then to skin, clean, and dress the rabbit Katy had planned for supper. Andy told Clara where the morels grew. "I'm a surveyor," he said, "and my job takes me all over this part of the county. As I come and go I pick up a little of this and that—a rock I can sell or wild groceries to trade with friends." She was stunned by his generosity in giving her the location of his mushroom find.

"I'll save you half of what I pick," she said, "but the way things are going, I won't be a bother more than once or twice a year. I work at a war plant in Pueblo."

He asked about the work and she found herself describing the days and nights, one indistinguishable from the other in the paint shop's dark and noisy cavern, cavernous in feeling even though it was at ground level; about the hunger they had for color after days and nights of gray primer and khaki and the gray paint they sprayed. He listened with such stillness, such intent interest, that she allowed herself to give details she would ordinarily have left out. Katy sat and listened, too, and Clara began to talk about San Pablo and Spanish Town, and about living in the Mexican area of Pueblo. She looked down at her hands and was relieved to see that she had left the wedding ring back there.

The afternoon breathed out and began to rest and fan itself cool. Katy's children played with the jar rings, quiet in the heat. Andy explained his 4-F status. He had had polio as a child and the disease had left him with a limp and a weak lung. "I'm not a fighter by nature, but I didn't want to be turned down. The country is in a total effort, and I'm limping around the landscape measuring the distance between one post and another and picking all the mushrooms that grow between them."

They sat still for a while and listened to the sounds of the house. Katy talked about her brothers-in-law who were in the service, and how she, too, felt helpless, not being active in the war effort the way Clara was. Then she said to Andy, "You collect scrap, don't you? I heard you go into old mines."

"I do, yes. I do that, at least."

Clara remembered Father and Oliver and her hand went up and she said, "Be careful . . . please be careful," and was embarrassed then.

To cover her embarrassment he smiled at her and said, "The weather's been nice up here this week."

"It won't be easy for me to go back," she said. "I miss these mountains, the uncut sky. You both feel left out by the war but I feel buried alive in it." They looked at one another and each gave a helpless shrug and they laughed.

Oliver came home and they all sat down to Katy's rabbit and Andy Percival's morels. The sauce was made with fresh butter Katy traded with her neighbor, who kept three cows on wasteland near the river. "These children will grow up with expensive tastes," Oliver said, looking at his small daughters. "They'll be as fussy as Father."

Sometime in the course of the meal, something in Clara let go, and she was suddenly overwhelmed with a relaxation so deep that there was nothing she could do to keep her head up or her eyes open. The three days of walking mountain terrain again, the sun, the air, the easy drone of voices, comforting and soft as rain outside a well-made house, stole her resistance and she sank away down into a delicious lulling darkness.

She woke up in the near-dawn on her bed but still dressed, thinking she wouldn't see the young man again, Raggedy Andy. He had had many experiences in his life, some unpleasant ones, but he had probably not met a girl who fell asleep on him in the middle of a sentence.

But he was back the next day, Clara's last, with a catch of mountain trout and a basket of sand plums. He seemed less comfortable this time and Katy's children, quiet the day before, were whiny and demanding. Katy asked him to stay again, but he said he couldn't, and took his measure of butter and packet of sugar and turned to leave. Then he turned back and asked Clara, "Do you ever get to Denver?"

"I could if I needed to. We sometimes trade shifts."

"My father's in the hospital there. I visit every month. I'll be going down there in two weeks. If I wrote to you . . . would you come?"

She said, "Perhaps I could come." Then she said, "Yes, I will."

Clara went back to Pueblo the next day, wondering why she had agreed to make a round trip of 224 miles, hitchhiking in the backs of farm trucks, to see Andy Percival for an afternoon at a hospital.

It was his warmth, his friendliness, and a quality that made her smile in the windowless paint shop and her cramped room in the boardinghouse. The thought of him evoked something of sun, wild plants, mountainsides, and the slow talk that had allowed so sweet and trusting a sleep that even at a shift's end, she could smile in remembering it.

5

*W*hen she got back to the plant and began to study her possibilities for trading shifts, Clara realized there would be more lies to tell. By now the girls on the floor had gotten used to coming to her for tradeoffs and the happy over-the-shoulder "I'll pay you back" had been unrepaid for so long they had begun to take her free time for granted. Except for illness at home, the married women took their shifts without extras. It was among the single ones that the blossoming and withering of love was charted in the number of hours traded for free evenings or weekends. Clara, who had let people think she was married and with a husband overseas, would have to think of a convincing lie, especially if there was to be more than a single trip.

So Seth Coleman, missing brother, was brought back and put to bed in a hospital in Denver and Clara had to be silent about the redheaded man she had met and whose unaccustomed letter caused some interest at her boardinghouse.

Dear Miss Coleman,

I hope you liked the trout and plums. We are in a drought now, and I am eating hay and pine needles. I boil the hay and eat it like spaghetti. The pine needles I fry like shoestring potatoes.

My father, Arlo Percival, is in the TB hospital in Denver. I plan to be there on Saturday, August 28, and after I make the visit, I will have some time there. I will plan to come by 12, and wait for you. You could get to the hospital anytime between 12 and 4, and I will be there.

Sincerely,

A. Percival

Clara read the letter and read it again, smiling at the picture of Andy with a plate of hay, but something was missing in what he had written and it wasn't clear to her what it was until she was riding in a feed truck on her way to Denver. To the right the sun was coming up, red and hot. When the light allowed reading, she took the letter out of her purse again. What were the signals? Where were they buried? "I plan to be there . . . make the visit . . ." It came to her that had she written to a friend about visiting Mama, she would have said "be with her." Had she written about visiting Father, she would have put the words as Andy had, impersonally, "make the visit." This recognition brought a smile and she remembered what

Cervantes had said: "*Cada uno es hijo de sus obras*—every man is the son of his own works."

The truck took her to the stockyards and she caught a trolley to the hospital, getting there three hours early, which allowed her a nap in the waiting room. He was early, too, a shock, his gangling body and the bright red hair. They were both nervous and silent. After telling each other how their trips had been, they stood and stared, smiling but ill at ease.

"Have you eaten?"

"I had coffee and some bread."

"We can go for something after." Then he blurted, "I don't like my father."

"I know. It was in the letter."

"Where? I didn't say that."

"No. It was in what you didn't say."

"I have to tell you—if we're going to be friends, I have to tell you."

"You don't have to say anything. I didn't like my father either."

"There's more. Go over there and sit by the window." She sat with her back to him. Trees had been planted at the side of the building and they drew her eye. He stood behind her and spoke. His mouth had gone dry and she heard him trying to lick his lips. "My father is a confidence man, a swindler, and a jailbird. He's the man who sells you the gold-plated river-stone as a nugget, the phony oil stock, a share in the Brooklyn Bridge." When she didn't say anything, he spoke more urgently, "He's been in jail. More than once."

"But that's not—"

"Let me say it all. My father is missing something, something you need to be an ordinary, decent person."

Clara couldn't think of a response, so she sat still and looked out and wondered if everyone in the world sowed poverty or violence, lived in it, and raised children who were ashamed of it. The thought made her sigh.

42

He said, "You can turn around now." When she did, he was looking down. "You can say something—"

"Denver is a long way and traveling's hard now. You said you come here every month. Why?"

The question seemed to surprise him. He thought for a second or two. "I don't know. He's all the family I have. He's the only person in the world who has been with me or known me through my life, when he wasn't on a scam or in jail."

A group of other people had come into the room at the words "in jail," and Andy flinched and stopped speaking. At that moment Clara felt a rush of love, a warmth she had known only once in her life, briefly, for a boy who had spent a year in the gulch with his family and then had moved away. The intensity of this feeling filled her with confusion and dread.

"Well, now you know," Andy said. "Do you still want to be here?"

She looked up at him and said, "He won't try to sell me a salted mine, will he? I'm an assayer's daughter."

The words were what he needed. He looked at her out of his wretchedness and then smiled and put his hand on her shoulder. "Come on, then."

The sick man was propped on three pillows in a bed in a row of beds facing another row. The white-shirted, white-sheeted figures looked like corpses. At each end of the ward the windows stood wide open; the breeze blowing through the ward made the bedsheets seem alive. Andy pulled up two chairs ceremoniously. "Hello, Dad." The man in the bed turned to look at them.

Even in illness the man had a command, a handsome, rugged presence. His hair was iron gray, a sweeping mane curving off his forehead. His features were strong but regular, his eyes deep blue, wide and trusting as a child's. They couldn't be father and son, Clara thought, studying his face. Then she saw that the shapes of their faces and jawlines were the same. It was as though in the journey from father to son the features had shaken

43

loose. The voices, the starts and stops in speech, were also the same, but Arlo Percival's voice, even in sickness, had a certainty that Andy's lacked.

Wretched and ill at ease, Andy asked, "Well Dad, how are you?"

Arlo Percival acknowledged his son with a nod. Then he turned his eyes on Clara as though he were seeing recovery itself. He began to inquire about her, listening to her answers with an eagerness, a joy, that showed he understood and valued her in some deep way they shared. He had discovered her, seen past her simple clothing and ordinary looks and identified the princess she truly was. Who discovered princesses in the clothes of goose-girls or Cinderellas? Princes do. Kings.

She chatted and laughed and found herself thinking of the ballrooms in the story of the twelve dancing princesses, underground palaces lit by chandeliers whose candles made their silver glow. Then she remembered the candlelight glowing on the silver in a cabin in which there was no food. She thought of Don Quixote's golden helmet of Mambrino. Father had talked about family pride and heirlooms but his people wouldn't take his body after he died, or inquire about his children. Mr. Percival's sphere wasn't one of family, but one in which certain special people, illuminati, moved, seeking others like themselves, the single, few, farsighted individuals who . . .

As Clara crested his wave, as he began to tell her how he was using his influence on a state senator to get a private room, as suddenly as a bubble pops in the air and is gone, the spell popped and vanished. It had all been moonwinkle, star-shimmer, like the sudden appearance and withdrawal of the fairy kingdom in *A Midsummer Night's Dream*.

Beside her Andy shifted miserably and she turned to look at him and saw misery pinching his mouth and pulling at his forehead. A nurse came with something for Arlo Percival to drink and the two visitors could see her admiration, the kindling of her eyes, as she approached him. He took the glass, toasting the nurse, then Clara, holding them in a glance intimate as a lover's. Andy rose. "We have to go," he said in a flat voice.

"Well?"

They were standing uncertainly in the street. "It was wonderful," she said. "It was a trip to Merlin's castle." He stared at her. She went on. "Let me tell you about vaccination; we had to learn about it at school. Jenner found that having cowpox conferred an immunity to smallpox. My father gave me an immunity to your father. Your father does it well—the con—but he doesn't believe it. My father believed it, and tried to con us all. It didn't take with me. I'm immune, really."

"You didn't fall for it, the line . . ."

"No."

"But you understand why I wanted you to see him, why I asked you to come."

"Tell me."

"I can't, not right now."

"Let's eat, then," she said.

She knew where Denver's Mexican neighborhood was, and she took him to a restaurant there. Andy had never eaten Mexican food and there were no menus.

"What do we do?" he asked.

"You showed me your spells; these are some of mine."

Albóndigas, tamales hot in their cornhusks, black beans. He was cautious and then he decided he liked the subtle alkali taste in the corn, the heat of the chiles, the tang of cumin, and he ate, discovering his hunger.

When they were finished and replete, they sat back in the close near-darkness. "I'm glad you asked me to meet your father," she said.

He looked away. "I was afraid you would fall for it."

"Don't be afraid of charm," she said, smiling.

He belched deeply, looked horrified, and then they laughed. "Charm." He had begun to relax. "Charm means magic, something that takes the will away. It wasn't only that he shamed me by getting arrested. I've seen him lying in the street. I've seen him in shackles and in jail clothes. I loved him. He got away with the money I earned on my first job and on my second, and I loved him even while he was taking me. He has more power old and sick than I do young and well. I had to show you because . . ." He stopped and took a breath and went on. "I keep forgetting the power he has because he turns it off when he doesn't need it, when we're alone. He loses that glow, and I think maybe age and being sick have done what even jail couldn't do. Then a new mark will come in, someone to impress, someone to sell the mine he hasn't got, and he's off and running again. He could be on his deathbed, and if the mark walked in, he would—"

"Why *did* you ask me to come?" she said.

He gave her a look as wretched as the one he had had at Arlo's bedside. "I saw myself liking you. I saw us together. I kept thinking about you, and I had to find out if he could deceive you—if you were a mark, or before your disgust at his being a jailbird could hurt me too much."

"Your father's been in prison," Clara said slowly. "My father made prisons for other people. Your father makes the world look lucky and rich; my father made it look mean and poor. It's funny because they both would call themselves realists."

He grinned at her. "You're right."

"Where's your mother?"

"I don't know. I remember a redheaded woman and sisters— two sisters, but then they were gone. I think he wanted to keep me, to train me as a partner."

She swallowed a laugh. "How did that work out?"

46

"My timing stank and I'm missing some physical essentials. Con men need a certain kind of grace, a presence. It wasn't my limp or my teeth or my size, it was all of it together. I looked like a liar, and funny is no look for a lover or a con man."

She faced him straight on and said, "Oh, yeah?" grinning. A glow came into his face, moving across it before the blush made it brick red. They sat for a long time until the dinner crowd began to fill the other tables.

6

*T*o the workers on her floor, Clara had undergone a sudden change. She began to be miserly about her time, working double shifts at the plant to accumulate off-time for the monthly trips to Denver. She had a compulsion about these trips, an intensity no mere brother-in-law would inspire. Winter came and travel got even more difficult. Snows wiped out the road between Pueblo and Denver and the wind blew them in again over the cleared places. Sometimes there were nightmare whiteouts on the plain. In the hospital, the open windows kept the patients blue-lipped with cold. The nurses walked their wards in heavy coats. There was a stir of eagerness on the ward that winter. A new miracle drug had been developed that would cure tuberculosis, the doctor said, and it would be used as soon as there was enough of a supply. By some marvel, the old man was slowly improving on his own. As the months went by and Clara continued coming up to meet him, Andy became easier and more relaxed. Clara was less so. She liked Andy's gentleness and humor. She liked his touch and his kiss, which he gave her in greeting and good-bye, but he had begun to talk about engagement, marriage, and when she thought of it, whatever passionate feelings she had evaporated and left her fearful and beset with vague, disquieting dreams. She could go nowhere for advice; the people at work and at the rooming house thought she was married. Who would understand the complexity of her situation?

She wanted Andy, yearned for him in a blurred, frightened way. She knew she loved him, yet she was relieved that they could spend only a few hours together. Defense jobs were frozen, and she was forced to stay where she was. To Clara, the prospect of sleeping with a man meant surrendering to him. Mama's story wasn't the only one. Accounts of drunken beatings and jealousy came and went through the plant. Now and then a woman on the line would come in hiding a black eye or bruises on her arms. "He was drunk and I answered back, and I should have known. . . ."

Drunk or jealous or wedded to anger like Father, that was men. The women she asked, "Why don't you leave?" would stare back at her as though she, a married woman, should know the reason. Andy drank little, he was kind and not jealous. She watched him, looking for the signs of weakness other women mentioned: overgenerosity, rage, stinginess, drinking, rigid piety, jealousy, suspicion. None of those things was evident in him.

At that time, a woman at Clara's boardinghouse became ill. Her daughter, who was working in Denver, wanted to come

49

down to care for her. The two women approached Clara. If she would take over the daughter's identity, papers, and job up in Denver, Lena Sanchez would come on the line at the paint shop under her name. Job boards were rigid but informal changes were made often, even though the charge for getting caught was treason. The war had turned, and no one thought that swapping jobs would menace the national security. Andy was delighted and Clara could give no reason why she shouldn't proceed with the change. The two women looked alike; both were tall and dark haired. The workers close to them in both places would accept the change. With their heads and faces covered, and the bulky protective clothing, it wasn't difficult to masquerade successfully, and, soon, to feel natural in the deception.

Arlo Percival didn't learn of the move until mid-December. "Living in some barrio rooming house—why didn't you come to me instead? I can fix you up at a swell hotel, rent-free."

"Fix her up with nothing. Don't help us," Andy growled.

After they left the hospital, they headed for the heart of town and the big stores, now with their Christmas displays.

"We don't want anything from Arlo," Andy said, still irritated. "No favors, no help. He's up and walking and that's okay. I visit him because he's still sick and because—until now—there was no one else. When he leaves the hospital he'll get a room some-where and we'll go back to the way it was. I don't want to owe him anything."

The streets were full of people. They came in sight of the Denver Dry at the center of a Christmas crowd. The stores were showing wartime creativity, tinsel made of shiny paper instead of metal, mirrors instead of lights, displays from delicately carved wood and paper.

They had planned to stop and study the windows, but Andy's annoyance moved them beyond the store and down the street, talking as they walked. "We know him and he's not a danger to us," Clara said.

Andy tossed hair out of his face in his familiar gesture of denial. "We say we won't let him get to us, but believe me, unless we keep our guard up, he'll find a way, a way you'd never have thought of, a way that would ruin any favor he could do. That favor will give him power over us and leave us ashamed, apologizing, hiding, or paying."

Clara had begun to draw into her coat. His anger reminded her of her father's rages. She slowed, then stopped, stymied, remembering her father's voice, his words, seeing his face, not wanting to be with this man, with any man so angry, so blind in his own anguish.

"You've been poor, and you think poverty is the only shame there is," he was saying. He had quieted down and then he stopped beside her, taking her misery for embarrassment. "There's worse shame. There are the looks people give you when they come to get the money that was promised them, or the deed they thought was theirs. I told you I'd seen him in shackles and handcuffs."

"Where was that?"

"Here," he said, and pointed to where they had been. "Sixteenth Street, a block down from where we were."

She began to listen to him again, to the anguish in his voice, and she wondered if she could ever confide in him any of her own, more subtle story. With his father's criminal past, would Andy be able to understand the denigration of a sneer, the hateful lingering on a word, or the poison of delicate sarcasm? Helen of Troy?

"I was nine then," he said. "We were walking up from Arapahoe. Someone called his name and all of a sudden there were police. They pushed him down; he was lying on the ground, and they used the handcuffs. Everyone was staring. They put us in the wagon."

51

"What happened to you then?"

"He went to jail; I went to an orphanage."

They walked on in silence. She felt sympathy for Andy, but at the same time she was weighing living a life with him, trying to reconcile the reality of herself as a trained, certified teacher, a woman who could work in a factory, too, if need be, or tutor as she had done, with the woman Mama had been, in a poor cabin halfway up Placer Gulch. After the war they would need teachers again. Andy wasn't a violent man and she wasn't dependent as Mama had been, staying out of need, in even greater need.

"How long were you in the orphanage?" she asked.

"Two years." His answer was almost too soft to hear. "When Arlo got out, he got me back and I stayed with him up in the gold camps. He tried to train me as a helper, but I always botched things up. Bad timing, he said. He'd leave me one place or another, depending on whoever would take care of me. He'd be gone—weeks, months—and then he'd blow back and we'd take off. I'd be so glad to see him I'd forgive all the rest." Andy stopped and stood as though trying to decide if this were the right place, the right way to tell her what he so needed to tell. "Then he got caught again on some stock thing." They started walking again. "In court they say the 'People of Colorado versus Arlo Percival.' I was set to be a character witness at his trial, but I froze up and couldn't say anything. The People of Colorado . . ."

It occurred to Clara that Andy must be saying these things for the first time. The words had a rusty hesitance, drying up and then coming out in spurts, too loud. Perhaps he hadn't put some of those sights into words before, not even in his own mind.

"So he was back in jail?"

"Yes. I got placed with a farmer in Arvada, Higgins. One day Higgins took me to Denver in his wagon. We were outside Union Station, waiting for a loading, and it was a little after dawn. They had a bunch of prisoners for transfer down to

Canyon City. People were watching them. The criminals were in canvas pants and those undyed muslin shirts—jail clothes, and they were all chained to one another. I started to move away, but Higgins was standing there staring. Then he came, Arlo, near the end of the line. It was sudden, so sudden I thought I was seeing things. He had trained me not to make any show of recognition until he gave me the high sign. As he passed, he winked at me. Higgins thought I had made a face or something. He nudged me and said, 'Don't mock them in their misfortune.' I didn't see Arlo for five more years."

They were almost at the capitol without knowing how they had gotten there. They turned around and started back. "No help from Arlo," Andy said. "None."

Arlo Percival was released from the hospital and moved to a place near Union Station. He got a job in a war plant and began a series of gambling games that ran twenty-four hours a day. He was caught. He got thirty days in the city jail. He did the punchboard: sixty days. He did the pyramid scheme: ninety days. Andy kept on with his visits to Denver, a nineteen-hour train ride down and back on a freight car, passenger service having been curtailed by the war. At the time, he was moonlighting for a company that was buying up mine sites. The trip got him a six-hour visit with Clara, who was so frightened of being tied to anyone that she sometimes froze in the middle of an embrace. She knew that his traveling was a sign of love stronger than any declaration would have been. She wanted to yield to him but couldn't.

In June, the invasion of Europe began and the gear-up put everyone on longer hours. "We ship while the rivets are still hot and the paint's still wet," the poster said. Andy came down again and met Clara right off shift, in overalls and hairnet, sweating and exhausted. He had a ring. He had asked his miner friends to pound together two dozen tiny nuggets, and these he had had soldered into a backing.

She turned it over in her hand. "I can't wear your ring. Here they think I'm already married."

"Wear it on a chain around your neck."

"How did you know my size?"

"I guessed. It needs to be big and loose, right now. I know that, too."

She wanted to yield but couldn't.

But she did begin to tell him about Father and his scorn, about the words and silences with which he made the women ugly to themselves. "Even now, when I see him in my mind, it's looking down at us, at Mama and me, as we scrub."

Andy listened quietly, and whenever the words deserted her or she felt herself slipping into complaint and her face heated, he said, "Go on."

"It sounds so petty . . . so small. . . ."

"Go on."

She realized that had the man listening been Father, he would have made a contest of it, comparing his griefs with hers, as though there were some advantage in the suffering, a conferring of rank, a tribute to be wrung from her.

Andy had none of this. He said, "Now I understand why it scares you to be married. But listen to me, Clara. Not every man treats people that way."

Father, having won the contest, would have used it to prove that the world was a sewer. He would have felt vindicated by whatever tale of suffering he had heard.

So Clara judged Andy as he listened, weighed his listening, sifted and measured it, and slowly, like a nervous invalid in a summer river, let herself slip, inch by inch, with caught breath and trepidation, into water.

In July, she got another long weekend and hitchhiked to Aureole. The driver of the beer truck expressed amusement. "What are you doing, lady, moving?"

Clara had a suitcase and two long, muslin-covered sacks, which she laid carefully over the space between the seat and the back of the cab. "I'm getting married," she said. "These are my dress and veil."

The veil was white, the dress a soft lemon color with a small, gray figure and a light gray sash. She had made the dress herself and it looked homemade to her when she tried it on. Andy had written to her to make the trip up instead of his coming to Denver for the wedding. Oliver and Katy wanted to have the party. Tessie Rubano was coming from Placer Gulch and the girls from Granite and Gold Flume, where they were now living.

"We can get married at the courthouse," he wrote. "Luckily, Arlo is doing six months in Colorado Springs or we would have to invite him, too. When he sees a courthouse, he crosses his wrists from habit." She knew his joke was an attempt to get past the pain that none of the wedding party would be his people.

But Andy's boss stood up with him and Katy with Clara. As they faced the judge, Mary Louise Coleman, four years old, went up gravely and took Clara's left hand. Oliver got the wedding picture on the courthouse steps.

When the party was over, and the cake and punch served and eaten, Andy and Clara left to register at the only hotel in Aureole still open. Andy felt Clara's fear, so instead of going up to their room, they took a long walk near the river and went up Pickaxe Hill, which overlooked the town. As the day passed, what should have been the long, contented, leisurely day, Clara faced the evening with growing anxiety. She went into longer and longer silences.

Andy said, "You don't want a wedding night, do you?"

She shook her head and began to cry.

At first he nodded and let her sit herself on a rock, but when the sobs grew instead of quieting, and lengthened into the long weeping that sounded like inconsolable grief, he began to be frightened. Should he touch her? Tentatively, he patted her shoulder, but the touch only made her shrink from him. He tried talking but she seemed not to hear. There seemed no way to reach her. She had been leaning on the rock, but her sobbing had so weakened her that now she lay down on the ground on her side, legs drawn up, arms protecting her breasts. When she could weep no more—it was dark by then—they made their way carefully down the hill. "Are you going back to Oliver and Katy's?" She shook her head. "You do want to stay married, then?" She nodded yes, keeping her head averted. Then she followed him dumbly into the hotel and up to the misnamed honeymoon suite.

Clara was married—as Mama had been and Tessie Rubano and other women she knew. She was now chained by law, and chained by love, because she didn't doubt her love for Andy Percival or her desire for him. Sensing it, knowing it, she knew that its depth would also be the depth of her self-abasement. Would he use Father's ridicule or demands for instant attendance, or would he use the jealousy of some of the husbands of Spanish Town or the war plant? Would he find drink, or some other cruelty, something worse?

She lay on the bed and wept again and thought that as ugly as weeping made her, he wouldn't want her.

"You don't have to have a wedding night," he said, "but I want you to see something."

"What?"

"Have you ever seen a naked man?"

She shook her head. He went away into the bathroom and came out again and said to her back, "Sit up. Sit up and look." Had the tone been bullying or hostile, she would have run away, left him. Instead, the voice was tender and even humorous. He didn't touch her. "Look at us," he said. "Look at how vulnerable we men are." As she looked, he became erect, and he said, "I can't appear dignified, not even when I want to."

She understood how he was standing before her, ridiculous to himself in his obvious need, a man willing to undergo the cold scrutiny of a sex-terrified virgin for as long as she would subject him to it. He turned around. "Here's the other side," he said. "I have one thing to say now. I don't steal. I don't steal money or love or bodies. I don't steal people's possessions or their souls."

They didn't make love that night. The night after, when she said it would be all right, he shook his head and said, "I've been alone a long time. I expect to be married an even longer time. I want it to be right. You're not ready, but you will be someday." They kissed and embraced, and the next day she went back to Denver and the paint shop.

A week later Andy came down, and the week after again. They had begun to embrace each other lying down, slowly learning the way their bodies looked and felt. "What's this?" His hand had found and was tracing the ragged scar on her thigh. She told him about the day they all cut broom, about the hailstorm and the attack by the unknown man. Lying with her husband and still terrified of sex, her proud self-defense now sounded excessive and hysterical, not courageous, and she ended feeling ashamed in spite of Andy's awe. Later, he said, "I know you got married against your wanting to be free. I know you did it out of love for me, because I needed that promise from you. I don't want you to feel enslaved. If you should ever want to stop being married, I won't keep you."

"It's not about being with any other man," she said.

"I know, and we are little by little *making* love."

A friend at the factory had a cabin near Morrison, and on another weekend, Clara and Andy hiked there and made love one rainy Saturday. The first time she was only glad to be able to do it, feeling little pleasure, but the second was less guarded and she began, hesitantly, to respond to him. It occurred to her that her pleasure in him was pleasure enough, the touching, the warmth, the loving. It was going to be all right. She cried with relief.

Andy was relieved as well. "I'd be lying to say I wasn't happy for that. Your body trusts me now, even if you aren't ready, and that's enough for now."

Late in September, in Denver, Clara got a letter from Aureole. It was typed, an invitation:

Andrew Percival
Invites
Clara Coleman Percival
To an Occasion
Thursday, September 29, at 7:00 P.M.
In Front of the Methodist Church in Golden
Dress Is Formal

Was it a wedding? Was it his idea to give her a church wedding? Golden was at the end of the trolley line, and she could make it if she left work early. She would wear the dress she had been married in, and the shoes. She would need to buy a hat.

As she rode to Golden on the trolley she thought about the complexity of her present life. The lie about being married to a soldier was becoming impossible now that she actually had a husband, a man obviously not in the service. She would have to move and become Clara Percival at an Anglo rooming house while she stayed Lena Sanchez at work.

The church in Golden was on a side street shaded by big, old maples. It was locked. On the next block was a gas station and she changed out of her work clothes in the ladies' room. Andy was in front of the church when she got back.

He was dressed as he had been for their wedding. He grinned at her and said, "Come on." Then he led her away from the church, east and then north, past the Coors brewery and the junkyard; there was no more town. East of where they walked were the railroad yards with two or three cars sleeping in the weeds of the siding. "Where are we going?"

58

"Keep walking."

They turned at a field littered with what the wind had blown there. "Keep walking," Andy said.

The day was cooling so the walk was pleasant. They began to climb a little hill. There was a footpath, but Clara was afraid for her stockings so she stopped and took them off. What was this to be, a wedding party in a hobo jungle?

Then, just as the sun went behind one of the mountains, they broke the crest of the hill to come into a protected glade. There were wild maple shrubs and aspen screening the glade from the view of the railroad and the back of the town. Above them the hill rose sharply like a wall covered with vines. With the quieting of late afternoon all the sounds hushed except the comments of birds on last errands. The low sun dappled the glade with broken light.

In the middle of the glade someone had carefully arranged a low table. There were cushions at the two set places. Silver threw blades of fire, crystal rang with light. A white cloth lay gleaming under the settings. For an instant, mountains, table, silver, and crystal all erupted in burning gold, and then the sun slipped behind the other mountain and left them in afterglow.

Clara stared. Andy was watching her, his eyes studying this scene that could have been part of *The Golden Bird* or *Beauty and the Beast.* He walked to the table, bent, and lit the candles, then went to a large basket standing to the side. He began taking things from the basket. Soon there was champagne bubbling in the glasses.

Much of the meal had been wild-gathered. There was a mushroom soup made of boletes, spring-beauty tubers and pigeons with pine nuts, cattail roots with wild garlic. For dessert they had sand plums stewed with honey. Then they lay back and the moon rose.

Once again, Clara thought, Andy had stripped before her; this time his tenderness was the use of his father's genius for magic moments and prestidigitation, but in *her* service, surmounting his own fear and dread. He had always spoken with scorn of how his father traded on people's dream hungers and mythic wishes. He had shouted down the grinning ghost in him, the part of himself he hated, to give her this gift. They were in the spell of the evening, but when they undressed under the moon, they folded their clothes carefully, like the careful, prudent people they were.

7

Clara went back to Denver to continue as Lena Sanchez.
Andy came as often as he could and by November her story of a
Tewa husband in the Pacific had collapsed. To her surprise,
instead of condemning her dishonesty, the people at work and
the rooming house praised her cleverness and spunk. Her astonishment made Andy laugh. "The world forgives nerve when it
won't forgive funny looks or clumsiness. For once, my father's
game works to our benefit."

Clara had a free afternoon one weekday, and in a surge of
good feeling she went to the address Arlo had given them after

his last incarceration. A bitter landlady informed her that Arlo hadn't been seen for two months, and the suitcase full of valuable family heirlooms he had left as surety had contained half an old newspaper, a dented saucepan, and three or four jars without lids. He owed her money and he had cheated most of the other boarders out of larger or smaller sums in greater or smaller ways.

Clara had begun to overcome her fear, and her body had begun yearning. She wanted Andy. She wanted Andy in a home she made for him. They had walked a hundred miles, sat in the rooms of strangers, borrowed beds, sat up late in bus stations and train stations as surrogate homes. From Denver Clara could look westward to the rising swell on swell of hill to mountain, green to blue-gray, blue-gray to the white of the high peaks in a vast order like the rise and fall of fugal music, sound on sound, theme on theme. The theme was "Come home, get up and come home."

The war ended in Europe, and rumors went around that jobs would be unfrozen. Then the war ended in Japan and the rumors went again, but it was over a year before Clara could leave the plant and trade back Lena Sanchez's identity for her own.

Andy was rooming in Aureole. The landlady said she would consent to their double occupancy, and Clara moved, happy to be with him and back in the mountains. But she looked for work all over town and came back disappointed. What jobs there were had been posted for men. People said that February and March were the bottom of the year, and she soon wore out all the possibilities of the *Ute River Voice*'s classified page.

"Wait till things pick up for the summer," Andy said. "We've got the money."

On a Sunday in March, the landlady came home from church and said to Clara, "I don't know if this would interest you, but one of the ladies from Callan says that the one-room school in Gold Flume needs a teacher."

Clara stared at her. "Where?"

"Gold Flume. The job isn't posted yet, but it will be. I don't suppose you would be interested."

Gold Flume was a dying town at the other end of the Ute Valley. It was thirty-five miles from Aureole and past Granite and Bluebank, past Placer Gulch and Callan, farther even than the Callan School. Clara all but ran to the courthouse on Monday to apply. The clerk stared at her. "Lord may mark the sparrow's fall, but the whole damn valley knows it before the thing lands. *You* wouldn't want a job like that, would you?"

The valley was between snows. There were winds from the south during that season, and the whiteness quilting the mountains was still deep, but in the valleys, old patches of decaying snow lay in pockets where the sun didn't reach. Mild days would entice the sap in trees to rise and sudden temperature changes, as much as fifty degrees in six hours, would freeze the sap and explode the tree from inside. There was a feeling of dry exhaustion in the ground from which no green yet swelled.

Andy and Clara took the train past the towns in their familiar slackness and ruin. Placer Gulch looked weed-grown and abandoned. Callan had smoke from only a few stove-stacks; the Little Annie workings were the same, but Whiskey Gulch had a new working and some of the old mines had been repaired. "It was the war," Andy murmured, "and the bomb. We started to get molybdenum, uranium, strontium—the ore was all in the tailings out on the hillsides, there for the taking. Now that the war's over, who knows?"

Callan School was still standing, crippled and diminished, its windows gone, its students drained away to Denver and Pueblo and islands in the Pacific Ocean. The derelict made Clara sad and so did the starving valley, which they now saw with the practical eyes of potential inhabitants. The train would be late in winter—there would have to be a snow-family to stay with, although school would close on the days of deep snow as it had in her own school days. They murmured these things to each other, judging, weighing her wish against practical possibility.

Gold Flume lay cupped at the end of the valley. Strands of the Ute River ran past it, through the fingers of the mountain basins. The town was compact, held in by the mountains, a mining town like all the Ute towns, living boom-bust and hand-to-mouth, first and grandest on gold, then silver, then on a succession of lesser minerals, poorer and poorer, the shine fading, dimming, and now gone dark about the eyes.

The town itself was a single paved street running east and west from the train station platform. A half-closed hotel with a faded sign stood east of the station. Andy and Clara got off the train and looked down the two-block main street to where it ended at the field the schoolchildren used at recess. Their glance took in the entire town. Directly to the east was the school, which stood on a rise that ended at the foot of the mountain behind it.

They walked to the deserted school—it was Saturday and they noted the businesses of Gold Flume: a bank; a WPA post office, which was the newest of the buildings; a small grocery; a feed store; a hardware and lumber yard, closed and abandoned; a firehouse; a drug and dry-goods store; and five saloons, three of them closed. "A town that can't keep its saloons going is no town for me," Andy murmured, but she saw he was joking, trying to keep her spirits up.

They came to the school yard, stepping over the old snow patches up the path to the square, stolid one-story structure of local dolomite, like Callan School's but grayer and much smaller. There were steps up to a porch. Although Clara wondered how Andy was seeing all this, everything she saw excited her. She would be teaching a regular class. There would be the possibility of continuity and watching students grow. The school was part of its mountain and part of its town, a solid building one could warm in winter, and it had friendly windows on three sides. She didn't dare look at Andy's face. They had gone up on the porch with the hesitancy of uninvited guests and they turned to the view of the town and the way they had come.

A woman was walking up the worn path, also avoiding the bordering crusts of snow. Miss Willa Optegard, she would be, the teacher. It was easy to tell by her quick, purposeful movements. Although the day wasn't cold, she was bundled in a man's heavy mohair coat. She looked up at them from the bottom of the stairs, her glance going from one to the other. Clara spoke.

"I'm Clara Percival. This is my husband."

Miss Optegard looked perturbed for a moment, but Andy smiled his disarming smile and said, "You ladies get on with it. I'll walk through town and see if there's a checker game on at the firehouse." They saw the teacher relax. Andy negotiated the stairs carefully; his bad leg made going down more difficult for him. He turned at the bottom. "I'll be back in an hour or so. Take your time."

In silence the women watched him make his way down the worn path. Then Willa Optegard squared her shoulders and faced Clara. "I don't know nothing special to tell you about the school. It's the only place I been, so I don't know no other thing." Her voice was soft but slightly nasal, a countrywoman's voice. "I heard you had the college and got you a certificate and that's why I thought you was a man. . . ." Clara heard sorrow in her voice and saw it on her face. Willa went on, softly. "The children is mostly good, some is slow, and one or two's bullies. You have them from the gulches, and some of them's pretty strange till they get to be with folks a bit."

Clara felt a pang at the phrase "from the gulches," but she also heard kindness in what followed. It dawned on her then that the words had a ring of finality in them. "You're finishing the year out, aren't you?"

"No, ma'am, they ain't letting me do that." Then Willa Optegard looked down, and then her hand went to the buttons on her coat, one, two, three, and the coat came open and there was the little belly beginning. "I don't have no gold band. It wasn't no love, either. It was Kester French, drunk. He's forced other girls, too, and the town knows what he does, but . . ." She trailed off.

"But *you* have to go."

"Yes'm."

"Were you raised around here?"

"Chinaman's Gulch."

"You went to this school, didn't you?"

"Yes'm. Miz Eliot kept school in my time."

"Where will you go?"

"Denver. They got places for girls in my fix."

"The towns should keep their own."

"This one is." She looked at the floor. "It's keeping Kester French."

Miss Optegard showed Clara how to work the school stove, then, and how to close the shutters, and where the tools were for washing the big windows. She got the roll book and began to go down the names, giving a short description of each of the twenty students presently in the school. Some of the names evoked affection, some regret.

"You write a new page each year?"

"Yes'm."

"How many of these pages are yours?"

"There's six. Six years I been here. Do you want to look at last year's?"

"No. This is the county book, so you can't take it, but why don't you sign each page and then copy all the names?"

Clara saw the green eyes widen, catlike, in her small face. Its planes had been flattened by early hunger. The eyes went brimming. "You ain't got time for all that."

66

"Then you'll have to start right away, won't you? While you write, put a word or two about each one. That way you'll remember them all."

So they went name by name from the beginning. Seventy-eight children. "This one here, he's pure gold," Willa said, "and this one here, he's fool's gold," and they laughed together.

Andy came back and they sent him out again. He came back again with sandwiches. "I was on my way to the grocery and as I passed a house a lady called to me, a Mrs. Bordereau. She said she was sorry you were leaving, Miss Optegard. She told me to wait a minute and she came out with all this. Elk, she said, and the bread's homemade, and here's pie." Andy's gentleness made them aware that Mrs. Bordereau must have given him her opinion. Not everyone agreed with the school board. After lunch he disappeared again and Willa went on with the names.

By the time they finished, Andy and Clara had missed the afternoon train. Miss Optegard left them at the school, thanking them and holding the composition book tight against her chest. She would be gone before classes began on Monday. "It means I'll be wanted right away," Clara said.

Andy nodded. "I know. This town is one big recording studio. I'll tell you this, though. This school has your name written all over it, and by now Town knows that, too, and is deciding on it."

"What do you think?"

"Why don't you stay the week and decide whether you'll help out till they find someone or take the job? Come home Friday and tell me."

"How would you feel if the answer was yes?"

"Well . . ." He tossed his head. "I wouldn't want a weekend marriage. I walked around town all day and I met some people and talked. Places are cheap here, and with the cost of living, I wouldn't have to moonlight. I'd still have the county car. I think we could move here and have a good life, schoolmarm and surveyor."

She was still heavy with Willa Optegard's grief. "This may be a beautiful place to live. It's beautiful to look at, with the mountains all around, but the people . . ."

"You mean because of what they're doing to that little woman?"

"Because she has to go and Kester French stays."

"Kester French? He's the man who showed me around."

8

*I*t had been more than five years since Clara had been in a classroom. She had forgotten the difficulty of facing twenty children in all eight grades, disappointed at the loss of an almost-parent. She saw their fear of change, their resentment at its force. She fought a desire to apologize for their loss of Miss Optegard as she stood before the accusing faces.

The students ranged in age from six to fourteen, but Clara knew at least two were older than that. One of them was Milvin French. Miss Optegard had been obliged to teach the son of her rapist.

Willa Optegard had been a good teacher in many ways. Clara could tell by the way the children came into the schoolroom. Their grasp of history was a bit shaky and they had little real feeling for poetry or literature, but their dates and facts were in place, and they had a respect for the importance of school and for its seriousness. When she saw the three textbooks available, Clara realized that her predecessor had done a good job with what she had had.

But it would be almost impossible to correct the effects of Willa's indifferent grammar. Her errors had been enshrined by the class in her honor. At last Clara said, "Miss Optegard spoke in her way and I speak in mine. I will correct you in my way and I want you to use that from now on."

Six of the children were immediately identifiable as Gulch children, idiosyncratic and even bizarre in their dress and habits, speaking a kind of home-talk that was almost a private argot. They did indeed smell, and they were crusty with scurfs and manges, their hair bushy with nits and uncombed. The older ones dipped snuff. Clara learned she had to confine them to answering factual questions only, because their responses to the thinking questions she favored were so often wild or mystical. Had she been as strange as any of these, as filthy and odd-sounding?

She came home every day that first week spent, shocked at the difference between her dream, the long-cultivated, long-held dream of being a teacher, and the grinding realities of the profession's daily pursuits. The work was exhausting, draining, full of pitfalls.

With so many of the children related to one another, Clara knew she would have to learn all of those links, or their enmities and alliances would be unintelligible. The groupings—Town child, Ranch child, Gulch child—were only the beginning. The town had its classes, too, small as they were. The men connected with the railroad had the only substantial houses in town and there were four or five prosperous ranchers who had flourished with the war's demand for beef. Peter Tavistock's father was town telegrapher, a fact Peter had made known to her on her first day. Jennie Bogard was a Ranch girl, Orval Bordereau a Town boy, son of the woman who had made sandwiches for Willa at her inauspicious good-bye. Clara had to learn who ate biscuits with deer fat for lunch the way she had, and who ate baked bread with slices of meat and slabs of pie. There were school-yard rivalries about things she could only guess at, and school itself formed a kind of shadow world of numbers and letters pulled over the real world, an intrusion of one order on another, more real one. Was school to some of them what it had been to her, a refuge, an island of order and direction in a chaotic wilderness?

The years of reading to the laundry workers had convinced Clara of the value of reading aloud, and she gave them half an hour of history in the morning and three-quarters of an hour of literature every afternoon, encouraging the children to bring some handwork with them to do during the reading. To her surprise she had to teach them how to do that—sewing, carving, weaving, knitting. She didn't stop to explain the words in the stories but read for pleasure only, and her first moment of reward was to find a group in the play yard one afternoon in late April enacting "The Speckled Band," with Orval Bordereau as the snake.

She hadn't imagined striking the children when they were inattentive, noisy, or bullying and was amazed to learn that they read her behavior as unconcern when she simply corrected them. The expectation was for the slap, the switch, the ruler, or the strap, depending on the seriousness of the offense. Miss Optegard was praised because she had been fair and her hand a slow one. Where had they learned to equate concern with such punishment, she wondered, as though words had no real meaning? Milvin French was a bully and a disruption to the classroom. Her criticism made him laugh and everyone kept pointing to the strap hanging in the corner, Milvin no less than they. "Ain't you going to whip me?" as though he had been done out of some reward. She told him to sit in the corner facing the wall. "I want to convince you that bullying and violence are wrong," she said, "but how can I do that by bullying you?" He stared at her with the absolute confidence of a person for whom there is no lower level to which he can fall. "And what if I won't do that?"

"Then we'll all have to find a way of restraining or ignoring you, because you cannot be allowed to disrupt the class." Milvin's bullying continued, so she had each child in the class discuss his or her feelings about Milvin's behavior. The difference in how everyone saw him and how he had thought they saw him was so appalling to him that he consented to exile in the corner rather than their icy, honest appraisals. It didn't work well. In the end she whipped him and felt wretched, and he took the whipping with a smirk of vindication. "I don't believe in the strap," she said, "but my father was a violent man and I have some anger in me, too. Don't test my justice. If I ever got started, I don't know that I could stop." Whether because of that speech or because he had broken her resolve, Milvin was less of a problem thereafter.

Andy had found them a cabin on Third Street, behind the bank's old stable. It had been a miner's cabin and its two rooms reminded Clara so painfully of the Coleman place in Placer Gulch that she had to nerve herself every night coming home to it and every morning waking up in it. She also had to keep this from Andy because he had given up convenience and pleasant rooms in Aureole to make the move and thought the place being warm, dry, cheap, and in Gold Flume was all they needed. It was at the narrowest part of the town and dark after 2:00 P.M. with the mountains shutting off the light of the sun.

He was a good husband, a generous, tender man, and his consideration as a lover was rewarded slowly but deeply by an increasing response from her. Her fear didn't leave suddenly, as she had hoped it would, but in shreds, thinning out and tearing like cobweb in rain, from its center outward. Yet when it snowed and the cabin smelled the dank smell, the mouse-grease smell of stale kerosene, Clara felt all her resolve weaken.

In May, one of the Gulch boys came to school after a three-day absence, limping and yellow with suffering, both eyes discolored, his lip split. Clara kept him in at recess and at her look of inquiry he shrugged. "He was drunk is all. I can hide if I want, but this time there was Ma." He got no sympathy from his schoolmates, who laughed at his raccoon eyes. She tried to speak to them about compassion without further humiliating the boy, only to meet their closed faces.

At home in the fumy cabin she complained to Andy. "My school should have given me a framework for this, a means of understanding it, a kind of height over it—" She was thinking of the cool view an eagle might have over its range, one that took in the scurry of a vole, the lift of a mountain. Andy sighed. "Which did you hate more, that man beating the boy or the other kids laughing at him?"

"Both. I tried, but I couldn't get them to feel anything. What's the good of the arithmetic, the literature, the science, if they stay savages?" She began to clear the table, then turned to him, dishes in both hands. "A boy made me whip him the other day and everyone approved. They have a hunger for justice, or what they think it is, but they're afraid of softness and change. Nothing I learned in school prepared me for innocent savagery."

"Does anybody know how to see this problem? Would any of your professors be able to help?"

Clara sent out letters for advice and waited. Every day she taught the school subjects and also showed the children how to wash, using a tub she had bought and kept under the eaves of the privy, how to brush the teeth, to comb the hair, how to use

73

kerosene for scurf and head lice, and oil for chilblains. She pulled ticks from them, explaining how they should inspect their bodies during the season, March through June. In her letters she tried to make the words she used neutral, to shame no one:

The father of this child doesn't value schooling. The boy is a bully and a behavior problem. I can't keep him after school because he's needed at home and would be whipped. I had to whip this boy to get him to obey. I do not like to do this. Do you have some approach to this problem?

Another letter:

I think the father has incest with these girls. I think their brothers know, or participate. How can I protect the girls? What can I do when the other children laugh at their situation? A boy was badly beaten by his father. The other children laughed at his bruises. How can I teach them compassion?

There was no answer to the first letter. The answer to the second was harsh:

You are not a priest or a minister. Your job is to teach the school subjects. The incestuous family you describe is depraved and probably beyond salvage. The boy must learn obedience. Teach the children to mind their own business and not embarrass the girls and the boy by looking at them. You were wrong to draw attention to the boy's bruises.

She read the letter and handed it to Andy. "Idiot," he said. "What do you want to do now?"

"I've been thinking. School will be out in another month. I want to make home visits. I could use the pretext that I'm new and that the school meetings were snowed out."

74

"You wouldn't be going up there to tell some half-loony prospector not to beat his kids, would you?"

"No, I'd just see them and let them see me. Mama would have valued such a visit, I think."

"Well . . ." He seemed dubious.

Andy had news of his own. The old workings on Hungry Woman Mountain, the mountain that rose above Placer Gulch, were being revived. He had also begun doing private surveys after hours. "I'll take you on those Gulch and Ranch visits," he said. "It'll get me familiar with the country."

She wrote letters to all the parents and as soon as the school-house door was locked for summer vacation in June, she began the Town visits. Part of her reason for going, she realized, was that it gave her the impetus to leave her dank, dark house.

The Frenches were the biggest family in Gold Flume, and the poorest. They, and those Matskes and Legrands into which the French women had married, lived all together in five wrecked buses out of town on the east side. A slow thread of the Ute, obstructed and stagnant, wandered through tailings and ash pits on that side, and there was a footbridge to get over the marshy bog to their island. The compound had no water, even by pump, and the buses were barricaded behind a half mountain of junk.

The women of the families, mothers and mothers-to-be, aunts and grandmothers, sat on crates, chair frames, and over-turned pails and watched Clara cross the stream. She came closer and was given no greeting and after a while took a crate and set it near the women as they sat smoking.

"I wanted to meet you," she said. They made no response but stared at her, nine or ten unblinking, unwavering pairs of eyes. The words of introduction she had planned dried up in her mouth. She understood that they assumed her visit was for some official purpose and therefore meant trouble for them. Around them, unintroduced, people came and went, old men and children. The women silenced barking dogs and screaming youngsters with well-aimed stones. The school-age children had vanished, and only when Clara's visit was over did they reappear, defiantly or cautiously, from one of the buses. She told the women some of what she had planned for the coming year. She asked their opinions. They had none. After a while she showed them the books she had brought. "They're stories the children might like to read over the summer." The books were the new pocket books developed out of the needs of the war. She had bought them in Aureole and, at twenty-five cents apiece, she could supply one to every family in her school.

The two she had brought were a Bret Harte for the boys and a Grimm's fairy tales for the girls, and she held them out and looked into the cluster of defiant and disinterested faces. Before she could say anything, the oldest of the women rolled her tongue into her lip and spat through the quid. "Ain't no use for none of that."

So Clara brought back the hand that held the books, got up, and said her good-byes, feeling their scorn behind her as she made her way toward the wobbling bridge. There was a space of about twenty yards before the bridge where the way was hidden by undergrowth and piled junk. She stopped there, overwhelmed by the atmosphere of the place, the careless, hopeless filth of everything, the smells, the vacant-eyed, slack women. There was a sound from the side—rats, maybe, but then there was a voice: "Teacher—Miz Percival—" It was Frances Legrand.

"Yes, Frances?"

"Wait up a minute—"

Clara knew, by then, that Frances's mother had been deserted by Bobby Legrand and had moved with Frances back to her people in the compound. Frances had the Frenches' long, bony nose and fine, mouse-colored hair, but there was a grace in her, a quickness from some other source. She was twelve years old.

76

"Them books—"

"Do you want them?"

"Yes'm—I like reading. I could keep 'em clean and nice and bring 'em back in the fall—"

Clara realized that the girl wanted the discipline of borrowing and returning. "Do you want both of them?"

"Yes'm, if I could."

"If you read these and want more, come to my house and I'll give you others."

"That's Town, your house."

"It's not a quarter mile from here—"

"We don't go to Town," Frances said, took the books gently, and disappeared into the tangle of underbrush and wreckage.

"I thought being a Gulch child was all there was to poverty," Clara commented to Andy that evening. She could still smell the rat-sweet, maggot-sweet odor of the Frenches' compound clinging to her clothes and the memory of their stares at the edges of her eye. It came to her, before she turned from the thought in distaste, that there had been some merit in Father's demands for graciousness and order, as cruel and absurd as he had made them.

"The Frenches' poverty was different from yours and from mine," Andy said.

Clara wanted to tell him all about the morning, but her feelings were too complex. She described the family and the area and something else she had noticed: "Body and head lice are gray down there, near the river. They are brown up in the gulches."

"Adaptation," Andy said, and grinned playfully at her. "Darwin knew it all."

Three days later, Clara sat in Sally Bordereau's small, fussy parlor in the wealthier, cleaner part of town. "You'll stay to dinner—Orval senior should be back soon."

"I need to be home soon to fix Andy's dinner," Clara said. There had already been cake and tea.

They talked about Orval junior, a placid, peaceable boy. "He's improved in his reading just since you've been here," Mrs. Bordereau said. "After dinner he reads to us, and he never did that before. Later we talk about what he's read. He said you taught them all how to do that."

"I brought this book to help him keep up over the summer," Clara said, "but if I'd known that, I would have come with a different one." She left the Bordereau house in a sweet glow.

Some of the Matskes had married Frenches, but there was a spirit, an energy in the family that the Frenches didn't have— they thought Clara had come to pick up town gossip and they were disappointed when she failed to pursue the line, but she did learn more about the relationships guiding the town, and the learning was provided in high merriment by the five or six women sitting around the kitchen table.

"Visiting all the families?"

"Yes, it's the quickest way to get to know the students and their parents. Next week I'll be visiting Mrs. Tavistock."

There was a long silence—embarrassment, Clara thought— and then one of the women said, "Our sister works over there, cleaning house." There was silence again, and suddenly they all burst out in a wave of laughter. "The damn woman's gone through our whole family and can't find one of us to satisfy her."

9

The Tavistocks were the only people in town rich enough to hire a servant. The house was three stories of ornate but weathered wood. It stood on the east side of town and had been built for the railroad owner, in case he visited in winter and needed a protracted stay, and it commanded the back of the station where the telegrapher's office was located. The days of the railroad empire were over, and the house had been derelict before being taken over by the telegrapher and his family. A boggy area, a fence, and thirty yards of vines and bushy growth separated it from the French compound.

As Clara came up to the house, she noticed how much had been done to accentuate the house's separation not only from the Frenches, but also from the town itself. The high wrought-iron fence surrounded the house on three sides, the fourth being the beginning of Prospector Hill. Vines had been trained up the fence and there was a heavy gate that cried on its hinges like a rack victim when Clara pulled at it.

Everything inside the fence had been marked out, corseted. A walk laid with little stones at the sides led to the house and the square patches of lawn were all demarcated with stones as well. The veranda steps were narrow and had heavy railings; the door was narrow also. Clara went up and knocked. She remembered the gossip over Daisy Matske's table the week before. "She has family money, the missus, so they live in that big wreck like it was the family mansion back in Boston, Massachusetts, or some-place. They couldn't keep the servants they sent for, so they're stuck with us."

The woman who answered Clara's knock was wiping her hands on a rough towel. "You must be the new schoolteacher. Come on in. Her Nibs is upstairs. I'm Ella Matske, and Tod Matske's my boy. My sister Daisy told me about your visit over there. I think it's good, you doing that. It's good for the kids."

The lively, chatty woman made Clara feel at home but as she laughed and answered one of Ella's questions, Clara glanced up, and in the dimness of the hall staircase she made out a figure standing on the stair. "Oh—"

"I've asked you, Ella"—the voice was penetrating, used to command—"to announce people, not to socialize with them."

Ella disappeared into the back of the house. Mrs. Tavistock came down, a heavy, small woman with a large head and strong features. She motioned Clara into the parlor, and in that motion, half dismissal, Clara realized that the woman was according her a position she didn't feel Clara deserved: I am seating you in my parlor, but you actually belong in my kitchen. Not even Mrs. Sanders in San Pablo had played the grand lady in that way. Clara became aware of her hands and began to hold them in the way Father had described as genteel.

Having settled her guest in the ornate parlor and ordered tea, Mrs. Tavistock considered her duties as a hostess discharged and made little effort at conversation. Clara was thrown back to the hints Father had dropped about genteel behavior in Virginia: One appreciated the appointments of a room but did not discuss them. Before tea, one engaged in small talk. "How long have you and Mr. Tavistock lived in Gold Flume?" Clara began.

It wasn't the right question. The woman answered, her voice intense and bitter. They had come here fifteen years ago, and promises had been made. There was a hiss in the words: "seniority," "advancement," "mansion residence." No one knew that the telephone would eclipse the telegraph and that private cars would increase at the expense of train travel. Here they were, fifteen years in this . . . place, a place they had planned as a *stopover.*

Tea came. It was an elaborate silver service, but Clara noticed it was badly polished and without the strainer. Her father's eye, complete with mote, took it all in. "If one can afford silver," his voice rang in her head, "one can afford silver polish." Oreo cookies lay in the plate. Father would have thrown them across the room. "Are these tea cakes? I thought they were doorstops."

But they drank and Clara made the usual murmurs of appreciation, coming at last to the purpose of the visit. "I teach your Peter and Lucinda, but you and I haven't met. When I replaced Miss Optegard, it was so sudden that—"

"The slut was pregnant. Schoolteacher! An illiterate slut was teaching our children," Dorothy Tavistock reddened with indignation, "a woman who couldn't speak a sentence without drowning in the grammar. Did you ever meet her—see her clothes? Gulch, Gulch born and bred. Her fingernails! Did you see them?"

The Gulch again. The woman was so angry that she failed to notice her guest's expressions, the pallor and the blush that followed it, and by the time she did look, Clara had recovered herself. "I replaced Miss Optegard," Clara persevered, "and I began to teach Peter and Lucinda. It seemed to me that I should know the parents of my students. It's nice to meet the whole family together, but that's not always possible. I'm happy that we arranged this meeting."

"It is appropriate that we talk," Mrs. Tavistock said. "I wanted to tell you that Peter often returns from school in a ragged and bruised condition. He is fighting at school and I want that stopped."

Clara took a breath to answer, carefully. "I know he fights. I don't allow that in school and I often talk about the problem with the children, but there's no way to stop it outside of school. To some degree Peter encourages it. His manner is lofty, and he never lets anyone forget that his parents have a high position in town."

The woman stared at Clara. "Am I to understand that you are blaming Peter for being bullied?"

Clara only said, "I don't think things will continue this way. Peter is on the edge, between fighting the bullies and joining them. This isn't a criticism of him. Many boys become bullies because they are frightened of being picked on." She stopped herself from saying, "My brother used to be . . ."

Mrs. Tavistock made no response, but an iciness settled in the room and Clara saw that her hostess had interpreted her frankness as a violation of etiquette. There was still the book to give. For a moment she hesitated, thinking that she shouldn't give it, that the situation had gone wrong and anything more would make it worse, but she had given books to everyone else and she had selected a book of stories that both Peter and his sister, Lucinda, might read with pleasure. "I brought this for them . . . to help them keep up their reading skills over the summer. . . ." And she laid the book gently on the tea table next to the tray.

Dorothy Tavistock's expression froze and there was a long silence. "This home is plentifully supplied with reading matter," she said.

Clara, stung, was tempted to ask why she didn't see any. She picked up the book and put it in her purse, rose with the standard words of leavetaking, and made her escape, thinking as she departed that she might have done better, much better, but thinking back on it, she didn't see how.

The other Town visits were friendly and easy, and the sting of the Tavistock visit faded. In July, Clara and Andy got horses and went up the gulches to the Bodas, the Covingtons, and the Markhams. The Bodas ran stock and did a little halfhearted mining on Little Annie Creek. Mrs. Boda was a dried-up, skittery woman whose English was so thick that even Clara, experienced in understanding heavily accented English, could barely make out her meaning. Clara taught two of the Boda children, Cyril in the elementary grades, a grim, silent child, and Sulo, the older boy. He was a glowering presence in the classroom, diminished here in the presence of his father, a man the size of an ox. When Clara introduced herself to him as the children's teacher, he walked behind Sulo and planted his hands on the boy's shoulders, digging his fingers into them. It was only when she gave the book that his suspicions were somewhat assuaged. "To read until school starts again."

"Yes," the man said, "yes," and the family went faint with relief.

In all those outlying places, the gulches or the ranches, it was the most ordinary politeness to be asked to stay for a meal, but

Clara wasn't asked there. She left as soon as she could, hurrying to meet Andy, who had been waiting just off Bodas' holding.

A week later they rode up Whiskey Gulch to the Covingtons, and there Clara met Mae Covington and realized why Mama had had such a hunger for bangles and bright clothes and shiny things—habits and choices for which Father had often laughed at her. Isolation had silenced the Bodas; it made Mae Covington talk on and on. Clara had wanted to hint to Mae that she might dress the twins less garishly because the children teased them, but seeing Mae, she didn't have the heart.

They visited the Markhams and afterward rode slowly down the gully of Chinaman's Creek, listening to the summer. Birds streaked here and there, crying their identities and warnings across the landscapes. Insects flew up from the horses' hooves. Water was flowing somewhere, a clucking sound against small stones like augurers casting signs. The voice in the mind droned on.

This was Clara's familiar landscape, her chosen home. She noticed the ripening of raspberries and buffalo berries, the Oregon grape and the alpine currant. For all the beauty that was here and all the grandeur of these places the Gulch families, her own included, were sad and isolated. They were like the stunted trees that are gray even in summer. She wondered if such a crippling could happen to the family she and Andy were making. How had it happened to all those people, each so differently? How had it happened to her parents?

In August, she visited the ranches. Ditmarses' went up Fourway Mountain and rested on the saddle. There were so many barns, outbuildings, and houses, it was like a settlement. Clara had seen towns smaller than the Ditmars ranch. There was a mood of lively interest in her visit. When they had lunch, the fathers and mothers, and the top hand, whose son was also at school, it was a huge picnic. Mrs. Ditmars laughed. "Your timing is perfect—on a ranch this is the only two weeks' lull we get all year."

So she found the Bogards at leisure also. They weren't as wealthy as the Ditmarses, but they were closer to town on a smaller, prettier piece of land. Alice Bogard was a few years older than Clara, and two of her four children were already at school. She laughed when Clara noted it. "We were considered essential to the war effort, and I guess that included starting a family early. I sometimes fell asleep standing up!"

Clara liked Alice Bogard. Her face was sun-tightened and there were wrinkles at the outsides of her eyes and a mouth that liked to laugh. When her husband Carl took Andy to see the ranch, the two women went up to Alice's sewing room, which Clara saw was full of books. They began chatting about what they liked, Alice favoring history and biography, Clara fiction and literature. Alice kept a list. "I'm going to do that, too!" Clara was writing as she said it. "I liked Willa Optegard," Alice said, smiling, "but I'm so glad you're here, now."

"When do you come to town?" Clara asked her.

"Most Saturdays," Alice said.

Clara broke her first rule. "Stop down at our place when you come and we'll trade books."

"Come up here in two more weeks and we'll go out after chokecherries." Then Alice said, "I know you're not supposed to socialize with parents while their children are in school, but that's so long to wait and too much to ask in so small a world as ours is."

Later they went out to join the men. Clara saw that Andy was enjoying Carl Bogard's company. "He's got interesting ideas about how domestic animals change the habits and ranges of wild ones. And he knows lots of local geology. I asked him to come with me next time I go up Hungry Woman."

That fall, Milvin French and Sulo Boda didn't return to school. Kester French attacked a girl in Bluebank and was then found dead in Crow Creek near his own place, drowned in six inches of water. The sheriff came from Aureole to investigate, noted.a general relief at Kester's passing, and pursued no clues beyond Kester's proven drunkenness. The Frenches complained bitterly at the sketchy questioning of the girl's brothers and the town's disinterest. What had he been doing in Crow Creek's narrowest, rockiest place? The town took no time forgetting Kester, and the Frenches retreated even farther behind their barriers.

"I have news," Andy said when he came home one evening. It was late fall and they had a fire in the cabin. "It's good and bad. The good news is that there's a refinery coming in near here. There'll be jobs for people and a new chance for this side of the valley. The bad news is that it will be high on Placer Gulch, at your old place, and by the time they're through, there won't be much left of it. Let's borrow a camera and take pictures before the place is changed and gone."

They were too late. A week went by, and another, and by the time they borrowed the camera and went up the gulch, earthmovers had gone up from the bottom and down from the top and wiped out the Coleman cabin, the yard, and the road. Mama's hideaway cave had been uncovered and blasted open, so that it gaped like a looted room. Only the Rubano cabin on the other side of the gulch had been spared. Tessie had been away, helping one of her daughters with a baby, and when she returned, the view across the gulch had been changed forever. At the top of the road was the graveyard. Clara, Tessie Rubano, Katy, and her sister Jean went up the next day to ask the engineer to save it. "If you would move the road over just a few yards—"

"Lady, I seen the grave markers"—he looked scornfully at the combination of bricks, name-scratched stones, cuts of wooden shoring beams with numbers and names burned on—"but the head office looked and this place wasn't registered nowhere as a graveyard site, so we've got orders to go through it."

"Give us a day to—"

"Sure. We ain't scheduled to do this until next week."

They called the head office, and an executive said a man would be sent out and some adjustment made. Andy had found a county statute that said if nine or more graves were on a site and/or three or more families were represented, the place had the legal standing of a graveyard. There were fifteen graves representing nine families. But during the night the earthmovers had gone in, and when Clara and Andy went up to take measurements and survey the site, it had been erased. The graveyard was now a turnaround for the ore trucks going into the refinery.

Up at the Bogards' she told Alice, "I couldn't even picture it the way it used to be. None of the landmarks were left."

Alice stared at Clara. "What was your maiden name?"

"Coleman."

"Was your father an assayer? Was he a difficult man?"

"He was an assayer, but not difficult, impossible."

"I think Carl's dad knew him."

Grandfather Bogard did indeed remember Winston Coleman and Marlena. He had done some prospecting around the gulch and he even had a few pictures from those days. "May I see them?"

They began working their way through the collection. There were pictures of the classes from Callan School, and in one of them, Clara saw herself standing grimly in a faded dress with a torn collar. She was looking straight out. Clara didn't remember the dress or the day, but she was surprised at the coolness, the expressionlessness, in the girl's face. She almost said, "That was the year after the Knowing."

Later, Andy said, "I never had a home place. Bad as yours was, there are links, memories. It makes you a person, not just a floating mass. I envied you and Alice up to the snoot in pictures."

"Don't you have any family pictures?"

"None. Arlo traveled light, and pictures identify people, and identity is no good for a con man. For me it'll have to begin here, pictures and identity. I've been doing more and more pri-

87

vate work and in a year or two I think I'll be able to leave the county and go on my own. Then you can take my picture and put it in an album."

"Why wait? I'll borrow the Bogards' camera."

The pictures showed Andy in front of their cabin, then on the main street in front of the bank. He wore his only white shirt and tie. Clara posed in front of Gold Flume's schoolhouse and then standing in the shade of the porch. A passerby took the pictures of them standing together in front of the church. Clara's face had a drawn, abstracted look, and there were shadows under her eyes. Alice Bogard had said that many pregnant women had that drawn look and those shadows.

10

*T*he people building the refinery began to come. Architects and engineers and their families filled the hotel and the better houses in Gold Flume. Construction workers parked trailers on the flats, brick masons and heavy equipment operators, steel and cement workers came. Aureole drew some of them, but many set up in Gold Flume and Callan, and the towns stirred, woke, and stretched. In Bluebank someone reopened the old grocery store and swept the corners for rat droppings. The Gold Flume bank got itself a new facade. The county library brought a branch to the deserted feed store.

Then, two Aureole men, veterans, brought a group of investors to town with plans for building a small ski area. They had bought up the west and south faces of Bad Axe Mountain and the west and north sides of Hurrah. South of town, the mountains stepped back and the valley widened, and just at that opening, a sunny but windy funnel, the builders hoped to place their parking lots and a big lodge. Andy was asked to do the survey for the area, mountainsides and plain. After the survey the planners asked him to stay on because of his knowledge of the miniclimates of both those slopes. He quit his job at the county and began to work on the locations of lifts and tows, placing them to take best advantage of late light and be out of the higher winds. "We'll be rich soon," he declared importantly to Clara. "We're going to buy this cabin," and he watched her face go stark before he began to laugh.

The population of Gold Flume had almost doubled, with ski area planners and refinery people, but the new people had no plans to stay and they didn't care about the mountains or the town; they had come from similar jobs in Stowe and Alta, and from Texas and Oklahoma, and they would be gone as soon as their parts of the projects were finished. Unlike Town people, they didn't try to keep their habits or their hungers secret, having no reputations to maintain. Their children filled, then overwhelmed, the valley schools. Clara's classes had ten more children, then eighteen, then twenty-six, coming in through the school year. The pressure forced Aureole to speed up its plans for a consolidated district. After the Christmas holidays, all the ninth to twelfth grades in the valley were to move to the new Aureole High School, but Clara would still be teaching in an overcrowded room.

To the Town children, the refinery students seemed the most worldly-wise and sophisticated of beings. The boys wore black, studded leather jackets, and chains instead of belts. Their hair was plastered to their heads and they chewed gum continually, milling away like cattle. Clara classed it with snuff and forbade it and had to withstand their glowering doom-looks and muttered curses. The boys were insolent and arrogant, the girls louder and more strident than Gold Flume girls, aggressive in their dress and gestures. In those days a Ranch child might still come to school on horseback; the older refinery boys rode motorcycles, which they gunned for long minutes before they rotated their black-gauntleted wrists and sped away, huddling girls glued to their backs.

Before Clara's pregnancy began to show, she wrote the required letter to the school board informing them. The county rule said that no teacher could be in the classroom after the fourth month of a pregnancy. The superintendent called the drugstore—the Percivals had no phone—and left the message that her letter would not be officially received. " 'We do not think your condition is sufficiently advanced.' Your condition won't be sufficiently advanced until the end of the school year. The Gold Flume board must have told the super they wanted you to stay. You suit the town, and they know it." Clara and Andy were doing the dishes, standing side by side at the sink.

"Does the town suit you?" she asked, and turned to him and put her wet hands on his shoulders.

He laughed. "It does, yes, it does."

They knew Gold Flume and its people fairly well by now— they knew who was dependable, who was neighborly, who drank in secret, who was cheating on a husband and who on a wife. They knew which neighbors would prosper with the new boom and which would stay as they were. Some of what Clara knew came from children who were too young to know which truths were to be guarded and which were not. They came to her with the daily talk she couldn't stem, and held it up to her as one would tell a story. "Daddy was drunk again and he puked all over.

Mama said with all the money it took he should try harder to keep it down." "Mattie shot a cougar in our chicken run last night but when she went to see, it was Bud French. She said, 'I'm sorry, Mr. French, I thought you were a cougar.' "

Andy saw a notice posted for a lease with option on the Steadman place. It was a homestead on what had once been a quarter section, a mile beyond the northwest edge of town. The county had built a road up and over Jackass Pass and the road had cut the original tract in two parts. The house and twelve acres were on the western side. Half the Ute ran there under the name of Jackass Creek. Andy and Clara drove up to the ranch immediately, expecting a crowd of prospective buyers. There were none. Although he had never met Andy and Clara, John Steadman knew about them. He sat them down and wound away the afternoon telling them about homesteading days and his grandparents. At dusk they talked business and by dark Clara and Andy had changed status. It delighted Clara that the criminal's son and the fantast's daughter were going to have a home, to be a family, to live in a place and belong to it.

Outside, at the car, she said, "It's two miles from the school and I can walk that." When no acknowledgment came, she glanced over at Andy, who was standing at the back, fussing with something in the trunk. "Andy?" He let down the lid and in the light from the window, she saw the glint of tears.

On the afternoon they were to move, an icy rain was falling and it was perilous underfoot. Andy strung a rope from the cabin door to the truck they had rented and Clara clung to it as she moved what things they had from the cabin.

"There may be more storm coming," he said. "Let's wait till things clear."

"Nothing doing. I've waited eleven years to have a home and I don't want to wait one more day."

"The truck may not make it if this gets deep—"

"That's why we should go *now*. There is a big fireplace up there and we have wood ready."

They were both carrying their table when a blue government car pulled up beside the truck. A man in uniform stepped out and came over. "Andrew Percival?"

"Yes."

The coat had no insignia. Clara looked at the car. Under U.S. GOVERNMENT she read DEPARTMENT OF CORRECTIONS and under that, in small, white letters, PROBATION AND PAROLE. Andy had seen it, too. "Damn," he muttered, "it's Arlo."

They put down the table. He turned to the officer. "We're getting moved—"

"If you could spare a minute, sir."

Andy gave Clara a helpless look. One or two people had gone past, walking gingerly because of the slippery street, but they would notice the government car and read its printing. The man must have asked directions at one or two places. Town would know all about this in an hour, giving the extra time because of the weather. Clara watched Andy sigh, lower his head, wrestle with acceptance, achieve it, and pick up his end of the table. "Let us get this under the tarp." Then they all went back into the cabin.

Arlo had been selling land he didn't own for the exploration of minerals it didn't contain to men contemplating retirement from the Chicago Police Force. "Cops are as gullible as anyone else," the officer said, and shrugged. "They had never been out of Chicago. They didn't have the money to come out here and see for themselves, so they relied on the portfolio of pictures and reports your father showed them."

"What land was he selling?"

"Ranch sites with mountain backgrounds so the buyers could run stock and mine for whatever minerals they wanted."

"And orchards for their wives to harvest?"

"Why not?"

"Bad land, desert land, and no water?"

"None. None at all."

They sat then, Andy glumly, Clara wanting to laugh a little at the victims' gullibility, that no one had thought to send someone out to check the site. At last Andy said, "Parole, right?"

"He's just done two years of a three to seven on four counts of fraud. He never used the mails, but it was interstate, so the jurisdiction was ours. If we can't parole him, he'll have to do the full fall."

"Damn!" Andy ground his fist against his mouth. "Damn him! I won't sign it. I won't take him. Send him C.O.D. to the con man's museum; the man must be the oldest crook in the system."

The officer waited patiently while Andy raged. Clara thought he must have been through this many times, waiting out relatives' angers. When Andy finally turned to her, Clara said, "Let's invite this officer to join us for some coffee. We'll have a room for Arlo now. He won't be a bother. If we don't sign for him, his imprisonment would be our sentence, not the government's."

Andy seethed some more, then he quieted, and finally he signed. Arlo Percival became their responsibility, like the house. Their triumphal afternoon ended in sulk and accusation. When they finally got the truck loaded and drove up to the Steadman house, their house, night had come.

"He's an old man now," Clara said. "Maybe he's slowed down and then he'll be a help with the baby and maybe he could work around the school."

"Doing what, buying secrets from the kids? Why doesn't he die and leave us alone?"

"You don't mean that. . . ."

He faced her and his look cowed her. "You still think he's a sweet old man with a little peccadillo, a lovable scamp who stumbles now and then. He's a criminal, a menace. He would take my savings and yours, take this house, use our reputations, convert everything to cash and be gone without a backward glance."

"We can't let him rot in prison."

They unloaded the truck in silence and then Andy said, "I can't stay here. . . . I'll call you," and left in the car. Instead of the celebration they had planned, Clara spent the night unpacking alone.

Andy was gone for two days. He called her from Aureole, wretched and reconciled. "He hasn't done it to you yet; I'd forgotten that. He hasn't taken your hope, your money, your name, and blown them away and laughed at you for running after the shreds. You'll learn, that's all."

The old man got off the early train and stood on the platform surveying the town. He turned around all the way, taking all of it in. Andy didn't greet him.

"Hello, Dad," Clara said. She thought he looked smaller but jaunty, prison-dapper in his tight, government-made suit. The prison haircut was a shave halfway up his head and it had destroyed the iron-gray mane she had admired at the hospital.

"Hello, Daughter. Is there a new generation on the way?" And he smiled that incandescent smile that included her among the vast joys he knew. She felt suddenly understood, approved of, wrapped in his sympathy.

Beside her, Andy muttered, "Jesus!"

"You look well fed," Clara said.

He nodded complacently. "I am. The federal places are inspected, you know. They have to give you so much air, so much exercise, balanced diet—" He took out a sheaf of papers. "You'll need to sign this, a receipt for me, and send it in. They do have a post office in this burg, I hope. I'll need a few bucks, fifty'd get me to Ocala—that's in Florida. I've got a business opportunity waiting for me down there. The Feds won't check on me right after you've sent this in, and when they get around to it, tell them the truth. I blew. If they pick me up down there, it'll be a federal slammer, not one of those Florida chain-gang county places. Colorado'll never extradite." Then he gave a self-satisfied nod.

"When will you be leaving?" Andy said with a piercing look at Clara, who had worked hard to make a room livable for Arlo.

"Tomorrow's train." He turned to Clara. "Daughter, you're getting lovelier every day."

If Clara had hoped for the old man's look of awe at their luck, their success or prosperity, she was to be disappointed. She had taken quick, covert looks at him as they started up the Jackass Pass road, a turn and then two others, coming into the little meadow where the house stood. It was late morning; a raw mist was beginning to gather in the valley. The first snows had come in September. Then they had had the long sweetness of Indian summer. She thought, It might snow again, maybe tonight. She pointed to the greater portion of the meadow and began to explain to Arlo that the Steadmans had sold the land on the far side of the road to a developer and that soon houses would be going up there, and a paved road.

"Who would live out here?" he murmured, looking blankly and then shrugging.

They went into the house. It was ranch style, a log house chinked with mortar. It had a big, central living room with other rooms added as the homesteader's family enlarged, fanning off from the original rectangle to give it a cruciform shape. Arlo made no comments. He had one bag, which Andy pointedly let him carry.

Andy's anger was chilling the air. Clara showed her father-in-law how the Steadmans had made the adjustments that allowed more light into the heart of the house. He looked, making no comment but seemingly oblivious to the mood his son was creating. After a short conversation with Clara about dinner, Andy went into his workroom. Clara took Arlo to the room she had prepared.

"The boy's eager to see my back," Arlo said.

Clara saw that dissembling wouldn't help. "The two of you are very different, and there's Andy's past," she said.

"Different is right." Arlo snorted. "I wouldn't stay in a house like this in a burg like this fifteen minutes unless it was to meet a mark." Against all reason, Clara found herself disappointed. He went on. "Trust the Cluck to get a house miles from anywhere and miles from anywhere you can *get* anywhere." He looked at Clara and shook his head. "When I was younger, I thought people got stuck in places like this. I never thought anyone would choose them. Lately it's come to me that people really are different, I mean beyond the different lies they tell themselves." And there was that smile, playful, intimate. "I like action," he said. "I like to go places and do things. I skate on thin ice. Now and then I fall in. So what?" He gestured toward Andy's workroom. "Gutless in there never wanted to be anything but safe. You"—and he winked at Clara—"you're a little different."

She felt the embarrassment of someone who has been caught at a forbidden act. She wanted to defend Andy, but a defense would dignify Arlo's description of him. She faced him with what she hoped was a pleasant look and said, "You may not like the hotel's location or its staff, but you did need someplace to go." There was no chastening, not even a wavering of his glance, only a great laugh.

"Not romantic, not a bit. Realistic, that's you, Daughter. You'd be a hard mark."

"Could you get to me, though?"

"Sure, anyone can be gotten to. Yours is probably helping folks, widows and orphans. You're trying hard because I'm kin now, and kin's important to you, too, but you'll check the house after I'm gone to see there's nothing stolen."

"Honesty is the best policy," Clara said, beginning to enjoy herself.

He laughed again. "Good God, Daughter, *nobody* believes that!"

Arlo had disappeared the next morning, even before Andy had filled out the affidavit and the paperwork on his parole. "Damn him! This is one more time he's made me lie for him, given me lines to read and marks to con for him!"

Andy grieved for two days and Clara watched him suffer. "Stop being sad," she said. "*He's* not. The prison people know what he is—you're the only one hurting, the only one who shouldn't be."

"What do you want me to do?"

"Take me out for a fancy meal at the new place in Aureole. Let's show them all!"

"Show them what?"

"Show them that sudden wealth can turn our heads and make us cave in to all the materialism we say we hate."

11

*M*ore and more students came. They filled all the chairs Clara put between the rows at the back of the room, but despite the crowding, she felt ever more isolated as a teacher. In the world outside, new methods were being developed, new materials coming into use. Gold Flume School had been set adrift with Clara as its only guide. Where was the world going? Andy surprised her with a subscription to a teachers' magazine, and she could barely read the articles without a pang of envy for what those teachers took for granted, and for the materials she saw advertised, the maps and numbering rods and abacus frames.

She began to think the class itself might fashion some of those things that would work even though they would be crude and even ugly.

It would be a job to make the numbering rods—they would have to measure, mark, cut, and finish upwards of four hundred cubes and rods. She gave the task to the older boys. Milvin French's brother Buster was still in school and idle. She could put him to work. Sulo Boda's brother, Cyril, was his age, and there were Orval Bordereau and Peter Tavistock.

The boys took up the work, and to Clara's astonishment, Cyril became the one they followed. The boy, barely literate after parts of seven years of school, listened to Clara's descriptions and seemed to wake from a sleep. Clara bought lengths of stock from the lumberyard in Aureole and gave them to the boys, and Cyril began to measure and then to cut carefully, allowing for kerf and the drift of the saw, clamping the stock together as Clara wouldn't have thought of doing.

She had expected Peter Tavistock to lead, his family being the social elite of the town. Sulo and Milvin, the school's principal bullies, had gone, and Peter was a big boy. He had joined the younger boys against the refinery group as she had predicted, but he was out of his element with tools. Cyril worked alone, asking help from no one and accepting it from no one. A rumor got around that Mrs. Percival was making baby blocks and Clara had to give a demonstration of what the rods and cubes were for.

Dr. Pratt visited the school one afternoon late in November. He was now one of three doctors in the valley. A shy, bookish man, he had come during the war. He had told Alice Bogard he was hoping to do some general medicine before he died of asthma. "He didn't die," Alice said, "so neither did Billy Bordereau fallen in the river. Before he came you would have had to use Doc Thompson, the vet, or neighbor women." Clara remembered Mama's dying and shivered. Dr. Pratt settled himself on one of the cramped benches and asked her how the children were behaving toward her now that the town knew of her pregnancy. Clara had not heard that word used in the valley. People said "in a condition" or "in the family way."

"It's been gradual, so no one noticed at first," Clara said. "The children began to hear rumors and then there was some sniggering and shame, but I began to talk about the baby and how I felt, and I've sent for some pictures of fetuses in various stages. I think as long as I'm going to be here and will be obviously pregnant, we might as well have a decent environment."

He grinned. "You are what I've been waiting for."

He described the girl he had just lost from a self-inflicted abortion, his third that year. The girl was fifteen. "You're going to know about it soon enough. When they're Gulch girls or people like the Frenches, Town shrugs and says, 'It's all they deserve.' This was one of the Hoven girls—you might have had her in your class."

Clara put her hand to her mouth. "Oh—she was sick—she was out sick."

"She was out infected and slowly bleeding to death. She hadn't told her family—they thought it was flu. I need a way to tell parents what's happening—we have to teach the children—" She was skeptical and he saw it. His voice gained urgency. "By the time they get to adolescence, there's too much in the way— yearning, myths, and nonsense. I want to come to the Christmas parents' meeting and tell the parents what I've seen and heard from their own children."

Clara sighed with relief. She had thought he wanted her to teach the parents, to stand in front of them and make a declaration. "I don't have all the parents at all the meetings," she said. "Some never come."

"We'll take anyone we can get," he said.

As she introduced Dr. Pratt and sat down, Clara wondered whether he would point to the Gold Flume teacher herself, vulnerable in her condition. She was suddenly frightened. What if the parents complained to the superintendent? She might be dismissed. Although she was only four months into her pregnancy, she was carrying big and, but for the convenience of the board, would have left the school a month ago. Willa Optegard had been removed after six years of service because of a pregnancy. The doctor's subject was sex, and the people of Gold Flume, conventional in little else, were deeply conventional in this.

The doctor went directly to his subject. He spoke candidly, using words many people in Gold Flume had never spoken, even in private, of infections, botched abortions, suicide. Clara saw the stir of bodies in the small chairs and heard boots scraping on the wooden floor, as Gold Flume made the motions of its discomfort. Their faces showed nothing. It wasn't facts that made everyone uncomfortable. Gossip about girls getting caught had gone on for years. No young woman who died in the valley was ever said to have died of anything but fever and never believed to have died of anything but complications of pregnancy. The problem was the doctor's vocabulary, the words denoting body parts and functions, in public, in mixed company. He went on as though he hadn't noticed their shifting and the scrape of work boots. He talked about the boys, too, about suicides done out of fear and ignorance. The restlessness increased. People coughed and cleared their throats. Some were pale. He spoke about the need for educating the children about the nature and function of their bodies. When he finished there was dead silence.

It occurred to Clara then that she had the power to open these people to some of their own hypocrisy. Their discomfort might be genuine, but many people were hiding ugly secrets. She knew who drank in secret, who beat his children beyond what even Town felt was right, who took his daughters or allowed his sons to take them. This room, crossed with belligerent stares, was holding its pride before it like a shield. Behind it was fear. She spoke. "The sad thing I see is that children are learning the facts of life from other children, spreading the ignorance even wider." Someone muttered, "Who'll tell all this to the Frenches?" and there was release in a wave of nervous laughter.

The Frenches never came to parents' meetings or church. They took no part in Gold Flume. The Bodas and the other Gulch people lived too far away; the Legrands attended sporadically. The afternoon of the meeting she had found Frances Legrand and Buster French hip deep in one another behind the boys' privy. Both of them were fifteen and should have been in the high school in Aureole, but they had been kept back so many times that their education would end for them at sixteen without their ever having left Gold Flume School.

She had talked with Frances after school. The girl, sullen and angry, was defensive of what she called being In Love. Love. She had been lying on hard ground—only Buster had had a soft bed—and they must have gone at it quickly, furtively, without a tender touch or a stroking hand or a whispered word, eye into eye.

"It ain't a sin—Buster's going to marry me."

"I don't say it's a sin, but I say it's foolish. How can Buster marry you? He has no job. You've grown up at the Frenches'. Do you want to move in there?"

Frances looked up at Clara with the mourning, desperate look of children unready for growing up. "He *has* to marry me. He says we'll go to Denver, and until then, he'll get on at the refinery."

Clara couldn't imagine any sensible employer hiring Buster to handle expensive equipment. Frances was brighter than Buster; what did she see in him?

"Frances, Buster drinks. If you get pregnant, you won't be able to stay in school. Is the sex that good?" Frances looked at Clara in amazement and then shook her head, slowly. "Why do it then?"

"Buster wants it. He *needs* it. Men need it, and Buster chose me."

Clara didn't have the heart to say, "Over whom?"

Clara looked at a rancher near her, whose jaw was working with disapproval. She looked down the row at other ranchers and at the wives, stolid and silent beside their men. Which of them had been in Frances's fix a few years before and had forgotten it or had lied it away?

Dr. Pratt was still arguing earnestly, intently, with Bud Bordereau and the Ditmarses. Clara agreed that there should be some simple information given the children, but how could a curriculum act on a mind like Frances's, like Buster's? Could any teaching bridge the jealousy, lust, frolic, yearning of those years, or the yearning to stay in ignorance that girls like Frances had? Arithmetic was hurled against the walls of their resistance, Clara wrangled English. How could she touch spirits as different as Buster's, Orval's, Cyril Boda's? Lucinda Tavistock was shy and sensitive; her arrogant and angry brother, Peter, would defend against words aimed at his fears and needs. Then there were the refinery children, who knew all the facts and functions and names with a crude heartlessness she found embarrassing. She wondered how she herself would have responded to the subject when she was their age, hardened against the sacrifices and surrenders that love is. She thought, At that age they want justice, not mercy, and they don't know how to surrender without abjectness.

She wanted to try to make the parents remember their own school days. Weren't teaching and learning like a war? For hours or days, students are either allies or enemies. The campaign often goes slack and everyone is mired down in facts. What a struggle it is to awaken feeling, to get the students to see into the lives and motives of the historical figures they studied, to grasp the harmonies of arithmetic and its beauty, to understand the ideas of the great writers. She could say none of this to the parents, so she sat and listened to Dr. Pratt and then drifted off into a fantasy. Her child would know . . .

After the meeting she walked home in the dark. Andy was worried about her falling and made her take a powerful flashlight, but she rarely used it. She knew he was frightened about this baby. She had felt the fear first as reserve, then withdrawal. Perhaps he was repelled by her morning sickness, her drawn face. When she asked him if that was true, he said, "God, no, it's fear. I don't want to be a father, or to lose you. That's shameful, isn't it, small," and he shook his head. "If you talked about this, the words would come out in a little buzzing voice, like an insect, because it's a little, buzzing thing."

The December night was cold but not windy. There would soon be more snow, but for the moment the winter's long shackle had loosened. She stopped at the first overlook, a little pull-off on the Jackass Pass road, and looked down at the town, now mostly dark. She was still hearing Andy as he spoke slowly. "It was so hard to take off my clothes in front of you that first time. I was showing you a naked man, but that naked man was *me*—knock-knees and my skinny polio leg. The face had been bad enough, I thought. Then there was Arlo. I told you about him. I got the courage to do that, too."

She had understood. "We're going to be a family and we'll have the courage to do that, too."

"Yes," he murmured, "I guess we will."

The months passed but the board made no attempt to remove Clara from her position. A few parents looked askance, but the children were used to the pregnancy and seemed eager for the birth of the baby. Even the bullies accorded her a rough gallantry when she asked for help.

On May 29, school ended and Andy left Gold Flume for a convention in Denver. His college friends would be there and

105

he could get some relief from feeling closed away in a valley while the rest of the world grew and changed. He had offered to stay behind, but she knew he was tired of her baby plans and preoccupations.

Clara had just lowered her hand from saying good-bye when she felt the first small fluttering cramp of labor, which she took to be the baby's moving. She took up the ladder and began to caulk the corners where the roof met the chimney. The cramp came again. She thought of a possible reason, dismissed it, and went back to caulking the roof. When the intervals became shorter, she stopped work, got down, and called Dr. Pratt. Andy had taken the car and the doctor told her he would come and drive her to the clinic in Aureole. When he arrived and examined Clara, he said they wouldn't make it. Clara remembered that Alice Bogard came to town on Saturdays, so Pratt called the drugstore. The pharmacist's wife found Alice and both of them came up and helped deliver a healthy, full-term baby. By the time Andy reached Denver, he was the father of a daughter.

Clara had seen babies born in Spanish Town and had long night-thoughts about Mama bearing hers in the dank, unheated cabin with no water. But it wasn't until she lay with the tiny girl in her arms that relief of the old terror she had kept at bay with work and denial overwhelmed her and she began to tremble and sob.

"Women get emotional at these times," Dr. Pratt said, but Alice, who knew something of Clara's past, silently went over and held her while the trembling spread itself and then spent itself and diffused into triumph, and then into sleep.

When Andy called that evening, the party line all picked up on Percivals' ring and cheered him with the news. Alice told Andy she would stay with Clara. "The party line's still talking to him, no doubt, even though I excused myself and hung up." She chuckled. "They'll fill him in on all the details. Can I help you stand? You might want to clean up a little."

"I don't want this baby to grow up the way I did," Clara murmured as though she had not been listening.

Alice nodded. "There's little chance of that." Her tone was matter-of-fact, but her eyes were serious.

Clara was murmuring, "She won't be demeaned or laughed at. Her clothes won't shame her. Her father's scorn won't humiliate her. If she's got a love of learning, she'll be encouraged, and when she goes to college, it won't be as a beggar or starving."

Alice's older children were in high school. She smiled at Clara and helped her up. "It's a healthy baby," she said. "It's a good start."

Andy came back the next day. "I couldn't stay down there. I couldn't pay attention to anything. I'll try next year, maybe, but this is what I need to be listening to now."

Julia Percival had begun to cry.

12

*W*hen Clara started back to school, she took Julia with her, and when the baby cried, Clara left the class to Orval Bordereau and went out in the sunny backyard, and facing the mine-scarred heap of Prospector Mountain, nursed and changed her.

Frances Legrand was showing. A little belly, high and firm, was beginning underneath the light dresses she wore.

"Do you know you are going to have a baby?" Clara had kept her after school on a pretext.

Frances muttered something.

Clara continued closing the windows and lowering the blinds. She listened to the vagueness and passivity in Frances's voice and wanted to shake the girl. "Does your mother talk to you about this?"

"She don't know."

"Can't she see?"

"She don't look."

"You know the rule, Frances; when you get noticed, you'll have to leave."

Frances had started to cry. "I want to stay in school."

Clara drummed her fingers. Frances liked to read, and school meant order, limits, a measure of peace. "I'll keep you here as long as I can. What about Buster?" Buster was still registered as a student, but he never came. At fifteen, he was free to leave.

"We'll be married as soon as people say I have to go." Then she dried her eyes, confident that with Clara's support, everything would be solved.

Clara had no heart to wake her up. "You can't stay in school and be married," she said.

Frances gave her a penetrating look, and Clara felt her face go hot. She had been in the classroom and she had been pregnant. She kept her own baby in the schoolroom every day.

"It's the rule," Clara protested.

Frances faced her with all the courage and self-delusion of her fifteen years. "I'll wait till I can't be here no more and then Buster and me'll get married and then he'll get on at the refinery. That's good money and we'll get us a trailer like them refinery people's got."

Buster would be sixteen with a wife and baby and no one who knew him would hire him, and he had no friends. There was no use arguing with Frances. Clara took a breath and said, "Winter's coming and you'll want to be wearing big sweaters and working jackets. Shut Buster's mouth. Tell people you're overeating. I won't notice anything, but don't wear those tight dresses."

"I get sick mornings," Frances said.

"It stands to reason," Clara answered, "overeating the way you do."

When the refinery people had started to come, Clara petitioned the county school board for a new school. The board said it would give her temporary buildings, but when the ski area began to grow and hotels and shops opened, the school board voted a new building. That winter, Clara went to Aureole three times for meetings with the architects who were designing it. They were not eager to hear from her, but she knew she would feel responsible if the building lacked convenience and access because she hadn't been there to speak of those things. Then, the board informed her officially that she was to be the new school's principal. There was to be a room for each class, six grades instead of eight, with six teachers and an office and a telephone and a gymnasium-auditorium with equipment for sports and plays. There would be inside bathrooms and running water. There would be closets for storing equipment. There would be privacy, warmth in winter, a janitor, and paving against the dust of spring and fall and the mud and slush of the colder months. Above all there would be company, other teachers, younger teachers who would know all the ways of doing things she could only read about. Had the paradox she had struggled with in teachers college been resolved? Would the new generation of educators be able to reconcile the ideas of child as savage with child as angel? Were there new ways to aid memory and strengthen concentration, link idea with action, sublimate cruelty?

When Clara next saw Alice Bogard and described it all, Alice clapped her hands, laughing. "Carl's got a new system for spraying the stock and he isn't a butt-patch to you for excitement. Go look at yourself in the mirror, Mrs. Christmas Morning!"

———

Frances Legrand carried high and small and she was in the eighth month before she drew stares when her loose shirts gaped open. One day in February, Clara was in Aureole shopping between snows. Her cart was loaded. She saw Dorothy Tavistock with a full cart moving purposefully down the aisle. It was too late to pretend not to have seen her. "How are you?" Clara said, and smiled.

Mrs. Tavistock pushed her cart past the question and came too close. "I've heard that there is a young woman at Gold Flume School who is in the condition. It comes of a poor example by the schoolmistress."

Clara's answer came without thought. "When I first became pregnant, I wrote to the school board and it chose not to receive my letter." As she heard herself, she was irritated for defending what needed no defense. "We don't allow pregnant *students* to remain in school." She had prepared this answer months before and hadn't had to use it until now. She smiled and added, "On the grounds, I suppose, that they know too much already."

Dorothy Tavistock moved on, and Clara knew she shouldn't have said what she did. Relations between them were strained, so it was silly to ruffle her. She had wanted to say, "You remind me of Squire Western's sister in *Tom Jones*," but thought better of it.

"What's put *you* off your feed?" Andy said, as she got in the car.

"Peter Tavistock's mother. The duchess of Gold Flume."

It was a week after that Clara was walking home, carrying a bag of books and Julia in a little papoose sling Andy had helped fashion. She was walking briskly in order to beat the dusk home. Another snow had fallen and drawn away, but the northern and eastern sides of the hills were still heaped with it. The abandoned mining road skirted the town and then petered out for the path Clara's own feet had made up the hill to the Jackass Pass road.

She had started up, parting with the road that sank away below her, a cindery, flat level with some rusted narrow-gauge rails where ore carts had once been loaded. She heard sounds she thought came from the deserted place, shouting, someone's cry. She thought the sound might really be coming from farther down the gully—sound travels unevenly in the mountains; rocks deflect it and an upslope wind might carry it from as far away as town. She went to the verge and looked down. There were people there, and in the almost-dusk, Clara saw Cyril Boda, Dalvin Moore, Frances, and two boys whose backs were to her but whom she knew. One turned a quarter profile—Peter Tavistock. It wasn't a group of young people, it was four boys and a girl. Frances was facing them, her hands in front of her, and she was in a half crouch, a stance of defense and terror. She was too ungainly to run. "Buster will get you for this!" They had begun to move in on her, rapt as cats.

They were so intent on Frances that they didn't hear Clara move down the shaly bank, even though she had Julia and her books and moved clumsily. It flashed through her mind that such clumsiness was uniquely female, a vulnerability that the boys sensed and were exploiting in Frances. She was coming to the group on its left flank, and she came on with a cheery pretense. "Hello, Frances, Peter; hello, Cyril, Dalvin; hello, John. Frances, it's a good thing I ran into you. If you don't mind leaving your friends for a few moments, there's something I need to discuss with you." Without stopping to receive an answer and still talking, Clara pulled Frances up, blocking the boys' view of her as she did so. Then she turned back to the boys, still standing dumbfounded in the positions they had been caught in. "Perhaps you shouldn't wait—this may take a while."

Frances was almost stumbling. Her hands were fisted with fear and rage.

"Frances—"

"Buster will kill them," she whispered vehemently.

"Buster will do nothing," Clara whispered back. "If you stay quiet, you can be out of the eighth grade by the time the baby comes. Get noticed and you'll be out of school and I won't be able to help. What were you doing up there?"

Now Frances was sulking. "They said they were going to take me to a cabin where Buster and me could live."

"You didn't really *believe* that, did you?"

"I thought if they could let us have the cabin we could live there and I wouldn't have to stay at Frenches' and we could be together."

They had come to the edge of town, which was losing itself in the dusk. "Listen to me," Clara said. "A thing has to make sense before you agree to it. Where would four boys get a cabin they had a right to give you? Why would they want to show it to you alone?"

"I only wanted—"

"Never let what *you* want stop you from thinking about what *they* want or what makes sense." It was all Clara could do not to shake Frances until she relinquished the passive, dreamlike dullness of teenage romantic surrender. Was Juliet so limp and milky? "I'm tired," Clara said, "and it's late. Don't let them try to get you alone again. Don't let them offer you a gold watch that's really brass or a promise to take you somewhere. Come on, I'll walk you home."

Frances shook her head. "No one's there, and they"—a backward toss of the head—"know it."

Clara followed the gesture. The boys were still there, staying back but following. "Keep walking." In her papoose case, Julia had begun to fuss. Clara said, "Here's the baby's pacifier—put it in her mouth."

They came to the town, the street before Main. Clara spotted Abner Matske, loading his truck. She put a hand on Frances's shoulder, guiding her to where the man stood. "Hello, Abner. Can you take us home? It's Steadman's place."

"Sure," he said, but he gave them a quizzical look. "School project," Clara explained. "It got late." When they pulled out Clara noticed the street was empty.

Frances stayed the night. Her people had no phone, she said, and she wouldn't be missed anyway.

The next day after school, Clara was on Main Street and stopped by Andy's office. He said he would take her home at five. She went to the drugstore and chatted with Sallie Austin, the pharmacist's wife, who was pregnant. "My future student," Clara said, and they laughed together.

As they stood talking, the school bus from Aureole came and pulled up in front of the drugstore, and the street was full for a moment. Then the students began to disperse by twos and threes up and down the street. Clara saw Peter Tavistock and with a sign to Sallie to watch Julia, she went out quickly and caught up with Peter, who was walking by himself.

"Peter—"

He stared at her. For a moment, she thought he might run. All she had to hold him with was interest and habit. She asked him about school and he warmed a little. Aureole High was interesting, he said. It was "departmental" with a homeroom and a choice of classes. Other students in small groups passed them, giving Peter questioning looks. "Are you on your way home?" He nodded. "Would you mind my walking with you?" He shrugged.

It was a cold afternoon, almost evening at this time of year. They kept their hands in their pockets, with the wind at their backs. Clara said, "Frances Legrand is a good girl. She's kind and generous and she believes the things people tell her. That's all right when the people are honest."

He murmured something that sounded like "She's pussy." Clara hoped she had heard him correctly. "No one is just anything," she said. "How would you like to be thought of as only what your penis does?" His reaction was all she could have wished. Shock. She had him. He had stopped walking and had to force himself to start again, trying for a swagger. She continued as though she hadn't noticed. "Did you ever hear the phrase 'Pick on someone your own size'? She's not your size, Peter, she's

114

your age, but she can't defend herself because she doesn't know how." He had started walking again, faster, dropping the pose of nonchalance. "She needs a brother," Clara said, working to keep up, "not another attacker."

"She's got brothers," he said.

"Do any of them look out for her?"

"They practically sell tickets."

"So you figure if no one values her, why should you?"

"Well, yeah. Why pick on me?"

They were almost to his house, crossing the bridge behind the depot. It occurred to Clara that the house had been built near the railroad but would be saved from the fumes and smoke because of the prevailing winds. All the smell and smoke went southward, over the town. "Why pick on you? Because you're bright and you have a future few other boys in this town will be able to have. You'll graduate Aureole High and I don't think any of the other boys will do that. You'll probably go on to college and they'll be stuck here and, I'm afraid, so will Frances. She's more than pussy and you're more than penis. Think about it."

They were at the fence and the complaining gate. Clara smiled at Peter and said good-bye, walking into a wind that brought tears. Back at the drugstore Sallie and Andy were chatting, and Julia was trying to walk.

A week later, Clara got a note from Mrs. Tavistock, who informed her that she would visit the school that Wednesday afternoon. The tone of the letter was command, not request, which made Clara smile. If the visit concerned Peter's sister, Lucinda, it would be very welcome. Lucinda was one of the brightest students Clara had ever known. It was a pity that Peter was Mrs. Tavistock's only interest. There was more to Lucinda than a good memory and a gift for connecting ideas. She had all the signs of a real love of learning, a hunger for the thing itself apart from grade or approval of the teacher, of fame or popularity. That love was rare, so rare, she wanted to say to Mrs. Tavistock, that we sometimes walk right past it without recognition.

When Dorothy Tavistock arrived, Clara was ready with a sheaf of Lucinda's papers. Clara opened it and handed one of the papers to the mother with a smile. "Lucinda's grades are excellent, which you already know, but they don't reflect all there is to measure about that girl. Her mind—"

Mrs. Tavistock cut Clara off immediately. "I'm not here to speak of my daughter, but of my son. You were seen accompanying him through town, lecturing him publicly in the street and all the way to his home."

"I walked him home, yes."

"He says you forced him to walk with you."

Clara was briefly annoyed, until the humor of the thing dawned on her. "How did I do that?"

"You had him by the arm, I assume."

"No, I didn't touch him at all."

"You were shaming him before the entire town."

"I had no idea that my walking a student home was a mark of shame. Most people would see it as a sign of regard."

"But you bullied and scolded him. He told me so."

"I did speak of his behavior. Since he's in high school, I couldn't call him into my office."

"His being in high school means that he is out of your jurisdiction."

"I hope Aureole High confers no special status or removes its students from contact with ordinary people."

"My son demands an apology."

"How do you see me doing that? Publicly? By letter? Any apology would involve a discussion of his behavior, which I found reprehensible, and about which I spoke to him. I would do so again and do so to anyone I saw misbehaving."

"I'm going to demand you be replaced as teacher and principal of Gold Flume School."

Clara tried for dignity and achieved a chilly sound she didn't know she had in her repertoire. "The board meets in Gold Flume and Aureole on alternate first Thursdays of each month."

Mrs. Tavistock left in a temper without asking what her son had done.

She told Andy about the visit. "What's the whalebone-stayed battlewagon up to now?" he asked. She hadn't told him about Frances or the boys, but her worry about Mrs. Tavistock brought it all out. He listened intently, then answered, "She hasn't got *you*, you've got her. If she tries anything, you can drop the word about her baby boy's doings."

"You don't understand. Parents have immense power in our schools. The whole system is based on trust and just the appearance of loss of that trust is enough to sink a teacher."

"The way I see it is this: At home one day, she'll ask the kid. She won't be wearing those tight corsets there, so some blood will get to her brain. That will enable her to figure she's got no case. Tell me about the new school."

"They start building in the spring," she said. "We move in the fall."

Mrs. Tavistock didn't pursue the matter. The board meeting came and went and the spring parents' meeting took place without her. By then the plans for the new school were available and people saw what it would look like and were impressed with its size and features.

But Clara's heart sank when she looked at the architect's drawings. There was neither the welcoming character of the present schoolhouse, nor the dignity and loftiness of Callan School. Its tan tiles were elementary school generic, as though Gold Flume were interchangeable with any school in Denver, Chicago, or Boca Raton, Florida.

But Clara visited the school every week through the spring and summer as it went up beside the old schoolhouse, which was due to be demolished. Foundations were dug, cement and rebars placed, framing, inner walls, and windows came. The architect visited the site and Clara begged him to use the warm, native stone of Callan School. He refused, and the garish tan tile went on instead. "Friendly spaces," he said, and the school ended up looking like a store or an office.

In June, Frances Legrand fell or was pushed out of a moving car Buster French was driving and had her baby at 4:00 A.M. on a shoulder of road between Bluebank and Callan. Someone took her family to pick her up. Clara, out of school for the summer and busy with the construction and her own second pregnancy, didn't hear about it for a week, by which time Frances was out of danger. Two weeks later, the girl went walking with the baby, Lorus, in Gold Flume. She held him like a shield as she went, the way she had held her books in front of her narrow chest. She was holding him that way when she and Buster were married in Pastor Frailey's parlor. Frances's aunt was witness. The Frenches never went anywhere in Gold Flume but its grocery and its saloons.

13

*T*hree teachers had been hired. Dean had a large family, settling in Gold Flume; Lorraine was a spinster, whose move was like a retirement; Anna was in her first position out of teacher training. Clara had hoped for more spirited people. Only Anna had any glow. None had expected that Principal C. Percival would be a woman.

In August they got the classrooms ready, selected furniture, and ordered supplies. Clara's excitement caught and overwhelmed even the stodgy older woman and everyone opened out in her eagerness. The long hall was turned into a gallery in which Clara ordered furring at three levels and chalkboards at three levels for messages and the paragraph autobiographies the older children would write for the younger. She put up her yard-stick and its poster: ONE YARD: 1,760 OF THESE MAKE UP ONE MILE. She put up her poster showing one hundred dots, one thousand dots, one million dots. She showed the compass points and the school's aspect, sunrise and sunset points at the solstices, and cutouts of the pint, quart, gallon, and liter. She made a place for a word of the week, a saying of the week.

Clara had continued to correspond with the children she had taught in Spanish Town at San Pablo, and to them she poured out all her joy about the new school.

The new term began. There were forty-three in three combined classes. There was a school office with a secretary, and Clara's own office. She had closets for storage, a workroom; there was a library, and she would be able to fill it with books the children could borrow.

The secretary was a Bordereau cousin, a young widow still bleak about the eyes and slow to warm to the children, knowing they would grow up and leave. "She's efficient, anyway," Clara told Andy, "and the first- and second-grade teacher is a jewel."

September went into October unseasonably warm. Rain fell, the first rain after August in memory. So strange was the heat wave that people were dusting off the talk about atomic energy having changed the weather. One noontime the secretary came into the workroom, where Clara was planning class trips, and said that Cyril Boda was in trouble again, fighting. Clara went to the front desk and there he stood, blood pouring from his nose. He was pale, sweating, and disheveled. "Cyril—" He looked up at her, a familiar look of incredulity and awe. Cyril was ill, very ill indeed. Clara had moved close to him before she thought to wonder what might be ailing him or to worry because of her pregnancy. "Cyril—" He fell into her arms.

He was feverish and foul-smelling. He said, "I wasn't fighting, Mrs.—" and then he was out. Clara didn't remember shouting.

They called Dr. Pratt. He told them he thought it was typhoid fever and that Cyril was too sick to be taken home. The family had no money for the hospital in Aureole. He began to call around and Lennice Janes said they would nurse Cyril at their house. Pratt waved a hand at the office. "And we're going to have to clean up everything in here and watch everyone with whom he had contact."

The health department came from Aureole and tested and gave inoculations. People worried; rumors flew back and forth, and some came down with wild and vague complaints, stomachaches and headaches and rashes. Clara stopped in at Janeses' and saw Cyril, and found him improved. With penicillin, the long course of the illness had been drastically cut. Cyril admitted he had felt ill for a week before collapsing at the office.

"Why didn't you tell anyone?"

He stared at her. His father would have beaten him for being lazy. Dr. Pratt rode up Chinaman's Creek to Bodas' with three health officers and they must have talked long and hard because the old man came down to Janeses' with a smoked haunch of antelope, a bushel of his wife's dried apples, and later, a quilt she had made.

In Aureole for the weekly shopping, Clara met Lennice Janes and they stopped to talk in the aisle. "Doc wants him to stay another week or two because he's still so weak."

"How is he as a patient?"

"Fine as a patient, not real good as a guest. He puts me off some."

"He's not rude to you—"

"Oh, no, but there are things folks say when favors are done for them, you know, a word or two to show the favor is appreciated. I go into his room mornings with a tray. Anyone else would say good morning and thank you. He never does. Even his friend has trouble with that."

"Friend? What friend?" Clara asked. Cyril had always seemed to be a loner.

"You had him, the Tavistock boy, Peter."

"Peter?"

Clara hadn't seen the two together except for the single time they were circling Frances. It amazed her even more that Peter had enough consideration to visit any sick person.

"Yes, it's Peter," Lennice said. "He comes almost every day. He gets off the school bus and comes right over. Mostly, they just sit, the two of them, but lately Peter's been teaching Cyril to play chess." She smiled at Clara's surprise. "Yes, he comes and stays for an hour—it would be hard for me to sit that long without talking. Cyril misses him when he doesn't come—don't tell me how, but I know it."

Then they nodded over their shopping baskets and walked on, but Clara reported it to Andy in wonder.

He grinned. "Ma Tavistock probably doesn't know her baby boy is visiting the likes of Cyril every day. I heard Sulo pulled a gun on the last health officer up there."

After school on Monday, Clara walked down into town and stopped at Janeses'.

Lennice came to the door, wiping her hands on her apron. "He's up with Cyril now, but he'll be leaving soon. I know you're dying of curiosity." They went into Lennice's kitchen for coffee and sat for a while, talking. They got up when they heard Peter on the stairs.

Clara was standing behind Lennice and Peter stopped halfway down the narrow stairway, seeing her there. "Do you want me to walk you home again?" Clara asked. He flinched. "It's all right, Peter. I know you complained to your mother."

"I shouldn't have done that." His tone was quiet, the words without drama or bravado.

"You're a good friend to Cyril when no one else has been."

"I wasn't at first," Peter said. "I am now."

"How did that happen?" Clara's tone was sympathetic. Peter relaxed.

"The things you said."

"I didn't say anything about Cyril."

"I know," he said. He had come down to the last step and his foot was dangling over the edge, but he didn't want to lose the height. "Cyril really likes Frances, but he doesn't know how to be with girls. I just wanted a feel. I knew it was different for him, that what I was doing wasn't the same thing he was doing, even though it looked like it." He was struggling with describing a complex emotion—a thing he had never attempted before. "You said she was a real person, and I thought if *she* was real, so was *he*." He was rubbing the banister beside him in his discomfort, a child's gesture. Clara was at the bottom and Peter didn't want to come any closer. They were conscious of the silence. Lennice had gone back to the kitchen. Peter said, "I hung out with Cyril to get other people's goat. Then you said that stuff, so I came over here, once. I guess you'd say I saw him and he saw me." He was trying so hard that there were lines in his face that wouldn't be there again for another thirty years, until effort and disbelief had become familiar to him. "That never happened to me before. He's hard to figure and hard to know, but we're *friends*. Yeah—I'm teaching him chess."

"I know. You've done him a lot of good."

"Yes," Peter said, "I have." His words acknowledged the fact without falsity or pride. Clara contemplated kissing him and let the mood pass.

The fall that year was fine and long with a snapping frost that gave tang to the rose hips. They heard elk trumpeting and had weeks of the rifle-shot impact of the clash of rutting mountain goats. Later there were the real shot sounds of hunters taking to the hills and there was the month-long influx of sportsmen that had held the bank, grocery, and dry-goods store together through the rest of the year.

Clara delivered Joseph in a break between April snows, in Aureole's new hospital. Faye Matske would take care of the children while Clara was in school. Andy had gone into an office on the new bank building's second floor. His survey clients had doubled, and he wasn't dependent on the ski area anymore. "I'm where I always wanted to be," he said, "my own boss, and getting smarter, and I can still pick mushrooms." There seemed to be less time for that. The children were growing; the town was growing, too.

In bed in the dark, they talked about their days. They were good days, mostly quiet, mostly peaceful, but they were moving more quickly, picking up speed. The ski area was bringing new wealth to all the valley towns.

14

*E*very spring, Clara had tried for a garden. The growing season was short and the climate so dry that the snows more often
evaporated than melted. She had planted patches of the herbs
and flowers mentioned in the Bible and Shakespeare. Most of
them died, but she brought the Gold Flume children up on the
last day of school every year to see the rue and rosemary, the
mint and sorrel, the aloe, clove, and balm.

Then there was a two-year drought. At first no one was
alarmed. These valleys were accustomed to long dry spells,
which were what made the snow so perfect for skiing. In winter

the snow fell and settled like ash, light as a blind woman's touch, and the skiers seemed to rest on nothing as they dipped and swooped, their skis making only a whisper in their ears as they went. When the snow melted in spring it carried little water. In those two years the heavier spring snows hadn't come and the early summer rains were scant. Everyone saved wash water and bathtub water. People's treasured lilacs died, and the mountain mahogany and the gray-green scrub oak went to wood and withe in the dust of the summers. The river, slick as oil, slowed until it was barely moving and on its receding banks, shocking as a nakedness, algae and curds formed like crumbs on the lips of a slattern child. The earth pulled in and went so dry that water poured on it ran away uselessly. Clara's few remaining herbs dried to paper. She had nothing to show the children that season. In the fall there were now a hundred and fifty students and six grades with six teachers.

One Saturday morning a few weeks after Thanksgiving, the house was so noisy that Clara didn't hear the knocking on their door until the visitor began to pound. Andy had been nailing a bracket for wall shelves and Julia was bossily commanding Joseph in some game. When Clara finally heard the visitor and opened the door, the man was almost ready to go away. It was Mr. Barnes, the president of the new parents' group. "Christmas present," he said.

It was an iron deer, almost life-size. "We got together and got it for you to make up for the plants the kids won't have this spring."

She put the deer on the east side of the house. Andy said he wanted to shoot the thing out of season. The next year, even though the drought had broken, the parents' group gave her a birdbath. She liked it and put it where she could watch the sporting birds from the kitchen window. The next year the piece was Snow White and Andy exploded. "It's awful! Send it back!" Clara was pregnant again and tired.

"I can't tell the parents their taste is atrocious. The kids love the visits and I'm able to get some of them to read things they wouldn't otherwise, because the figures inspire them."

"What happens next year? Will I feel like I'm living in an amusement park?"

"You won't even see them. I'll move everything into the blind spot on the northeast side. You'll never know they're there."

But the deer, the birdbath, and Snow White were the beginning of a tradition. There came a windmill and then a black jockey in iron, which Clara had to fix by painting out the stripes in its clothing and giving it a Union Army uniform. She planted a screen of lilacs between the house and the display, but between snows and in the autumn it was possible to see the growing collection—ducks, a sundial, an Indian. The area had the fussy, coy look of a doting grandmother's mantelpiece. Clara didn't mind, but Andy did, and it became one of the things dragged up in their fights, which always started about something else. At first Andy was alone in this judgment. Julia and Joseph and then their third, Thomas, loved the little figures and the birdbath and took their friends to play there.

Julia was a questing, testing little girl, eager, angry, full of suns and storms. Clara, who had been watchful and quiet as a child, didn't understand her daughter's temperament. Andy, who had grown up denying his eagerness, saw in the girl all that had been stifled in himself, and he praised her natural intelligence and even the willfulness that was so much a part of her. "If she doesn't get her way, she howls," Clara complained, "and she isn't a baby anymore."

"She'll learn to control that on her own," Andy said, and smiled at his daughter's excesses.

Julia loved her celebrity in town. When she was three and four, she would dimple with pleasure at people's fussing over her, and the yard ornaments and school visits were evidence of her special status in her wide world, which was Gold Flume. At the grocery store there was always an ice-cream cone or a lollipop waiting for her, and when she was eight Pastor Frailey let her work the pedals on the organ and twice let her take the collection. This honor he had allowed no other child. She made the most of it, too, giving sad or baleful looks at nongivers down the row.

When she had come into the new first grade, she had fully expected her status as Principal's Oldest Child to be respected by the teachers and other students. She had been the first child in the new school, having visited it in its construction even before the teachers, and she told everyone so on their first day there. "I know it better than anyone except the *architect*." She used the term with obvious relish and was disappointed when the teachers didn't allow her to run off and consult her mother at will.

As she went into the second and third grades, her natural enjoyment of her status and position became more brittle and tense. She forced things and people, demanding their attention in ways some saw as charming and others as intrusive.

Behind her, Joseph toddled, then ran, adoring. He was impish, and while Julia guarded her prerogatives, he cared nothing at all for status and position and won affection without trying for it. Thomas was a quiet, sweet baby, as unlike his brother and sister as they were unlike each other. Clara had hoped that knowledge of her own family would deepen her insight into the question she asked herself at school: What is the nature of the child? The issue was only complicated by her new understanding that personality seemed to come already formed, and that she could only channel or try to modify what was already there. In her reading, no definition of children, ape or angel, showed their vast variety of response. Everyone said children reflected what was done or said to them with all the fidelity of a still pond reflecting a summer cloud.

New teaching methods came. Clara spent parts of summers at courses that explained them, but no one talked about personality or a reconciliation of the old paradox.

By the time she was in fourth grade, Julia was a dominant personality at school. Her teachers said she was bossy and made friendships only among the children who would follow her spirited, capricious leadership. Clara waited, yearning for the silent companionship she and Mama used to have. When they did the supper dishes, she would try for Julia's confidences about school and friends. Julia's problems were not what Clara's had been, but neither were her joys. Clara had never told Mama about being laughed at for her clothes or her smell or her chilblains, but she remembered the delight she had in running home to tell Mama—what? Studies? Reading? What had they spoken of so deeply in the sweltering intimacy of the summer kitchen? Or the icy mornings at the washtub? Clara knew that Julia wasn't having an easy time. People were always reminding her, panderingly or invidiously, of her status as the principal's child. Clara was proud of Julia's ability to make friendships of her choice, not to have to live on the edges of other people's good times as Clara had been forced to do, turning the jump ropes but seldom jumping. Julia could be bright and charming when she wanted to be, and unlike Clara as a child she didn't have to be silent out of shame.

But Julia was not a reader. Clara read to her children every day, but Julia showed none of the eager joy for words that Clara remembered from her own childhood. The difference puzzled Clara and saddened her.

When Peter Tavistock was in his sophomore year of high school he had begun to visit Clara at home. He gave the excuse of needing help at school but actually he was yearning for someone to talk to, to wrangle with in the wide range of his interests, few of which were discussed in his classes. He had a strong intellectual curiosity and an original cast of mind that delighted Clara.

As he opened to the human factors in his reading he became more interested in the language of the political movements he studied. He made Clara ransack her memory for the words union organizers and company mine owners had used during her childhood. How did they define themselves? Were the prospectors different from the company miners? How did they describe themselves? He took a trip to Ludlow and studied grave sites at Telluride and Central City. Granite, of course, had been a company town; Bluebank had been settled by claim-jumpers, independent prospectors, and bootleg miners whose midnight holes weakened the horizontal shafts of company mines.

In his third year of high school, Peter began to be interested in war. He hated its violence and death, its destruction of carefully made moralities, but he was fascinated by the phenomenon. Did war have a special language? Did it promote special ideas? If the South had won, how would our speech be different? When he asked his high school history teacher, she told him such speculations were fruitless, and he came fuming up the Jackass Pass road to Clara, full of righteous anger. By that time, his sister, Lucinda, was in high school, too, but she was deep into her artistic interests and too appalled by the very idea of war to talk about it.

Peter began to study tactics and strategy, particularly of the conflict in Korea. Germany had won the First World War on Percivals' living room floor, with maps and charts spread out to the kitchen, as he tried to postulate the world that would have resulted. Clara missed those afternoons when he graduated and went away to college. He said he would write, but she didn't think he would.

By then, many of her first students had faded from Clara's world. Sulo Boda, then his brother Cyril, had disappeared to the gulch ranch. Some families had moved; Old Man Markham, about whom Clara had written for advice, died and two of his maimed daughters drifted away. Frances Legrand stayed married to Buster French and had four more children. She and Buster moved, temporarily, they said, then permanently, into the French compound. Buster joined his brothers and uncles at the sad bottom of Gold Flume's social order: jail, sporadic work, blame, neglect, violence, and forgetting. The men haunted two of the town's six saloons, the women sent their children to the grocery store to keep from going to town themselves. By the time her first child, Lorus, started school, Frances was unrecognizable as the girl she had been. She was now a slack-jawed, collapsed woman, the eagerness Clara had once seen in her soured into hate.

The refinery builders had moved on, but the engineers stayed, and with the ski area increasing, there were lodge owners and ski area technicians, a doctor, lawyer, and dentist in Gold Flume itself, and the people who operated the new motels and restaurants. These people moved into the new development on the far side of town and Clara continued her school visits there. Some of the houses were well furnished, some almost empty, the families living in wealthy surroundings and sleeping in bedrolls on the bare floor. It was a new kind of poverty to Clara. She had never imagined a poverty that hid itself, secret want in a fine house. "Wait until Peter comes home for the summer," she told Andy. "He'll be interested in studying this. He knows Cyril Boda and other Gulch people, but this kind of poverty will have aspects that may surprise him." "There's a secrecy the ordinary kind of poverty doesn't have," Clara wrote to Peter, "a secrecy that makes everyone else, even the well-disposed, potential enemies."

Peter surprised Clara by answering her letters with full and eager descriptions of his new world—Negroes, Mexicans, Jews, open homosexuals—"It's like color when you've only seen black-and-white movies—their lives are nothing like mine, their world nothing like Gold Flume."

Clara wrote back, "Don't forget that while your new culture has a wide spread, ours has a deep one. We live with social differences that city people rarely do. How many bank presidents in city communities know their letter carriers and children's teachers socially and see them in other contexts than at work? The problems of social distance are increasing for us, also." Now there were Bodas, Frenches, and also the new doctor, the lawyer, the dentist. The Ditmarses and the Bogards, original homesteader families, looked poorer, shown against the new wealth of the town. Because of this separation, Clara asked the parents' group to hold school events, a barbecue in summer and a sleigh ride in winter, to help people come together informally.

When Joseph started school, his teachers threw up their hands at his antics and fell in love with him. He was freckled and redheaded like his father, and Clara was glad of an orthodontist in Aureole who might help him later with his teeth. Thomas was dark like Clara, even darker than Julia, but from the beginning, nothing could overwhelm Andy's partiality to his daughter.

"You can't criticize Joey for what he does, when it's the same thing you praised Julia for doing," Clara argued.

She argued in vain. Andy dismissed Julia's tempers and imperiousness, was kind and patient with Thomas, but Joey, full of joyous spirit, drew no praise or approval from him. Clara wondered why this was until she happened to see Joey standing with his friends one day. It was that smile, that radiant, we-two-together smile that was Arlo's trademark and Joey's curse, shutting him away from Andy's trust and, therefore, from his love.

Peter Tavistock began to question staying in college. He had a deferment from military service, but he thought about going into the army. The Korean War was over. Peace talks were under way in Panmunjom. He wrote, "I'm going to be a historian. This is my chance to see what history really feels like, smells and tastes like. If only I can get over there!"

He was soon writing to Clara from basic training. He asked for books, and these she sent, along with cookies she baked for him.

She looked forward to his letters because the voice in them was so clearly Peter's own. Great questions were bracketed with petty annoyances. He had witty and penetrating descriptions of army life and the places of his training. When his request for Korean posting was approved, he sent her his APO address with a hand-drawn cartoon of his imagined presence at the peace talks, guarding the U.S. delegation but also interrupting at key moments with the crucial word here, the necessary guidance there.

Once in Korea he sent fascinating descriptions of the country and its people, of villages at the perimeter, of Tokyo and Seoul and the devastation of the war, which his reading and study had never made real to him. "I want to see history clearly, to think about it while it's still news, while I'm experiencing it, so that thirty years from now, standing in my mothball-fumy uniform on Veterans Day, I'll be able to see the difference between what I knew and what history has agreed to have happened."

Clara sent him clippings and articles about Korea and wrote some of her experiences in the changing town.

A mother came to my office yesterday. She was furious about a book in the school library, a love story written for teenagers. The characters in it meet secretly, kiss and do a bit of petting, but the girl realizes she isn't ready for more. They break up. The mother said it was obscene and demanded I take it off the shelves. "Books are supposed to ennoble people," she said. She told me the school was supposed to ennoble children the way church does. I told her that in some ways I agreed. I had been "ennobled" by books and reading, I hoped, but there were other things education should provide and one of them was a recognizable presentation of the world. I think you and I have talked about this now and again. Is childhood a training time for life, or years through which some inborn holiness and innocence are to be prolonged? When I asked her that, she only stared at me and demanded I take the book away. Please include this paradox in the history you write. I want pages 365 and 366 in Tavistock's *American History 1929–1979* to deal with it. You may use my name in the footnote or not as you see fit. A huge new development is going in across the road from us. Details to follow.

The spring was mild that year. The school windows, those that could be opened, received the fluttering of a May wind that reminded Clara of the milder springs down mountain in San Pablo and Pueblo. Because of that, she had evocations of those days, of a younger, more restless self. Lena Sanchez had smelled this fragrance on the wind and wondered about the war and what was to become of her. Clara sometimes remembered with amazement that she had been such a person and had done such things. The children Clara Percival wrote to in San Pablo were now young adults. It was a spring day that smelled just like this when they had stood by Arlo's hospital bed . . .

"Clara?" It was Alice Bogard, putting her head around the doorway into the office.

"Alice—Oh, Lord, I was back years ago in another body. Are you down shopping?"

Alice didn't answer. Her pleasant, freckled face was unsmiling. "I brought you a copy of the *Voice,* and I want to sit here while you read it."

Clara knew from Alice's look and manner that the news was bad. She began to play for time. "I never get to this until the weekend."

"I know that," Alice said gently. "It's why I brought it."

"I remember when it was a two-pager," Clara murmured, and started looking down the front page. Let it be this—"Oh, *this,* yes. . . ." It was news of the new development, roads already begun across the Jackass Pass road from the Percivals' house. "Rename the road? Good Lord, isn't Jackass Pass Road good enough for them?"

"Turn the page," Alice said, and her voice, toneless and flat, brought Clara's head up.

"Alice—"

"I don't know any other way to tell you about this—"

Clara turned the page:

KOREAN CONFLICT CLAIMS VALLEY MAN

Peter Tavistock, son of Dorothy and Millburn Tavistock of Gold Flume . . .

"But the war is over!" Clara protested. Alice didn't answer. Clara tried to read the article that followed. Peter had gotten transferred to a unit guarding the DMZ. Occasionally patrols traded fire by mistake or got lost in storms or fogs and wandered out of their limits. Peter had been with his unit on such a patrol, and they had encountered Korean troops and he and two other soldiers had been shot. The two were injured, one seriously. Peter had been killed. An investigation would be made into the details. Families had been notified. . . . "The words are not letting me get away," Clara said. "I can't stop this from being true, can I?"

Alice shook her head and they sat together in silence for a long time.

"He was on his way to another future," Clara said to Andy that night. "That's what I can't let go of. Kester French built the roadway to his death, but Peter's service was a stopover, a digression—"

"He was a likable kid," Andy said. "I remember him up here banging the table over the Battle of the Marne. I don't think most people knew how bright he was. It's a damn shame."

Clara didn't start crying until she had her hands in dishwater. It was Mama's old mess, weeping into the suds, having to dry her hands before she could blow her running nose.

That evening, she read Peter's letters again. She had kept them in a shoebox on her history shelf. There were about thirty letters and they covered a three-year period, college, military training, then Korea. Reading them in order, Clara saw into a depth she had not penetrated before. Peter had grown and changed in those three years, but not steadily or evenly like a dawn breaking. His growth had been in strands, themes, like a creek finding a new bed, then filling in between the new and the old courses. As he read, thought, explored, he changed the outlines he had previously made, widening some, rounding others. His experiences had been working on him, but he hadn't been passive under them. He had been working on himself all the while, trying to shape what he was living into a coherent system, philosophy, belief. It had been a conscious effort. To do this work, he had had to trim, to change, to invent and mold—Clara wondered if this was her model of the child, born neither ape nor angel, and not passive but busily working at experience to organize it, to give it meaning, good or bad.

Whatever deeper thoughts Peter's letters inspired, they were full of his sense of discovery. It occurred to Clara that whatever Peter had been writing to his parents or to Lucinda, these letters would be different and it might mean a lot to the family to read them. Clara called the *Ute River Voice* the next day and asked when the families had been informed. They told her the visit had been made four days ago. Clara thought it over. She had been Peter's friend, and though she and his mother weren't speaking and only nodded coolly to each other as they passed their shopping carts at the market, she knew she should pay her condolence visit and let the family read the letters.

15

She waited until Saturday, made the chicken casserole she usually brought to such occasions, put the letters in a nicer box, and drove down to the Tavistocks' old mausoleum of a house.

Because the house was past the far end of town, Clara hadn't come that way since she had walked Peter home almost seven years before. In summer, the place had been screened by hedges and foliage, only its third floor showing. Now it stood stripped of its protection. She stopped at the end of the buckled street and saw that the entire eastern hillside that bounded the house lot had been staked out for the new highway that was to link the four towns and continue over the pass. The east side of the house would look out on that highway, separated only by a stream and a swath of scrub. The house would be forty feet from the passing cars and trucks, fully visible to them, and because it was set low, no fence or shrubbery could mask or protect it. Loaded semis and trailers would labor up the grade, making all the urgent sounds of their gear changes. There would be road litter, papers and worse thrown and blown down into the Tavistocks' careful yard. It was a modern punishment for house-hubris, a tear in the illusion of mastery and safety.

Clara parked the car in sight of the house but not in front of it. Dorothy Tavistock didn't belong to the sewing group or the altar society or any of the other gatherings of Town women, but Clara had half expected some sign of visitors with their loaves of bread, apple spice cakes, casseroles. There was no sign. The house was as daunting and unwelcoming as she remembered it.

Balancing the casserole and the box of letters, Clara pushed the shrieking gate open and went up the walk to the door. She knocked, then waited. Just as she was considering knocking again, Lucinda opened the door a little way.

Lucinda had changed in the five years since leaving Gold Flume School, more than a physical change. Her shyness had been transmuted into reticence, her stiffness into dignity. Clara held out the casserole and box of letters and said, "Lucinda, I'm so sorry about Peter." Lucinda nodded but said nothing. Her eyes had dissolved in tears.

Behind Lucinda in the parlor, Clara could hear the soft sibilances and rise and fall of subdued talk. People had come. "Visitors?"

"Relations from back east." Lucinda made a gesture of vague dislike.

"I'll just leave these—" Clara said, and began to step inside.

At that moment, Dorothy Tavistock's grieved voice came raised from the other room. "Who is that?" Lucinda turned away from Clara and went inside. Then Clara knew that no one from town had come, except, perhaps, the pastor. Dorothy Tavistock felt that no one in Gold Flume was her social equal, so Clara's affection for Peter wouldn't be seen as honoring him.

She stood uncertainly at the door and then Dorothy was there. "So it's you," she said. Her eyes had been emptied with weeping, but hate moved across them like a darkness.

Clara stood clumsily, hands full. She had expected hesitation from Dorothy, even annoyance, but not the hate she saw. "I have letters," she said in explanation.

"I'm sure you do. I have letters also. He compared me to you in his letters. He told me to get to know you, to learn from you, to be more like you. Why did you alienate my son's affections? You had no purpose with him after he finished as your student."

Clara stood, thinking she had no answer the woman would want to hear.

Dorothy's voice rose. "I told you to leave him alone. I told you once to leave him alone!"

The stridency of her tone brought three of the relatives out into the hall where she stood, and the hired woman came from the kitchen. With embarrassment's uneven perception, Clara noticed that it wasn't Ella Matske. Clara was still standing on her side of the threshold and she knew now that she would bring no healing or reconciliation with anything she did, so she turned and left, Dorothy Tavistock's voice rising behind her in mounting shrill accusation. Its noise drowned out the cry of the gate and then the sounds stopped.

"Wait!" Lucinda came running from the back of the house. "Wait, please."

"I can't," Clara said. "Just let me go now."

Lucinda put out an arm. "I'm suffering, too," she said.

139

Clara stopped and looked at her. "What can I do—it only makes things worse."

Lucinda followed her to the car and held the door while Clara put the casserole and letters on the floor in the back. Then Clara got in and leaned over to open the door for Lucinda. The smell of the still-warm food rose in the closed space.

"Chicken and noodles?" Lucinda asked.

"Yes." They laughed, and then Clara found herself in tears. "Oh, God, I'll miss Peter! He had such great capacity, and how much I wanted to talk to him about everything—his experiences, his hopes. I had a lifetime of talk stored up, waiting . . ."

Lucinda motioned toward the house. "He was their great hope. I don't know what they will do."

The two of them were quiet for a while, and then Clara asked Lucinda how she had been. "Are you still drawing?"

"Less than I was. I've gotten interested in three-dimensional forms—I've started sculpting."

They talked about Lucinda's plans after college. As much as she had changed, there was a good deal of the girl Clara had known in school, warming, in the presence of interest, into eagerness. She wasn't a pretty girl, but enthusiasm made her beautiful. They were enjoying the conversation when they suddenly became aware of the time passing. Parents and relatives were waiting. Clara said, "I had all those letters from Peter that I thought your mother would want to see—"

"She wouldn't, but I would." Lucinda gestured to the box. "I'll see you get them back."

As they said good-bye, the door of the Tavistock house opened and Dorothy stepped out onto the porch and began to look up and down the street. She saw the car and Lucinda closing the door. Her eye caught her daughter and the box of letters and she turned a stare of hate on Clara that was as unequivocal as a blow.

When Clara told Andy about the visit he said, "You're a full citizen of Gold Flume now. You're teacher here, a mother, and you've even got an enemy. Treat her well. With care, she could last a lifetime."

Peter's body came back to Gold Flume for burial. The pastor thought the town should have a memorial service or a graveside ceremony, but the family refused. The house, weathering and raw, exposed to the new highway, drew in on itself. Lucinda graduated and stayed away.

Two years later, Clara got a package and a letter from Chama, New Mexico. Lucinda wrote that she was working as a school janitor and doing art in her spare hours. In the package was a small, detailed sculpture. Of the three female figures, two stood close and turned toward each other. The largest was facing away from them, her arms thrown wide, her face turned up, distorted with anguish. She was a big woman, but her gestures had something of constriction in them. The second figure stood in an attitude of dejection, hands covering her face. The third and smallest was looking away, as abstracted as she was grieved.

The sculpture was in bronze, and untitled. When Clara showed it to the teachers, one of them saw it as a Three Marys. It was an honest Three Marys, she said, each sorrowing in her own way, the three united in their grief but in nothing else. The sculpture was small, no more than eight inches high and six long. "I think it's a war story," Clara said, but would say no more.

16

*J*ulia went into the new junior high that had just been opened in Callan and Clara felt lightened by her leaving. She confided that to no one but Alice Bogard. "We argued all the time. I hate cliques and work against them. They give most of the pain that's suffered in school, but Julia was always angry at me for backing the teachers who separated her from her friends. Maybe she won't bring these fights home anymore."

"Are you still hoping you and she will be as close as you and your mother were?"

"I know it's a dream, but I still dream it, that we'll be working away together, talking woman talk. Where would that happen? I don't know. She thinks I'm cold and forbidding, but I get along well with your girls and with Katy's, too."

Alice said quietly, "You and Julia are so different, I wonder if you see the same daisy or smell the same rose. I see you together, rankling each other without even trying. The very things you want her to do and be oppress her, and she, poor soul, comes to you offering all the wrong things."

Julia had dozens of acquaintances in junior high. Clara saw a kaleidoscope of faces and bodies running in and out of the house, playing records or trying on one another's clothes, this girl, that girl, in favor and out before Clara could learn their names. They would be in Julia's room, in group, giggling, and then they would all swoop away somewhere else, and the next week a new group, and any girl Clara remembered disdained and forgotten: "Oh, *her!*" and the look of exasperation.

When Clara complained, Andy shrugged. "What do you expect?"

"I don't know," Clara would answer, "maybe that she keep one or two special girls to be her *friends,* her confidantes. She's too willful, too mercurial—" And Andy would shrug again and shake his head.

Joey grew to look more and more as his father must have looked at that age, all pratfalls, hands, legs, elbows, but the smile and the gift to befriend was pure Arlo Percival, and Andy would glower as he watched his son laugh his openhearted laugh. He saw no pleasure, but only a con man judging his mark. Arlo had been gone so long, Clara wondered if Andy would remember what he looked like if not for Joey and his smile.

Oliver and Katy loved Joey and took him and Thomas rafting and hiking. "Why does Andy come down so hard on him?" Katy asked. "Because he smiles like Arlo," was all that Clara could say.

Clara loved Joey headlong. She loved his generosity, his joyousness, his easy laughter, and easy sorrow. He had a delight in adventure that wasn't mean or vindictive, only fun-loving, and

Clara watched Andy's jaw tighten and his eyes go hard when he heard his son's laughter or saw that incandescent smile.

Sometimes they argued. Andy forgave Julia her imperious will and was enchanted by her quickness. When she had fights at school he took her side, listening sympathetically to her accusations of this or that girl who was making trouble for her. Now and then mothers would call about the cruelty of the cliques or malicious words or about how Julia's supposedly best friends had come home crying. When Clara tried to show her daughter how her attitudes were hurting others, the denials were shot back out of Julia's pouting mouth. *"They* said . . ." *"She* was the one who . . ." and it was her sureness and will that kept her at the center of all the junior high intrigues, the groupings and regroupings of those years. Andy admired it, Andy praised it. The teachers said Julia was coasting through school on her intelligence alone, doing minimal work. When Andy heard this he would say that the school was limiting.

When Joey was ten, he discovered the practical joke. Clara and Andy endured whatever popped out at them or fell down on them, learned to live with rubber turds, plastic ink stains, plagues of rubber beetles, flies, worms, and roaches, lifelike vomit and broken eggs. Coronets of plastic flies decorated every potato salad. Thomas followed his brother like an awed dog.

One August afternoon the summer herb tour was being held in the yard. The children and some parents were walking among the yard figures. There were twelve now, including windmills and a sundial, and all of a sudden there was water everywhere. People ran every which way, trying to get out of the drenching. Joey had gotten someone's old hose, punctured it with holes, and run a series of small tubes through the holes. There was more to it, some kind of pressure-builder, and it all showed considerable study and application. Clara was surprised to see Andy, pushed well beyond annoyance, spank Joey hard. "Your father is a good man," she told Joey afterward, "he's honest and generous, and he's usually even-tempered, but don't shame him in public, because he can't take that."

He gave her his level look and said, "It's not fair."

"It's how he is."

"It was a good trick, though; it really worked."

"I suppose it was, but maybe some people had clothes ruined, and it certainly put an end to herb study for the day." She saw him taking that in, absorbing it.

"They're pranks and he's a normal imaginative boy," she pleaded to Andy, who was still seething. "They weren't done as insults to you."

"I don't care. I won't be pointed at in public," he said, "and especially not by him."

"Oh, Lord," Clara murmured to herself, "whoever thinks children cement the bonds of marriage has bedfeathers in his hair!"

That fall, on a November Sunday when hunting season's iridescent blue sky made going to church an act of consummate piety, Clara and Andy sat together in their pew and listened to the sounds of gunshots echoing through the hills. Julia and Thomas were sitting with their friends. Joseph was home sick. Just as the service was ending they heard a deafening fusillade of gunshots outside the church, followed immediately by the sound of shattering glass. Everyone rushed out the door. In the parking lot, shotgun blasts had destroyed the windows of every car. People went back to see and stopped, stunned, gaping at it all, and then someone ventured gingerly to his own car and began calling out to the others, "It's a trick. .... It's . . . they're *decals!*"

People poured into the lot, even those who had come on foot, and they saw that every car had a broken-glass or a bullet-hole decal of clear plastic. Shock and rage were followed by relief and laughter, then by wonder. There were thirty-four cars in the lot.

There must have been many pranksters in on the trick, which had taken organization, speed, and silence. They had done the decaling while people were in church, then they had shot the guns, dropping thirty pounds or so of metal sheeting and iron chain that everyone had heard as crazing and shattering glass. Unsmiling, Andy stood with Clara by their own bullet-riddled window. "That boy had better be home. If he didn't do this, he masterminded it."

Joey was in bed when they got home. Andy was furious, but fear of confronting his son in an outright lie kept him quiet. He could only mutter and look at Joey darkly. Three days later, the story began to emerge. It was impossible for five boys to keep one secret; one of them bragged. Clara had known where Joey had been all along. She had opened her son's closet when Andy had left the room and received a strong whiff of cordite from the clothing there. When Andy did find out that the plan had been Joey's, organized and executed by him, he went white with rage.

"Be annoyed," Clara said, "but this isn't grand larceny."

"The boy's spirited," Oliver declared when he heard about it. "There's not a malicious thought in his head." He told the story around the county shops and for years afterward would laugh at the memory of the prank.

Andy wouldn't hear his brother-in-law's defense of Joey and kept watching his son for evidence of criminality.

Thomas measured his sister's willfulness and his brother's spiritedness and he made as conscious a decision as Clara had herself. He hid. He became quieter, more deliberate. He was the gentlest of their children, one who could be brought to tears by a tragedy on the evening news. This gentleness also he pulled inward.

Clara thought that if there were differences between her family and others, the Bogards or the Bordereaus, one difference might be that the Percivals didn't reminisce about their childhood days. Clara told the children about Mama, her love of color and music, her dancing, her luxuriant auburn hair. She mentioned that Winston Coleman had come from Virginia and that the sideboard at home and the silver service at Uncle Oliver and Aunt Katy's had come from his people. That was all, or almost all. Andy went vague when the boys asked questions or friends talked about their childhood days.

In the winter of that year, two pieces of mail addressed to Clara came a month apart. They were postcards sent in envelopes. The cards and postmarks were from different places.

Daughter,

Hoping this finds you well. I've put your name down as next of kin. I'm in a situation here. If someone calls about me, tell him you have all the necessary evidence in a safety-deposit box.

A. Percival

The postcard was from Schroon Lake, New York. The postmark from Winston-Salem, North Carolina. The second said:

Daughter,

Can you send forty? Need is great. It pays to get arrested in the morning as lunch is pokey's main meal. General Delivery, Fargo, North Dakota.

Clara sent a money order with a note: "Dear Arlo, It's worth the forty to know you are still alive." She didn't tell Andy.

In the spring of Julia's first year of high school, Clara became a public figure. She was chosen Colorado Elementary Educator of the Year, and a long article in the *Ute River Voice* proclaimed: EXCELLENCE IN GOLD FLUME. The article profiled her career in the valley and quoted statistics that were surprising even to Clara. More Gold Flume students did well in high school than did the students of other schools in the county, more went on to college. Many credited their love of poetry and literature to her

147

special reading programs, poetry collections, Richest Student contest, and poem duels. Clara and Andy were given a three-day trip to Denver and introduced to the governor, and Clara spoke at a national convention of elementary school principals, receiving mention in the *Rocky Mountain News* and the *Denver Post*. The articles were full of overpraise and inaccuracy.

Her speech at the convention was received with the politeness reserved for the utterly irrelevant. As a grade school principal in a rural county, she still had control over much of the school's day, as did the individual teachers. The teachers at the convention were wrestling with racial balances. Clara had no such problem. The principals were worried about interracial fighting, local control, government fiat. Clara's problem was the harmonizing of widening social classes. At the social hours they ignored her or studied her as one would study a specimen from Civil War days kept in hibernation and awakened a hundred years later.

When Clara and Andy got back from Denver, there was a party at the school and Clara was presented with the articles from the Denver and Gold Flume papers all nicely framed. She had to hang them in her office and pretend to be pleased. She wished the articles were about the school itself. Then she could have hung them in the hall for the students to read and enjoy.

"Aren't you pleased?" Alice asked.

Clara shrugged. "It's nice to be praised, but not for the wrong reasons. I got tired of smiling and pretending. My reality was irrelevant there."

"What do you mean?"

"Gold Flume School sends kids to the junior high well prepared, but the trip that was supposed to have been a reward made me sad, and now I feel more isolated than ever."

That summer Clara took more classes at the University of Colorado, commuting home on weekends. History and geography had disappeared into social studies and were leached of facts, locations, and dates. Vocabulary lists in elementary school readers had been purged into two-syllable simplicity. She came back puzzled, meditative, and quiet.

The school year began, and there were two new teachers to convince. "Read the books to them. Read what you like yourself and don't worry about the vocabulary. Read them Dickens and Francis Parkman." They stared at her.

The development across the road was now ready for occupancy, and people began to move into the houses before they were fully finished. At night the place glowed with lights that dimmed the stars. Jackass Pass Road had been renamed Flume Heights Road, the development was called Flume Heights. When she could, Clara still walked home from school on the trail she had made herself, still experiencing the seasonal changes of light and dark, flowering, greening, and decline.

On this November day, imminent snow had brought them to full darkness and Clara had come as usual, carrying her flashlight but not using it, up the trail from the back of the school, letting the walk clear her head. Andy was home, his car parked in the lean-to west of the house. She went around to the back door because of the mud on her boots. Letting herself in quietly, she heard Andy's voice in a low murmur. He must be reading to the kids. She came very quietly through the kitchen, thinking to enjoy the scene and not interrupt. "Please remember," he was saying, "that we have a special position here in town. Because of your mother's work, people's eyes are on us."

What was this? She went close and peeked through the hinge side of the half-open door. They were sitting in the little TV room that Andy and Oliver had added on to the house. Julia, Joseph, and Thomas were sitting close together, and they looked small and a little cowed. Usually they fought for space, spreading themselves wide and complaining if anyone's body or clothing touched them. "That's not fair!" Julia shrilled. Clara winced. It was the tone Julia used that most annoyed her mother, a whining, petulant, and bossy sound.

"I know it isn't fair," Andy said, "but it's the way things are. Like it or not, you need to be more careful than other kids about what you say and do."

She wanted to go in and stop him. What he said was true, but she didn't want them to feel the town's judgment weighing down their days and squeezing the joy out of them. The Percival children were judged more narrowly than other children; they were both more and less privileged, but Clara had wanted them not to be so blatantly aware of it.

Julia made a face. "I'm not a kid anymore."

Andy nodded. "That's why I'm telling you this. It's not fair to have a special set of rules to live under, but your mother's position demands it, and you're going to have to face up to it. I'm not asking you to stop enjoying yourselves or struggle to please everyone. I'm asking you to be conscious of your behavior and consider your actions a little more. . . ."

She backed away from the door and heard Julia's voice, with its whine of discontent; Joey's voice, trying to sound helpful; and Thomas's voice, the sound of a child who only thought he had done wrong in some way. Andy's remarks had saddened her. Their position in town had come to mean so much to him that he must be seeing each member of his family as a potential hostage to it and still thinking of his own father as a wild card that could fall face up before the world at any time.

And nothing changed. Julia, who had felt hemmed in by the time she was in junior high, added unwilling martyrdom to her other defenses, blamed Clara, and hated Gold Flume even more. Joseph tried restraint but was as incapable of it as a happy drunk at a party. Thomas, the child least needful of such weights on his spontaneity, bore the lesson longest and became even more silent and introspective than he had been before. Clara never told Andy she had come in on his talk, but in small ways she tried to whisper to the children over his head, "You can laugh a little, you can shine a little. . . ."

17

*I*t seemed that no sooner had they built the new school than temporary buildings had to be added. The towns were booming, the ski area was growing; two blocks of shops had gone up on the north and south sides of the railroad tracks and the old depot was remodeled for a restaurant. Gold Flume School's enrollment doubled again.

Enrichment programs had come into the county curriculum, and the school got a film projector and a library of educational films. Clara felt like a pirate in a movie, sifting treasure in the chests of the hoard, but when the teachers tested the children at the end of the year, everyone was shocked at how little the students had learned from the films. They had seen them passively and made no connection between them and their other studies.

The television news was showing images of the civil rights struggle going on in the big cities. Clara had speakers come to the school to talk about the problems that were light-years from the valley towns but a nightly event on the news. Many of the parents were critical of her, and some protested strongly. There were no Negroes or Mexicans in Gold Flume, they said, and the children were having nightmares. "It's as much a class struggle as a racial one," Clara explained to the parents' group, "and we're near enough to that right here."

She told them about the five girls, fourth-graders she had come upon standing in a ring around a sixth. "She called us a name!" they screamed. The girl in the middle of the ring was Rio Markham, born to the youngest Markham girl, probably by her father. They lived in the old cabin on Chinaman's Creek and Rio was the last of the Gulch children in the old definition of the term. "Rio . . ."

The girl was mealy pale under her freckles. Her hair, braided tightly into two stiff ropes, seemed to pull her face even tighter. "She had that party—she wouldn't let me come. I asked her why not, when the whole class came, and she said—they said—I was a nigger. I only called them nigger back."

Clara had to decide whether she should start with the word *nigger* first or with what was behind it. Everyone had heard about the ski party. "Everybody got invitations but me," Rio murmured.

Clara was proud of Rio, standing her ground. Her sense of what was fair had overwhelmed her Gulch child's shame. All the new children had skis and lift passes they traded back and forth, but the Gulch children and the Ranch children and the poorer Town children weren't part of those enviable networks. "Well?" Clara turned to the party-giver.

The girl had a stiff, sanctimonious look. "She couldn't have come anyway. Those kids who live"—and she waved a vague

152

hand southward to where the ranches and the gulches lay—
"up there . . ."

"I know where Rio lives," Clara said coolly. "I was born and
raised near the top of Placer Gulch." Rio's face showed amazement. Clara let her steady gaze convince the girl. Then she
turned to the party-giver. "I think Rio deserves a big apology
from all of you, even those who didn't say anything but didn't
protest." They were all wide-eyed innocence. There was an
apology at last, but Clara didn't know if what she had said sank
into anyone's consciousness or was only to be forgotten, the
authority placated.

The parents heard her story with equanimity, and some of
them began to excuse the girls' behavior. Only a few looked
down or shook their heads in disapproval.

Clara said quietly, "We can't have that divisiveness in the
school," and took up the next subject. When a film about prejudice was offered, she sent for it and showed it to the school.

Stealing at school began to increase. Some of the teachers
dealt with it case by case, and some not at all, but when complaints began to come from all the classes, Clara raised it in a
teachers' meeting. "What's changed here?"

"It's the degree," one teacher said.

"The wealthy and the poor don't share much experience anymore," another said. "The children of the highway workers don't
care what they do. They're like the refinery kids, here and gone."

"Everyone steals; it's natural at that age."

"The rich ones come in with lots of fancy things, showing off.
Who can blame the poorer ones?"

"But the poor kids aren't the only ones doing it," Clara said,
"and the poor children of twenty years ago were poorer than
they are now, and few of them stole."

She had thought that when everyone had inside water and
plumbing, the ridicule and envy would stop. "We need to take
a stand."

153

She canceled a day's classes and had a full assembly. The sheriff came and read the law to them; Pastor Frailey spoke. One or two children volunteered their experiences with stealing and spoke of the lasting shame they felt. Some of the parents were outraged, and Clara had to defend her idea. "Children shouldn't be coming to school with valuable things and showing off, but a child should be able to wear the crown jewels to school without fear that they'll be stolen." Some parents expressed approval, but it was given in private; at the school meeting, many people said the matter should have been handled more discreetly. "Theft isn't merely a social blunder," Clara argued, wondering why so many of the parents took it so lightly.

By then, Julia was in her last year of high school in Aureole. From time to time she and Clara had achieved short, intense rapprochements. There was a failed prom in her sophomore year from which she came home weeping into Clara's comforting embrace. There was a play in which Julia starred that took careful study, and Clara coached her, sewed for her, praised her. But Clara felt that most of the time her daughter had set her up as a judge—an image shaking her head in disapproval in spite of all the reality she tried to heap against it.

Julia was home less and less, being whirled away more often in the complex choreography of high school social life. Clara admitted guiltily to Alice and defensively to Katy that her daughter's absence was a relief. Julia's overlarge presence in the family scarcely left breathing room for Joseph and Thomas. Now that she was often busy with after-school activities or staying at friends' houses or with Oliver and Katy, Clara was free to discover Joey's spirit and Thomas's subtle sense of humor, the outcome of all his years of silence and watchfulness.

"Their world is freer," Alice said. "They make claim to it earlier than we did."

"Our world was poorer," Katy said. "We stayed together because we were scared and poor and desperate and most of the world outside was against us. We clung."

"Katy, I've been asking Julia what she wants to do with her life—she's almost eighteen and she doesn't seem to know."

Katy smiled. "Most people aren't like you, Clar. You knew from the start you wanted to be a teacher. Most of us blunder around until we get interested in something or get tired of looking."

"What do you think of that?" Clara asked Alice.

Her friend grinned. "Katy's right, you know." She looked levelly at Clara. "You'd die if she didn't go to college, wouldn't you?"

"Yes."

"Because you had to fight so hard."

Clara nodded.

"It may not be right for her."

"How could that be? She's bright—she needs a wider world."

"But college will be different for her. You discovered it, claimed it for yourself. These kids we raise so carefully don't have the chance to discover much on their own. We give it all from the beginning. I know I did that. *College.* Martha dropped out to get married. Sarah never had the joy you told me about when you left the Prillers, that scary, eager trip to San Pablo, the discovering, the claiming . . ."

But Clara couldn't relinquish the dream. Julia might have no direction, she argued, but college would give her one. There, with freedom, choice would form into vocation. In spite of what everyone said, Clara couldn't believe that people weren't signaled, called by voices meant only for themselves. It had happened to her. Perhaps it didn't come at such an early age to everyone. Perhaps people stifled it or refused to listen—if there wasn't a call sent, how did people know where to aim their lives?

Julia took Clara's urgings and gave her passive, shrugged acquiescence. She would go. For the first time Andy heard her with misgiving, then with impatience. "Is she doing us a favor?"

They sent for catalogs, wrote letters, marveled over the profusion of classes and courses. Julia said no to this, to that, and finally yes to the University of Colorado. When Andy and Clara added up all the costs, they nearly lost their courage. "Be sure," they said, and took Julia to visit the school. It was huge. There were more people on the campus than were in the five towns of the Ute Valley added together. Would she be lost there? But when Julia was accepted, she seemed pleased. She called all her friends and talked for hours about it.

Two days after her acceptance, Andy came back from a trip to Aureole with a large package and a smirk on his face. It was the makings of a picnic, an echo of his surprise banquet in Golden twenty years before. "All of us this time," he said, but the boys had made other plans, and at the last minute, Julia also begged off. Clara was disappointed, but on the way up Jackass Pass she decided their being alone was a blessing.

It was a glowing afternoon, August turning mellow in the high country where the wild maple, last to bud and first to yellow, was lighting its fires. They went up the pass to the second hairpin and struck up-country to a little grove that Andy knew. It had been years since they had been there. "I didn't know the way was so steep," Clara said, "or the basket so heavy." They moved slowly, not feeling older but tiring sooner.

When they found the grove, they saw the place was littered with the papers and bottles of careless campers but not having the energy to go any further, they sat down facing away from the mess, more disappointed than they would let each other know. "Never mind, we can't see that well anymore."

"Speak for yourself. 'Age cannot wither . . .' "

"Then something else has. Fifteen years ago we would have made love in this grove. Now it's just champagne and an ache of bunions."

156

They spread the picnic, murmuring back and forth, in the comfortable code of the long married. Then Clara said, "I have a confession to make."

"Confess away."

"I once sent money to Arlo."

"Only once? I thought it was more."

"How did you know?"

"My dear girl, if you're going to lie and cheat, you'll have to learn some guile. You sent a money order and you sent it registered. I saw the return slip in the mail and the old con man's signature on it large as life. Forty bucks—you got off cheap."

"It weighed on my mind."

"Look out over those mountains and tell me how important it is after all."

They opened the champagne and toasted their accomplishment. Alone, they were free to brag, exult, and make declarations their children would have been embarrassed to hear. The day stretched itself out, dozing and easy, and it seemed at that height that their inward vision reached as far as the sight of their eyes, hill after hill, mountain after mountain, sufficient to itself, full of repose in the golden light.

The next week was all hurry and shopping, packing, sulks and good-byes, and taking Julia to Boulder to her first year at a university where her call would come and her way be made plain.

18

They were soon aware of Julia's unhappiness. Six times that first semester she called them, telling them her classes were vast and the lectures were to hundreds over a PA system. They counseled patience. After the required classes were out of the way, the numbers would shrink, and next year, if she still wished, she might transfer to a smaller school.

But when she came home for Christmas, Julia said she had joined some clubs and was finding her way in spite of the impersonality of the school. Clara tried to talk to her. What was she reading? Was she wrestling with paradox in her studies, questing as Peter had, puzzled as she herself had been? Had new interests come? What was her social world like, her friends, her roommate?

Julia would say she was too tired to talk, or it was too late, or she was expected somewhere with friends. "It's all boring, anyway," and she would shrug. When she went back after the vacation, she wrote that she had decided to continue at the university through the spring term.

When the term ended they thought she would find summer work in the valley. Clara was taking on bookkeeping work to help pay the tuition. Joseph would soon be in college, too, and needing money. She wrote to Julia:

> The tourist business has begun to extend into the summer. Hotels and motels are staying open, and some feature rafting and pack trips up the gulches. What about a job?

Julia called. "I'm going to stay here over the summer. There's work and I can take a class and be that much ahead. I'll need more money, though."

Puzzled, Clara asked, "What class would you take? What's the rush?"

Julia sounded vague. "Political action teach-ins."

"I don't understand it," Clara said to Alice. "She was never interested in politics. I wonder if she hasn't found a boy."

Alice was resting a backache against the sun-warm wood of her corral fence. She laughed. "Maybe it is a boy, maybe a cause. Our kids tried all kinds of things in college, the two who went. They joined all kinds of groups. Rob was a socialist, did you know that?"

"No, and you'd never know it now. Julia sounds so far away. She seems to be saying that whatever her interests are, I wouldn't understand them."

Alice looked out into the deep summer blue of the sky. "Carl's gone up with the herd to summer pasture and I'll be alone this week," she said. "Why not stay overnight, and we'll make marshmallows and talk."

"Slumber party?"

"Yup."

Clara and Alice had confided deep things and trivial things for so long that they knew each other to the heart. Clara thought about the confidences she and Mama had shared so long ago. Had it been what Katy said it was, a clinging in poverty, friendlessness, fear, and want?

"You're worried, aren't you?" Alice said.

"Yes."

"Then we'll make the marshmallows with your favorite, almond extract instead of vanilla."

Julia called later in the month. "Political action" wasn't a class but a teach-in, with speakers coming from all over the country. It was an exploration of the truths the government had been denying its citizens. She sounded exhilarated.

Then the calls stopped. When Clara called Julia's dorm, the phone was answered by summer students who didn't know Julia or who said she wasn't there. One girl said Julia might have gone to Chicago. Andy called the dean. No official trips had been planned, but there were dozens of unofficial campus groups, some of which had gone to demonstrate at the Democratic convention.

They drove to Boulder. Julia had not been registered for summer classes. There had been teach-ins all spring, but they were not part of the curriculum. The dean said he would make inquiries. They went back home to wait, feeling inept and unsure. A week passed, during which one of them was always home and near the telephone. "We ran away," Andy said, trying to reassure himself and Clara. "We left home like that, and we were all right."

They questioned Joseph and Thomas, trying to understand. "She didn't confide in me," Joey said. "She thought I was a nitwit, but she really hated this town. I thought she'd be happy at the university because it isn't like Gold Flume."

Thomas said, "She kept telling me that what we've been taught wasn't true, and what the government says is all a lie. The history in books is a lie, too, told by the colonizing power."

As they waited, frightened but not knowing what to do, a call came from Chicago. It was the office of the district attorney of Cook County. A Julia Percival was in custody. The charges were rioting, creating a public nuisance, obstructing justice, and resisting arrest. Bail had been set at five thousand dollars. Clara and Andy left for Denver that afternoon.

Julia was filthy, her hair matted. She looked skinny and skittery, and she stood before them raging at the police, using language that embarrassed and humiliated them. When Andy told her he had the bail, she assumed he meant to free her group, and they argued. Clara tried to explain that school money was being spent on court appearances and plane trips. Julia said she wasn't going back to school. "Their" school taught lies and deception. She was going to work with her group to further the work of truth and change.

They stood in the interview room, which was summer-close and smelling of unwashed bodies, and they listened to Julia present a picture of the world as far from their experience as Cathay or Trebizond.

Clara watched Andy deal with the courts, bail, police, a meeting with the assistant district attorney—could they get the charges reduced? She thought she had seldom seen heroism like his. He went steadily on without self-pity, this man for whom jail and public shame were emblem and metaphor of all his childhood nightmares and betrayals. He paid his daughter's bail, looking the way Civil War soldiers must have looked as they faced the unanesthetized amputation of their limbs—pain so great it bewildered. *Trial date, attorney, arraignment.* They were the ancient and familiar words said of his father. Julia glided past his pain to embrace the misery of strangers.

Arlo Percival had been chipper coming out of jail. Julia was angry, raging, arguing. To Clara it was one more willful choice. Julia said they had never understood her. Clara acknowledged that this was true. Julia said the individual was now irrelevant; now all action was political and the individual only real as part of a group or faction. Clara said that an individual had paid Julia's bail and supplied her with safety and food. Julia muttered rejoinders that Clara chose not to hear. They had a plane trip and the long ride back to Gold Flume, where the girl continued sulky and withdrawn. When Clara calmed down and asked Julia to explain, the girl's explanations were incomprehensible to her. Clara tried without success to line up her world of experience with Julia's, the way bullets are placed and turned under a microscope for ballistic study. The striae and blank spaces of their realities never met, never came to agreement under the questioning eye. There wasn't even the shared meaning of the most basic words: *work, class, power, history, teach.* . . .

Andy and Clara argued. Why hadn't Clara tried to be closer to Julia? Why hadn't she given Julia the example she needed, the teaching, the discipline? Clara raged back at him. "Do you want a record of all the times, all the ways I tried, waiting, urging, telling, showing, *begging* for her confidence?"

"You were her *mother.*"

"I still am, but she's not a blank wall on which I write any message—"

They defended, glowered, pulled up each other's secret shames, Andy's idealized, invisible mother, Clara's busy-ness, days too full of other people's children.

Then and later they were to drag the thing out and go at it again, like two punch-drunk fighters waking at the sound of bells in their own heads.

Julia spent the summer in Gold Flume, sulking around the house. "I can't talk to her," Clara said. "You try. Will she go back to school or get work?"

Andy had no more luck than Clara. Julia blamed the legal system—how could she decide, when she had to be in Chicago in September? They got the tickets and made the plans. Clara thought that by now the whole town must know about their troubles. Julia wouldn't be keeping the secret out of kindness to them. She thought their need for respectability was pretentious and hypocritical.

A week before they were to leave, Andy and Julia argued. Andy remarked about the cost of Julia's political consciousness. What was the *money* they were so interested in? Julia shouted back at him. It was only paper, printed and controlled by the power elite for the subjugation of the masses. The next day she was gone. Joseph told them she had taken whatever money she could find in the house and fifty dollars from him. Their car had been left at the Callan railroad station. Joseph's tone was awed. "She blew five thousand dollars bail money just like that." Clara had to go to school then, Andy to work, and coming home in the late afternoon, they went into Julia's room, the sunny bedroom with its view of the mountains.

Andy muttered, "I wonder if there's a place where the deceivers and the disappointers meet to plan the pain they cause. She'll meet her grandpa."

Clara realized then that his pain was greater than hers. In spite of all he knew, intellectually, he couldn't keep from a nagging suspicion that a seed of inherited flaw had been saved in his body, carried carefully from his father to his daughter—Arlo lived on in Julia, with Arlo's willfulness and without Arlo's charm.

They paid the state of Illinois five thousand dollars. It was almost one-third of Andy and Clara's combined income. It was given for no one's education or health, not to save or protect anyone or to give anyone pleasure or to take away a moment of anyone's pain. Julia had left without a backward glance. Autumn passed and winter with no word.

Julia's arrest and disappearance muted the sounds from the outside world. In Denver, rioters camped at the university. In Boulder they shouted down a speaker. Into TV cameras people screamed a junk shop of righteous grievance and political cant. To Andy and Clara, it all went like words swallowed in fog. The sound had been turned down by their own grief and bewilderment. The Vietnam War stopped for them.

But it had not stopped for the rest of the world. In May, John and Sallie Austin's son, John Jr., died in a rice paddy. The pharmacy was closed for two days and the whole town went to the church and then to the graveyard. Clara told some school anecdotes, and other people recalled funny or touching moments. Such a binding hadn't happened since Dr. Pratt's death in the avalanche that buried him on his way to a heart attack victim. After the ceremony, Clara walked over to Peter Tavistock's grave. At the edge of the graveyard, some wild roses were budding. She dug up a clump and set it before his stone. Later that summer at Abner Matske's funeral, she noticed that someone had pulled the shrub up and scattered the canes nearby. Peter's grave lay bare.

Late that summer a woman called saying she was a friend of Julia's. She had seen Julia at a political commune near Ojai, California. Julia was well but "nervous." Joseph and Tom got cards on their birthdays, and Julia said they could write to her care of general delivery, Ojai. Clara wrote, but there was no reply. "It's nice to know she's alive, at any rate," Clara confided to Alice, "and I'll get used to her being alive in places and conditions I know nothing about."

They were sitting on Alice's back porch after making jam from late raspberries. They had had a pleasant, desultory argument about the chokecherries just coming in. For years they had been studying the seasons of wild fruit, trying to predict their

164

ripest weeks. Alice got up, groaning with the effort. "This back-ache won't go away. Did you hear—there's a woman doctor com-ing to the new office in Callan?"

"Let's go down and stare at her through the window. I miss Dr. Pratt."

They went back inside to begin cleaning up. Clara told Alice that Thomas and Andy had joined the fire department. "He's a good man, Thomas is, and smarter than he thinks. He says when he's through school he wants to go on at the county, a heavy-equipment operator, like Oliver. He says he likes to overwhelm his problems with labor rather than transcending them with bril-liance, the way Joey does. Joey will go into the navy."

"You wanted college so badly for the kids—"

"Sin of pride. We don't have the money anymore."

"Sin of hope, and hope is in us to stay."

19

*D*enver was beginning its own boom, and the cliffs-and-canyons silhouette of its rising skyline was shown to Gold Flume in the background of the six o'clock news. Much of that skyline was the work of Ernest Reiber, the development tycoon. In the year Thomas graduated high school, Reiber announced plans for a theme park in the foothill suburbs of Denver. The park was to have a western motif and would be called Bonanza. People all over the state were buying stock.

"Well, old girl, should we take a flutter?" Andy asked Clara one evening. "If we mortgage the house we can recoup the loss, even the trips to Chicago. . . ."

She shook her head. "I'd be too nervous. The shares would become like a savings account, and what if they fell?"

"They can't fall; half the town's gone in on this thing. People you'd never think of as risk players are deep into it. The Austins have shares, and Carl and Alice, Anderson at the bank has shares, and so do the ski area people. We'd feel like fools if everyone got rich and we were left behind because of caution and cowardice."

"But we are cautious and cowardly," Clara said. "I'd be up all night, worrying. Did you say the *Bogards?* Carl? Alice?"

"Yup. Conservative Carl, accumulating Alice, even they. People who don't know how to read a stock market report are scanning the *Wall Street Journal* over their cornflakes. Your very own sons are making plans."

"Did they say so?"

"Joseph says that if he doesn't go into the service, he'll try to get on there as a laborer. Thomas can't wait to get through high school to go down there." Everyone's eyes were wide with expected wealth.

Alice often stopped in at Clara's after shopping and when she next came, they sat by the fire and talked, but their conversation was muted and Alice looked drawn. "It's range-feeding time. Storms can ruin everything, but it's more than that. The kids have left the valley and we realize now that none of them will be coming back to take up ranching. When that sank in, something went out of ranching for us. I'm worried, too." She looked out at the still-fresh snow banking Clara's yard. "We've borrowed money, too, quite a bit."

Clara was able to respond without surprise: "Ranchers are always borrowing—you've told me so yourself, against the calves, against beef prices for feed and equipment—"

"This is different. We borrowed to buy that Bonanza stock. When we thought at least one of the kids would come in with us, it didn't matter that we weren't big money ahead. The ranch has always fed us well and put a roof over our heads, but now Carl feels his age and doesn't know how it will be when he has to hire people to do what we've always done ourselves. It sounds funny, but we never needed to be rich before, and now we do."

When Clara told this to Andy, his face clouded. "It's crazy. It's crazy gold fever, Clar. I've let people in town think we've invested in the thing, too. No one talks about anything else, so when people ask you, don't say no. Maybe then, they'll stop trying to convince us."

"How much should I say we've invested?"

"You don't have to say. Just don't tell anyone we're not. People are selling stock they've had for years to buy in on this and the Bogards aren't the only ones borrowing to get more."

"You're scaring me."

"I'm scared myself. Last month I thought we might be foolish, but this stock business is swelling like a tumor. Nothing can sustain growth like that."

"Shouldn't we warn Alice and Carl?"

"Don't you think I've tried? No one's ready to listen."

Joseph wanted to join the navy but was inducted, while he waited, into the infantry. He trained in California, from which the expectation was that he would be sent to Vietnam. Clara steeled herself.

In February he came home on leave, and, when he returned to camp, was posted to Germany. "I'd be lying if I said I was sorry about these orders," he wrote, "and they can reassign me at any time, but so far so good. They may even give me some training that will be useful in civilian life."

Clara went up to Alice's, sat in her living room and cried with relief.

March came, and the heavy snows.

They would all remember it as an ordinary night early in April. Ski season was beginning to wane, with only the spring snow fanciers remaining. Gone were the college students and the church trip skiers from Oklahoma and Kansas. There was an easier, more relaxed atmosphere in town. Gold Flume looked almost as it had been, as it would be in its pictures.

Clara had been at her desk, planning her spring project; Andy was studying some paperwork. He would soon be needing someone in the office to handle that for him. The TV was on and the news was running only half-heard, so the bulletin was almost over before they were both shocked into awareness.

"Andy—"

"Wait!" The announcement was over. Andy began turning to the other channels that Gold Flume received, flipping past breaks and commercials. Then, they sat mesmerized and unbelieving. Reiber Construction was in bankruptcy. The empire had collapsed. The picture in Clara's mind was of the demolition of a huge building. She had seen pictures of such demolitions, the building suddenly gone to a painted image of itself, a scrim thirty stories high, and then the scrim falling light as a veil, in airy shivers, and only at contact with the ground the bricks becoming bricks again. The Reiber empire had folded in on itself and lay a ruin, and a cloud of dust was rising at the collapse.

Clara said slowly, "I'll need to call Alice—they'll be out working, maybe, and won't have heard—"

"We'll get the full story from the paper tomorrow, so we'll know more. . . ."

Andy had to go as far as Aureole for the papers, which were sold out everywhere else. In January, an electrician named Elton Yarborough had gone to the accounting offices of Reiber Construction. He was owed $148.48 for wiring an entryway sign to the Bonanza theme park the previous October. The disbursement officer had given him a check, which had bounced.

Yarborough went to the county courthouse in Denver and filed a mechanic's lien. In late February, one of the vice-presidents of the corporation got a call from Denver Industrial Finance. The five-million-dollar loan that Reiber had negotiated with them would not be put through because of a lien entered against the company. The vice-president told the finance company to wait a week until the oversight could be taken care of. The month passed. Denver Industrial called the Reiber people. The interest rate for the loan had been good only until the fifteenth of February. They could no longer make the loan at the old rate. The Reiber man figured the new rate, at a half percent higher. On five million dollars it was prohibitive.

A vice-president of the Consolidated Bank of Denver called Reiber. The bank's short-term note was supposed to have been paid by Denver Industrial Finance. Where was the money? Reiber said there was a temporary problem. The bank called Denver Industrial.

Two weeks later, agents of the Consolidated Bank of Denver appeared at Bonanza's building site with trucks and a warrant. They picked up tools, lumber, cable, and 136 cases of light bulbs. The employees on the site left immediately and began filing for back pay.

Clara and Andy read carefully, making sure they understood each part before going on. They explained it to each other, but Clara, in spite of the words, was seeing a breeze lift the curtain that had been a building, as the *whoomp* of the charge reverberated.

On the twenty-fifth of the month, potential investors and representatives of the First Bank of Dallas came on the site. They were working on a six-million-dollar loan for Bonanza and another six million for Reiber's other buildings in Denver. They saw that the work had been stopped and the area sealed off. They went back to Dallas and called the Consolidated Bank of Denver. C.B.D. called Chase Manhattan, which froze Reiber's account. Eighteen hundred employees immediately filed for

170

back pay, some of it owing since January. The scrim shivered and fell lightly as a veil, and the bricks became bricks as they shattered against the ground. Two days ago, the *Denver Post* said, Reiber Construction and Reiber Associates had filed for bankruptcy of a 216-million-dollar building empire. Elton Yarborough, asked for a statement, said, "Why didn't one of them guys pay me right then? They got that in pocket change. People been riding past my house shakin' their fists like I was to blame for all this."

Andy put the paper aside for Clara to take to the Bogards. "The town will go into another bust," he said. "Everyone but us and the Frenches was in on Bonanza." He looked weary all of a sudden, old in a way he must look to young people who hadn't known him when he was young himself. "I never wanted to live in a boom-bust environment," he said, shaking his head. "It's too much like living with Arlo, all flash and no substance. Maybe that's why I felt strange about all this. It stank of Arlo's grandiosity. *Empire.* The word alone is enough to make me check my wallet and lock up the family silver."

"The Bogards," Clara said. "Alice told me they had borrowed. . . ."

He came over and took her in his arms. "We'll go up there together," he said.

They hadn't heard the news. They had been midwifing three calves born early and had come home late and exhausted, had washed up and fallen into bed. In the morning, Carl said, he turned on the local ranch news for the weather and the cattle prices, assuming that the world around them wouldn't collapse in a day, the weather being fine and the prices holding. His only fear had been of a sudden freeze or a heavy snow.

Clara and Andy delivered the paper and left as one would leave a house of sudden mourning. They went home and came back again that night on the pretext of helping with the calves.

They brought things to eat, cooked them, and heard the extent of the Bogards' loss, money borrowed against the dream of hiring full-time ranch help, doing repairs, getting a hedge against all the ranchers' dangers of weather and disease.

"I'm going to have to tell the kids, because we may lose the ranch," Carl said.

Alice tried to comfort him. "We started out with debts this bad, and we climbed out—"

"We'll see," he said.

Alice got up gingerly. "I have an appointment with Dr. Hudson this week. It's my back again. I've been there four times and nothing seems to help."

"It's just strain," Carl said, with an edge of bitterness, "lifting those calves and bucking bales at your age. We're not kids anymore. When we started I could wrestle bull calves all day. I'm smarter now—but the energy isn't there anymore. If only the boys would—" and he shook the thought away.

Gold Flume, too, was under a pall. The Austins had counted on Bonanza money to expand their drugstore. They had borrowed heavily. The people at the bank were grim, and they were followed by rumors, a wind of whispers picked up and let fall, blowing down the night streets of the town. Had the Gold Flume bank gone into Reiber's debacle? Had the bank officers embezzled depositors' money to invest in the stock, thinking it was a sure thing? People stared and looked away.

"I started the deception to stop being nagged at," Andy said, "I never said we had invested, but only nodded and looked eager. Now I nod and look grim, but it feels wrong. And now the bank officers are all having to defend themselves against shadow accusations and suspicion. People want villains, and Reiber is too far away. People are asking why the bank officers didn't warn them against the archfiend from Denver. People are saying that the bank officials, Clint Anderson and Bill Cleveland, cooked the books. It's all wrong and stupid. People are shunning Clint and Bill in the street and the wildest rumors are going around. I think Bill will have to leave town. The bank did go in, but it was a bad investment, not a crooked one. The truth is that boom-and-bust is what we are—what we've always been. Why did Arlo stay so long in this area when I was a kid? It suited his style. Before the fancy changes, these roads were named Jackass Pass and Jackass Road. Jackass Road was where the miners carried out the ore and left the hole."

"Then no one knows how much was invested?"

"No, and no one knows how much was lost because no one has come out with an accusation. It's all bubbling and boiling in a whisper. Looks. Stares." Andy shook his head.

Clara shivered. She had one of the random connections in thought that made Andy say women were a separate species. She had watched him working. He had been coming home to sit up with office work every night. "You said you would get some help. It's eight o'clock most days before you're home."

"My mistress has been upset about that, too."

"Why don't you teach that stupid mistress to type and run office machines? With all the work you put out, it's a wonder you are balancing it at all. Tell her to quit buffing her nails and get busy."

"My mistress: seductive skills, A; office skills, F. Besides, her perfume makes the janitor's dog cough. What goes into the *Voice*: 'Wanted—brilliant and beautiful secretarial genius. Low pay, long hours; no chance for advancement'?"

"I've got someone for you."

"Who?"

"Chessie French."

Outside the window, four crows flew up from the creek, and Andy said, "See? Everyone is shocked."

But Clara could see he was thinking. "I would train her," she said.

Chessie was Frances French's youngest, one of those sudden surprises repudiating nature, nurture, logic, and cause-and-effect to restate the wild-card, random gifts of fortune. She was pretty, steady, aware, and intelligent, a girl whom Clara had seen go her serene way through grade school, acknowledging but not accepting the laughter and malice everyone heaped on the Frenches. When Chessie was in junior high, Clara saw there were jobs for her, and by high school Clara was studying ways to get her a college scholarship. The more she thought about it, the better Clara liked the idea of Chessie working for Andy.

She had thought of Chessie in one of those leaps of the mind, having begun with thoughts of the shameful rumors going around Gold Flume in the wake of the Reiber empire's collapse. Chessie had grown up in such a sea of scorn and ridicule. From the moment she was old enough to walk through town, she must have been aware of the looks, the words, the laughter no one bothered to suppress in her presence. Her brothers, cousins, and uncles were drunks and part-time criminals. Buster French, her father, was now a bootlegger and fence, when he worked at all. The family compound was now a full circle of derelict buses, buried in junk. Year by year its reputation had grown along with the rolls of stolen barbed wire, conduits, empty fuel drums, and rat-busy garbage. Their jury-rigged electrical system made the Frenches place one big fire hazard. Chessie, coming out of all that, had run errands since she was ten, baby-sat since she was twelve, and had, apparently on her own, learned to be neat, well-spoken, and utterly dependable.

"*You* keep the books. . . ."

"Yes, but Chessie can learn—I'll teach her."

"As long as I get the work done."

"It's practically done, now." Clara could see that Andy was allowing himself to be convinced.

"You're smiling," he said.

174

She nodded. "Something smiles inside when there's a chance like this. It's like the smile on one of those old Greek statues."

"It's a smirk, if you ask me."

A letter came from Las Vegas.

Daughter:

Keep this package. I was down in San Pablo and the old folks still remember you. *Don't open it.* TB has flared up again. Going south. If somebody shows up, charge them plenty. Tell them you had to buy other investors off.

The man who came for the package was a federal officer. When he began to explain his purpose, Andy excused himself and left the room. Clara gave the officer coffee and cookies and they talked about Arlo.

"He was a wonder, in a way. Ninety years old and still running scams . . . a rap sheet as thick as *War and Peace.*"

"He said he had been in San Pablo—he was scamming my old friends down there, wasn't he?"

"He told them he was your dad."

"But—I'm still in touch with those people—why didn't they let me know?"

"Embarrassment, probably. I don't think he got much. It takes a lot of energy to be a con man, which is why you don't see too many very old people doing it."

"Where is he now?"

"He's gone, Mrs. Percival."

"Escaped?"

"Died, and under odd circumstances, which is why I'm here. There was a package supposed to contain diamonds hidden in molten glass, which had been formed into something. . . ."

Clara got the package. "Size of a breadbox," she said, and handed it to the officer.

"Has anyone called about this, or come?"

"No."

The officer cut the double strings and pulled away the old-clothes wrapping. It was a glass paperweight. "Nice piece," the officer said, holding it up in the warm afternoon light. "Worth ten dollars of anybody's money."

Clara took up the paperweight. "You said he was dead. Is there a body?"

"He'd left San Pablo, as he said. It happened near Tucson. He was found under a bridge in what were . . . uh . . . odd circumstances. He had no ID. After what investigation they were able to make, they buried him down there, thinking he was a vagrant. The inquiry was sent out on a priority five, and I didn't get it for two months so he'd already been buried. If you want to exhume, I have the location."

"No," Clara said, wanting to add, "He hated it here," but afraid the officer would think her foolish. "Is this paperweight evidence?"

"It's evidence of the gullibility of about four hundred people. Keep it. I'm going to leave you twenty of my cards. Tell whoever shows up that the piece was taken as contraband by the government. We don't want his family inheriting some thwarted investor's anger."

Clara called Alice, planning to exult in the plans for Chessie and ask about her doctor's visit. She was also bursting with the news of Arlo. The line was busy. When she called again, Alice's voice was slow and seemed to stick to the words. "I was just calling *you*."

Clara began to dread. "What is it, Alice?" There was a pause.

"It's bone cancer," Alice said, "in four places."

Alice went on, giving a doctor's words about chemotherapy and radiation, but Clara was struggling too hard against the shock to hear meaning in them. "I want to see you," Clara said.

There was another pause. "The kids are coming up this weekend to help out, and I'll have the painkillers that will let me work as long as I can."

"I want to help, too."

"You will, but not now. Later I'll need to remember the books we read, all the canning seasons and the mushroom seasons and the talk we had, to go over it all with you before it's too late. . . ."

Clara put down the phone and cried. Afterward she was too restless to wait for Andy to come home and called him at work, and was oddly comforted by his gasp at the other end of the line when he received the news.

20

*T*hree days after Alice's halting words over the phone, Clara went up to see her and they wept together and went over the details: the spread of the cancer, the plans her doctors proposed, the symptoms, the tests, the findings. Alice was still able to work around the house and her daughters would come when she no longer could.

"And when can I come?" asked Clara.

"Come up on Saturday. Come up to sew and garden. I need to stop dwelling on this. . . ."

Later, Clara went down to the French compound to talk to Frances about Chessie. It was years since Clara had seen

Frances, but rumor kept her current. She had heard that Frances was a drunk now, bitter and foul-mouthed. For all her presence in town, Frances might as well have been a Gulch woman.

Clara was glad of the diversion from worry and sorrow over Alice, whose illness was made worse by her agonizing over the Reiber debacle. When she crossed the Frenches' footbridge, which must have been replaced many times since she had gone over it all those years ago, Clara felt altogether removed from the present Gold Flume. She remembered the small, quick little girl who had been Frances Legrand: "Teacher, Miz Percival— them books—" and the gentle, almost reverent way she had taken them. It was a sweet memory and Clara had used it, unfolding it now and then to hang before herself in times of need. She had kept it separated from the later memories of Frances, preferring that resolutely naive and credulous child.

The compound had added buses and grown. Like cancer, Clara thought, and had to stop and clear her eyes of tears, her mind of Alice's face. The litter had grown, too, and lines of barbed wire were hung with bottles and scrap metal, probably to warn the family of the approach of strangers or to scare away wild dogs. All the snow had melted here. There was no tactful covering of the mounds of rubbish. A clamor of tin cans, strategically placed, brought out an old woman who stopped defensively behind a fifty-gallon drum to stare at Clara. She was stooped and stringy, with a belly poking out from under her sagging sweater. Clara looked again and saw that missing teeth had caved in the face of a relatively young woman. "Frances?"

"Hi," Frances said. "Come on through and have a beer."

Clara started to refuse but stopped, nodded and walked through the narrow aisle in the litter. Frances's hand was still up, as though shielding her eyes from morning light. There was a defensiveness in her posture that reminded Clara how Frances had never been able to get beyond people's scorn the way Chessie was able to do.

"Come on up." Frances motioned to the gravel-filled container that made a step up to one of the buses. A makeshift door had to be moved so that Clara could follow. The interior had been gutted and fitted with a woodstove and some bed frames and tables. Clara wondered where Chessie slept. How did she keep clean in this tangle, years of it, winters freezing and summers baking? Clara, who had used her own poverty-blighted childhood as a yardstick by which to judge all the poverty she had seen thereafter, was shocked into the revelation that her life had been a magnitude's remove from what she saw and smelled here.

Frances went to a bucket in the corner and pulled out three tall boys, popped the tabs expertly, and handed one to Clara, possibly conscious of the closeness and stench in the bus. She said, "Let's take this outside—it's warm enough out there by now." Clara, whose eyes had just grown accustomed to the gloom, now saw three small children staring at her from places on the clothing-strewn floor. One of them had started to cry.

Frances paid it no attention, and they left, stepping down into the mud of the yard and around to the back of the bus. There was a cleared place with three benches that faced away from the compound and into the now-leafless tangle of brush and a few pine trees. It was sun-warmed, out of the wind, and perfectly clean of trash. "Chessie and me made this," Frances said, "and the boys and them don't know about it, just only Chessie and me and Grandma Daisy French and Grandma Legrand. Sit down." Clara began to sit cautiously. "Don't worry, these benches here'll hold you." Her words were difficult to understand, coming past her missing teeth.

They had their beer, Frances drinking deep, Clara sipping for companionship's sake. After a while Frances said, "Buster's gone again and I don't know if he's coming back or not."

"Who else lives here with you?" Clara gestured back at the other buses.

Frances began to count them all off, twenty or so, some of them people Clara had forgotten were still alive, old people and children, mostly. "You here about one of the kids?"

There was a way to help Chessie, Clara told her. She and Andy would train Chessie, who could work afternoons and Saturdays during her last year of high school and then for two or three years full-time, saving for college. Clara would tutor Chessie so she could go for a full scholarship. Frances listened, finishing her own beer and then another, and then the one Clara had started and left. Frances had once been easy to read, her emotions coming and going on her face unchecked, and this was one of the things that had made her so vulnerable and easily seduced. By now, the hard years had taken the trust out of her and Clara had no idea what her mind was saying behind the unchanged expression.

"Chessie's different, ain't she?" Frances said.

"Yes," and Clara thought, You were, too, but didn't say it.

"She'll do what she wants, but I'll tell her you come."

"I thought you should know what we were thinking, Andy and I."

Frances nodded, sniffed.

Clara looked at her and said quietly, "How have you been? I haven't seen you in so long."

Fortified by the beers, Frances began to talk. Her slurred words weren't maudlin or raging, but hard, simple, and bitter. She told Clara things about Gold Flume, about its people and the life the Frenches lived here. Some of it Clara knew, but knew in another way, a softer way. Some of it Clara hadn't known, and Frances painted the people of the town in colors darker than Clara had ever seen them. It was another hour before she got up.

Frances motioned to her and said, "This here's better," and led Clara by another way to the footbridge without thanks or good-bye. Two days later, Chessie came up the street to Andy's office and began to work for him.

Clara began to spend Saturdays up at Alice's, and at first their friendship seemed as easy as it had ever been, but both of them achieved this only by ignoring all that was foremost in their minds, the Bogards' losses at Bonanza and Alice's present dying. They talked about Arlo, about the development, Flume Heights, that was now across the Jackass Pass road from the Percivals' house. The company had widened and paved the road, and the development had arrived in explosions of dust and granite. Lines of trucks, poundings like an immense buried heart, had followed, then houses, rows of them, obedient and trim, eyes front. "I remember how it was when someone new came up Placer Gulch," Clara said. "Mama would clap her hat on and we would rush over to visit, happy, curious, and, Mama said, 'with a cake to get us in' to look and talk. Were they friendly? Were there children?"

"And now?"

"And now we have fifty new neighbors and it's all I can do to pass the place, it's so daunting. I *am* going to visit the ones with kids. I have sworn to!" And Clara was gratified to hear Alice's old laugh.

The second time Clara came, they discussed the bankruptcy at Reiber, edging closer to what was hardest. "That collapsing building was so huge that it's still falling," Clara said. "Six new people have just come to Gold Flume and started their young-sters in school for these last nine weeks. They were all engineers and builders from Reiber's Denver mess. The ski area hired them for its expansion. Did I tell you? The company's bought Grubstake, the whole mountain, and it's going to build another ski resort and a huge lodge; a whole valley will be full of chalets."

Alice looked dully at Clara. Death dust and ruin dust had clouded her vision so she couldn't imagine the change.

"Don't you see what that means?"

"No."

"It means that the ski area people bought stock individually, but the company itself didn't. It's growing, and that means the Reiber mess didn't hurt Gold Flume, because most of the skiers come here from out of state. Land prices are going to soar, so if your kids want to sell the ranch, and if they can hold out for a few years or so, they'll be rich in a way they never could have been by raising stock."

"Is that supposed to cheer me up? Carl and I put a lifetime into the ranch. You've grown up in mining—the land for you was something like an impediment. Earth was there to be pulled away, blasted and chiseled away from what you were hoping to find. For us—"

"Damn it, Alice, I don't expect anyone to cheer. The skiers are tourists; they invest nothing and they don't care where the water comes from or where it goes after they use it." Alice looked stricken and Clara gentled her voice. "The new people are a mixed blessing, sure. I don't like it that Flume Heights blots out the stars with its lights or that the name 'Jackass Pass Road' isn't good enough for them, but your family won't be ruined. The kids will be able to sell the ranch as they would have anyway, or they can make a dude ranch, or in any of a dozen ways come out richer than ever."

Alice's tears began to follow one another more and more rapidly until she shook them away. "This dying biz has turned me stupid and self-centered. We invested and borrowed. Some part of Carl wants us to lose the ranch as a punishment, and because I can't think past the summer and I don't have much energy, I'm not fighting."

"Fight, Alice. This is one you can win."

21

*T*he April ground swells with corm, bulb, and root. Snow-white flowers bloom from the lips of departing snow. The spring beauty comes complete, and the pasqueflower. The arthritic fingers of wild apple branches hold blossom clusters in their thousands. "Quiet," Andy says. "You can hear the branches pulling sap!"

Clara was grown and working in a war plant before she learned that willow, oak, and maple, which were shrubs in the valley, were trees elsewhere, taller than houses. In the valley, the green things had been humbled by the difficulties of growth and drought, cold, and short summers. Long ago they had learned not to hope so high or bud so early. The maple bush doesn't leaf out until June.

But the sweet cherry, the apple, the lilac, and the snowball bush are newer immigrants, and they haven't taken the password into the mnemonics of their genes. They are fooled every year into stretching and budding and leafing in the warm suns of March and April. They give and give, and just when their million blossoms are ready to burst wide open, the sudden freeze burns them black and shatters the sap-stained branch from the inside out, exploding it as from a lightning bolt. The freeze lasts a day or two and if the lilac still hopes itself green, the snow is yet to come. To the end of May, snow can drive through the valley, breaking branches, all those million lush shovels of leaves, and bowing the bush to ground and freezing it there.

Then came strangers from sea-level places, all the motel people, orthopedic surgeons, engineers, shopkeepers, restaurant workers, all needing places to live. They bought houses in the developments south of town on familiar level land that the river had made, and then they came to the development up the hill to the north, to Flume Heights. These strangers came yearning for the green they had left far beyond these mountains. They sent to nurseries back east for their rosebushes and their azaleas, their oak trees and elm trees and weeping willows, flowers and shrubs, domesticated as lap dogs and dumb-trusted away from caution, to bud and freeze.

Early in April the new doctor's wife planted a dozen red Countess Someone rosebushes. Tyrone Legrand, the garbage-man, took their blackened corpses away, coming across the road to snicker about it to Clara. "Roses! What will they do next? Did you see the weeping willow they got up that street? Truck come and put it in; I bet the dang thing's ten feet high. Weeping. They'll be the ones weeping." And it was so. The April snows broke every branch and freeze-exploded the sap so the tree looked burned.

185

"At least what you got here can't freeze," Tyrone had said admiringly, pointing to Clara's yard ornaments, twenty-seven of them now, at the east side of the house. "I remember when there wasn't only ten or so. I thought coming up here was dying and going to heaven, seeing all them toys, the moving ones especially."

Clara neglected the parent visits in May and June to spend her Saturdays with Alice. Carl was usually out and that was a relief, because he now haunted house and barns, grieving from chore to chore about his ruin. The time of the land was past, his children had told him. In ten years the condominiums and town houses would be creeping up these hills and gulches and the valley beyond. Their land was near town, well watered and sheltered. It was prime land, but soon the whole thing would be taxed beyond any rancher's ability to make a profit from cattle. So Carl walked, muttering answers to their invisible presences and to his creditors and to his wife, dying before his eyes.

Through the spring, Alice's pain was easily circumvented and she did her work, using different combinations of drugs to trick her body, but by July the amount she had to use to dull the pain was dulling her as well, and she lost the patience to relive old joys with Clara. She yearned for the slow opening of deep talk from a mirroring well of stillness, but desire without patience made her weep with frustrated need. In July she lost even the desire for remembering. She argued with Clara, with Carl, with everyone, envying all of them their youth, life, consciousness, most of all their freedom from pain. By August she was visibly dying, beaten back to the solipsism of the baby, her world no wider than her bed. Clara had been aching with the loss of her best friend for three months before Alice died.

"Why do you have to do parent visits at all?" Andy asked. "In the old days it was a necessary thing. There are more children this year—three hundred in the school, you said—"

"It's good to meet the mothers informally. It's good for them to know me so I'm not unapproachable, and this time I'll be meeting them in small groups. I'm going across the road Saturday afternoon for tea. Mrs. Treece is having it for the five new engineer wives, the ones who came in the spring when Reiber folded."

"Saturday . . ." Andy said, and then understood that it was Clara's way of filling the day she had been spending with Alice.

Andy had enjoyed Carl's company and respected him. He was fond of Alice, but he hadn't seen the ranch as a refuge or enjoyed the Bogards' friendship the way Clara had. After the funeral they went up to the ranch, but Carl rebuffed them. His grief had metastasized into grievance and spread even to friends. "It's too bad," Andy said, and was resigned.

But for Clara, the ranch was another loss. She and Alice had gone berrying along its creeks and walked its meadows for more than thirty years, and she had begun to dream of the land in ruins, with its glades and grasslands burned. On the night before her meeting with the Flume Heights mothers, she had another kind of dream: The Flume Heights houses had merely been facades. Their formal and forbidding doors opened on Fern Hill, Alice's broad north pasture. It was summer. Clara and the mothers began to run, racing up the hill to the sky-dazed meadow where summer flowers lay tangled in the long grass. By the time evening came they had become friends. All the mothers looked like Alice, but at the different stages of her life. The pictures were so intense that Clara woke happy in their afterglow, aware of the dream's metaphor.

There wouldn't be another friend like Alice, with whom there were years to be shared, but new friendships might still come, and she might see past the size and grandeur of these houses to the people who lived in them. Maybe one or two of the mothers would enjoy the books she did, or would like to hunt for wild herbs and forest mushrooms.

"Here I go," she said to Andy. "I will put on my new blue blouse with the frilly collar, and I will put my comb and handkerchief in my pocket, so I won't have to wrestle with my purse, and I will go over to Flume Heights and meet the mothers."

"Tea, huh?"

"Absolutely. Tea. Little cakes, too. Finger sandwiches."

"Is that like a knuckle sandwich?"

"*You'll* get a knuckle sandwich. Go enjoy yourself caulking the windows. I have to wash my hair."

22

At the side of Rosalie Treece's house the remaining orna-
mental tree had been eaten leafless by deer. The lawn lay baked
brown, as did most of the others along the row. Rosalie saw Clara
looking. "We can't get enough water for it. You water half an
hour and the pressure falls to nothing all through the development. Then it runs muddy."

"I don't think this grass is native here," Clara said tactfully.

"My petunias dried up in July," Rosalie persisted, "and I got
them right here in Aureole."

Clara smiled. "Oh, I know how to save *them*."

"How?" Rosalie looked dubious.

"You put your household water on them. We have petunias, pinks, and columbine, vegetables, too, and table herbs. The mountains are hard country, but if you take them on their own terms, they'll let you have lots of things."

"We water them, but . . . ."

"Use the water from your washer, your dishwater, and bath and shower water, and the water you collect when you run the faucets to get the water hot—all that—"

Rosalie was staring at her. "That would take buckets, carrying *buckets* of dirty water. . . ."

Clara saw Rosalie's surprise and distaste, felt a stab of loneliness keen as ice, and said, "It's habit. I do it for my vegetables, my flowers, and for my trees." She looked down and noticed a run in her stocking. They went into the house, making a tacit agreement to start again.

There were only two other women there. "Carly was sick and Ellen couldn't get a sitter," Rosalie explained.

The house was larger than it seemed from the outside. The close presence of all the other houses in the row had changed Clara's sense of size. There were deep carpets on all the floors and heavy furniture in scale with the rooms, low tables that were sheets of plate glass resting on stone columns, huge couches, breakfronts, many lamps. Even in the bathroom there were things put out solely for decoration, interesting in themselves. Clara found the rooms daunting, but the heavy carpets and drapes sucked up the chatter and laughter of the women, so their sounds made no more than polite ripples in the deep pond of the living room.

Rosalie Treece was younger than the others, married younger, Clara thought, and a mother sooner. Her children were in kindergarten and second grade. Mary Anne Van Dyke was the oldest, a large, plain woman with a maternal quality Clara found attractive. When Rosalie mentioned the dryness and starkness of the mountains they could see through the picture window, Mary Anne laughed and said that having been raised on a Nebraska

farm, the country seemed lush and green to her. Helene Singleton shook her head incredulously. "You drive forever to get any-
place, and when you get there, there's nothing. There's not even
a decent grocery store." The tone was aggrieved. Clara felt a
need to defend the valley towns, but she stifled it.

As Helene talked on, bitterly, Clara realized that she was the
focal point of the group. She was a tall, handsome woman,
dressed with casual elegance. At first, Clara would have said she
was beautiful, but as she studied Helene and tried to see where
the beauty resided, she realized that the effect had been made
not by nature, but by an incredible skill. Each feature had been
studied, then its faults shaded back, its good points brought forward, and the whole brought into a harmony that made her ordinary features seem beautiful. She had done the same thing with
her dress. Every line had been chosen to enhance the positive
features and subdue the negative ones. This was a study as rigor-
ous as any literary or mathematical one. It required, Clara realized, a disciplined denial of personal vanity, a cold-eyed,
clear-eyed assessment of features and posture. It gave Helene's
scorn an importance and validity it would not otherwise have had.

"The town has grown so quickly and changed so much, there
hasn't been time to build the stores and businesses for people
who live here," Clara began, and was annoyed at herself for
offering a defense.

Helene went past her. "And then there's that mess across the
road, which we have to pass every day—Rancho Glorioso, the
amusement park, we call it. They actually hang their clothes out,
too, billowing underwear and all. Why doesn't the development
have it zoned out?"

Had Mary Anne Van Dyke said that, Clara would have
laughed, and then they would all have laughed, but Helene's elegance had created a space around her and her tone had no
humor in it. "The development has no control over that house,"
Clara said. "The house was there years, generations, before the

191

development was built. Are the garden ornaments and drying clothes so visible from here?"

"See for yourself when you leave"—Rosalie laughed— "although I have to say our kids keep begging to go over. God knows who lives there."

"God does know, and so do I." Clara tried for lightness. "Andy Percival and I live there, and your kids are as welcome as they can be."

There was utter silence, and then Mary Anne gave Clara her steady, countrywoman's gaze and said, "What a wonderful way to get kids over their fear of school and the principal. How did you think of it?"

Clara began to explain the long-ago iron deer and the year-by-year additions, Andy's impatience with the tradition, Julia's joy and then her scorn. Mary Anne showed her understanding of the situation. Rosalie and Helene, city-bred, did not understand. "About the laundry," Clara said, "I didn't realize how much it showed. I can't put it west of the house—too many trees, and there's the creek, but I'll get Andy to turn the line poles so you don't get the broadside view."

And Clara suddenly knew, as sure as snow in May, that the minute she left, Rosalie Treece would say, "She waters her flowers with used bathtub water. She carries buckets of it in and out!" A terrible pang almost brought tears: Gulch girl. She wears her frilly blouse that's too fussy and hangs all wrong, a countrywoman with work-roughened hands posing as a school principal. Then she made herself think, I'm not here for their judgment. I'm here to get to know the parents of my school. She said, "Bad as the amusement park is, the kids come up every year and there are stories connected with everything, and some of them are quite good."

They stared at each other in silence. "I don't know why the school is so small," Rosalie said. "Our kids are in temporary buildings and they won't be heated well enough."

Clara talked about the sudden growth in Gold Flume. Then she said to Mary Anne, "I know where *you* come from, because you told us. I don't know where you are from, Rosalie," and she saw Helene wince. Was she supposed to call them "Mrs. Treece" and "Mrs. Singleton"?

"We are from Atlanta. We planned to settle down there, but . . ." Her words trailed away in the unexplainable reality of her present plight. How could we have ended up here, here in the bone-bare mountains of this inhospitable place? Rosalie turned to Helene: "You grew up in Washington, D.C., didn't you?"

"The Virginia side," Helene said.

"Helene designs clothes," Rosalie explained. "She designed and made the outfit she's wearing."

Clara said something that showed appreciation, thought of telling Helene more, and decided against it. Two of the three women had been in sororities in college. They had learned light conversation and social ease there. Clara felt another moment of loss.

Helene Singleton was staring out the picture window with bleak distaste. Her husband's job had landed her in a place she obviously hated, and with a talent she felt would go unused. She might have been a concert pianist in an Eskimo village. "Ten years ago," Clara said, "we had a retired man here. He was fascinated with bats and knew all about them. I asked him to come up and teach, and he did. His enthusiasm was so contagious that a number of the children went on into zoology because of it." Remembering that time, she felt herself relaxing. "There were bat lodges all over town—" She looked at Helene, wondering if her example had been understood.

Helene said, "Designing takes talent. Bats do not."

"I only thought you might share some of that talent with the children. The fifth- and sixth-grade girls are always drawing and doodling, and many of their ideas are about clothes. If you could

193

guide that interest . . ." It sounded weak in this overfurnished room, spoken to the elegant woman.

"No, thank you," Helene said coolly, and Clara heard the studied sound of a hundred sorority tea afternoons. "I'm going to be in business here," Helene said. "I've designed a line of ski-wear. Women have been skiing in men's clothing, sized for women, with all the femininity of baseball uniforms. If people like my designs, I'll be able to make the transition to New York with my other things."

Clara was awed. "Did you go to school—I mean to a fashion institute?"

The expression froze again. Clara wondered why she kept hitting cold walls in this woman whenever she moved.

"I went to *college*," Helene said. "Women in our family weren't encouraged to pursue careers. I was expected to be in college for the MRS. degree. They waste us. They waste our lives and our ambitions and our talents."

"They?" Clara asked vaguely.

Helene didn't answer, but bitterness had scored lines in her face that the makeup didn't blend or cover.

They ate the little finger sandwiches then, and Clara was subdued and careful. (What have I said? How did I insult her?) Rosalie asked about cultural activities for the children, and Clara thought that here at least she might show the valley to advantage. The library was rudimentary, she explained, but there was interlibrary loan, so any book was available with only a two or three day wait. "Now we have the educational channel on TV, too—and plays, operas, theater—" Clara felt herself breathing against the words, working hard. "I'm a *Hamlet* fan. I got the Olivier version for school, and we showed it last year in the gym. Lots of people from town came. The Derek Jacobi one ran on TV, and we have Richard Burton on cassette tapes at the library. That's three *Hamlet*s in three years. You don't get that on Broadway in a decade."

"There's no dance, no ballet?"

"Well . . . I've never seen a live performance up here, but some of us went down to Santa Fe one year for the opera, and people always go to Central City. . . ."

She was trying too hard. "Gold Flume isn't Athens," she said, "but it's not Yonville or Gopher Prairie, either. We have a professional chamber music group playing in Aureole every other year—and really, how many concerts and ballets did you go to in Washington or Atlanta?"

Then she looked up and saw the anger in Helene Singleton's face. She had hit a target she hadn't even seen with a weapon she wasn't aware of using. She almost said, "Oops."

"They ought to hire you for the Chamber of Commerce," Mary Anne chuckled, and it was, for the moment, all right again.

When Clara left, she was careful to note the unfolding view of her washline and the painted animals, plaster gnomes, windmills, and flapping ducks that Helene had called an amusement park. That night she said to Andy, "Your underwear has gone public. We'll need to turn the washline and I'm going to give my frilly blouse to the gypsies. We'll put in a line of willow shrubs on the east, but before that . . ."

"Don't those people wear anything underneath?" he asked.

"No one knows. They all have clothes dryers."

"They really got to you, didn't they?"

"She got to me, Helene Singleton."

"Singleton? I had lunch with Hugh Singleton today. He's new on the fire department, a nice guy. He's in love with these mountains. He told me how he had to take something quick, anything, when Reiber went belly-up. All of them were desperate, and they hadn't been paid in three months. He said he would have taken a job in hell redesigning their brimstone delivery."

"They must be husband and wife, then."

"Two kids, two little kids?"

She nodded.

"Well," Andy said, "he did twenty minutes on how they came over Victory Pass, how the mountains looked—I even remember some of what he said. 'I felt like I was in at the beginning of Creation, before God clothed the bones,' and 'The snow on those peaks was a part of the first snow that ever fell.' Poetic—" and they stared at each other in wonder.

After supper Clara took Andy to look at the amusement park and see how they could move the washline pole. Behind the Percival place the mountains lifted up and away. It was true that they had been scarred and laced with abandoned trails and played-out mines: Little Lonesome and Big Sarah, Martha's Cut, Bendimeer and Bendixen. They were all leaching yellow and fanning a spew of tailings from their silent mouths, but couldn't those people see how the light poured over it all and blessed everything? "The nights here used to be velvet-black as an emperor's pockets," Clara said, "and the stars used to tremble and catch their edges in the trees over there. . . ." She sighed. "We'll move the line and plant the willow, but by the time it blocks out the ducks—"

"Those damn ducks," Andy said, "and the damned windmill."

"—by that time the haters will probably be gone."

Because Elton Yarborough was owed $148.48, Reiber Construction in Denver had collapsed. Because of that, four women had been put together in a living room in Gold Flume, Colorado, two of them hating it and one perhaps becoming estranged from a husband who had fallen into his spiritual home.

Two days later, the blue dome lowered gray and spat snow, and a wind howled it down the gulches and beat the withering snow over the passes. It was just a dusting, but the leaves of all the remaining imported trees lay in their broken branches in black and frozen heaps.

23

The Gold Flume bank managers and their families left town and the question of whether or not money had been embezzled for Reiber stock was answered in the negative by the new directors. Still, the rumors continued to drift on like the stench of a dead animal days after its death.

The Treece children had come into school and the Singletons, but there were also Cyril Boda's grandchildren. "How many children and grandchildren did I expect to see through school?" Clara mused to Andy. "The Bogard kids left, Peter Tavistock and Johnny Austin are dead, Lucinda moved and never married. . . ."

"You teach two Bordereau grandkids."

"Yes, Frenches and Matskes, too," she said ruefully. "I'll retire in five years, and if I still have my health I'll probably do tutoring—"

"You may have to," Andy said quietly. "Land values may have gone up, but land taxes have trebled. We may be forced to sell off some of this acreage."

"I don't want to leave the valley."

"If we have to, we can sell the south seven acres. Did I tell you? Millburn Tavistock died the other day. For God's sake don't go down there with a casserole again."

Clara laughed. "What will Dorothy do? Live in that crumbling mausoleum all alone?"

"If she sells, she can get a fortune. That place is bad for a house but great for a saloon."

Developers bought the land the Frenches had been squatting on, and after a hard fight they were resettled near Bluebank. Chessie got the developers to haul the family's buses to the new site. The place was leveled, the creek given new banks with a sort of levee, and a street of shops sprang up almost magically. One of them was a fashion boutique, and in it a section of ski-wear. It was Helene Singleton's Nini.

Clara read about it in the *Ute River Voice:* HIGH FASHION COMES TO GOLD FLUME. The article said that the outfits had hardly been displayed before they were sold out. "Singleton has gone from the sewing room in her house to the old Phillips garage, where four workers will be cutting and sewing her fashions. We will be seeing the Nini logo, a big N with NI on each upstroke, reminiscent of a mountain silhouette, being worn by women skiers on our slopes and, as time goes by, perhaps worldwide."

"I met your nemesis today," Andy said, "the lady herself. At the Chamber of Commerce lunch."

"What did you think?"

"Nice girl. Homey type." He was grinning. "I don't know what I liked more about her, her gentle kindness or the self-effacing charm she radiates. Why don't you stick to your old nemesis, Ma Tavistock? Gone all spidery on you, has she? Not enough action?"

"I never choose my nemeses; they choose me."

"Wrong. Had you caved in, Ma T. would have liked you well enough. It's the same with this here new one. I've got to hand it to you, though, your nemeses are top-drawer."

"She is amazing, though—what she makes of herself."

"True, but don't get in a gunfight with her. The bullets will ricochet off her corners."

The long, golden autumn passed and the ski season began. The streets of Gold Flume were crowded with skiers and the beer halls threw open their doors, filling the streets with light and noise. The skiers had so much heat from their youth that it flowed out with their singing, their laughing, their drinking, and poured out into the icy night streets so none of the saloons needed to close their doors.

In November, the little McLean boy fell off a swing, breaking his arm and bruising his face and hip. His parents declared they would sue his teacher, Clara, and the school. There were conferences and sleepless nights, worry about lawyers, recriminations. At first Clara had been dumbstruck. "Children fall!" she cried to Andy, and then to the county's lawyer, Mr. Clayton. "They fall running or climbing or in any number of ways. What is 'due care'? We tell them to hold on when they swing. A lawsuit never happened to us before." She felt herself turning grim and fearful.

The boy recovered and the idea of the suit faded, but Clara and the teachers had been changed in small but profound ways. They were all warier, more defensive, and the worriers among them besieged Clara with their nightmares. Could a child slip on the wet floor in a bathroom? If a teacher put a scarf on a little child in such a way that he could remove it, and he did and got sick . . . Dogs were following some of the children to school. What if . . .

A Chinese family came and opened a restaurant in Callan. The black family of a construction worker came and there were racial slurs on the playground. Again, Clara stopped school for a day and called an assembly. This time she was prepared for criticism but took no pleasure in her preparation. "It used to be fun," she murmured, communing with the memory of Alice Bogard as she walked up the hill to home. In these months of early darkness, the gassy glare of reflected light from town now followed her up the hill. "It used to be such a joy!" Andy was a good listener and a wise advisor, but he wasn't good with plain worry or agonizing or things for which nothing could be done. Sometimes she had talked to Alice about family things Andy didn't want to hear. Then she lightened.

After three hitches in the army, taking college courses when he could, Joseph had come out a college graduate. He had majored in math and had been working with a small computer printing company, designing systems. He lived in Denver and seemed happy there. Physically, he was the image of Arlo Percival, complete with the mane of hair, the grace, the easy smile, and captivating laugh. Now and then he would bring young women up to Gold Flume, one, then another. At first Andy was suspicious, but it was the quality of the young women that changed his mind. In the beginning, Andy had muttered to Clara, "Why shouldn't he have lots of them? Women fall for charm, don't they?"

"These aren't pushovers off the farm," Clara said. "He's been in the service and in school for years—Arlo wouldn't have lasted under that discipline for seven minutes."

"I know. . . ." Something in Andy relented a little.

Then he came to ski with a girl named Barbara once, and

then again. "This is the one," Clara told Alice. Six months later Barbara and Joseph were engaged, and the next June they were married in Denver. At their wedding Thomas met Gudrun, Barbara's housemate from Norway. That Christmas, Thomas went to Norway to meet Gudrun's family. Clara and Andy traveled to Bergen in August to be at the wedding, agreeing wistfully with Gudrun's also wistful parents that the young couple, wherever they chose to live, would make someone sad. Thomas got a job in Denver as a heavy-equipment mechanic.

Julia had been moving, now west, now south, staying awhile, moving on. In the last years she had been letting them know where she was. Clara sent news of the weddings. After Thomas and Gudrun had married, Julia wrote a letter.

Dear ~~Mother and Father~~, ~~Mom and Dad~~, Clara and Andy,

It's true—I don't know what to call you. I've been away so long and had so many lives since I left Gold Flume that my time there seems to have gone small like a scene through the wrong end of a telescope. At the same time, I find parts of that life sticking to me even now.

It's because I'm a mother myself. Liberty was born, you would say, out of wedlock. I had the wedlock twice, and it was lock, all right, so now I'm staying with someone, and either of us is free to leave at any time.

We've lived in different communes, as you know, and in one of them we took Native American names. I kept mine after the commune broke up, so I use that now, and if you use it, too, the mail will get to me sooner. My name was SoulDancer, but it's so hard in this society to have only one name that I took another, so I'm Anna SoulDancer.

I started this letter to say something like good luck on the occasion of Joseph's and Thomas's marriages, but I don't believe in personal ceremonies, really. Things change without our doing very much. Why do we congratulate ourselves on inevitable birthdays, anniversaries, all of that?

"Why are we reading this?" Andy asked. "Why isn't the Soul-Dancer family reading it?"

We are having our victories. Young people are learning from us the things I had to find out on my own . . .

"She's having better luck than we did," Andy said.

. . . and while liberation may take longer than we had planned, things are moving and I guess that inspired me to write this letter. The West offers little if you don't like waterskiing or lying in the sun. I'll be moving away from California. Mexico is a place that appreciates single mothers. Women are respected there, and children are loved. We will go there soon and I'll write as soon as I get settled.

When Clara finished the letter she and Andy sat and looked at one another and then they started to laugh, first slowly and then in gusts. They laughed without knowing why, until their sides hurt and they were both in tears. "Your daughter"—and Andy hooted again—"your daughter certainly knows how to spread joy—"

"Stop it—it hurts too much to laugh anymore."

"SoulDancer? I wonder what that dance is."

"The dance you do when you stick your finger in the light socket," and they were off again. "Why are we laughing?"

Clara had written steadily over the years to Julia's many addresses. Now and then, Julia answered but always said she was too poor to afford a trip home. When Clara offered money for the fare, Julia said there were better uses for it. Liberty had been born when Julia was with a group called What's Coming near Oakland. There had been two pictures, one of Julia and Liberty when the child was about three, one of Liberty alone at seven or eight. Andy and Clara had never seen their granddaughter.

School was to begin again. Clara met with the teachers.

"Dare I suggest we shorten the poetry contest this year?" Sharla, the fourth-grade teacher, asked, looking around at the other teachers. "Parents are complaining about the difficulty."

Clara followed her look. Others nodded in agreement. "I've gotten complaints, too," Clara said, "but I always have. Memory work is difficult, and the vocabulary is unusual, but memory is the forte of the young. Why not exploit that gift?"

"What nine-year-old understands Gray's 'Elegy'?" Sharla was beginning the argument they had all come with for the last twenty years.

"None, I think," Clara said, "but there's a feeling awakened by the rhythm and flow of the words. Slowly, meaning emerges, and one day a girl may look around at her situation and say to herself, 'I'm wasting my sweetness on the desert air,' and in those words, that idea, a wisdom is there for her, to use and draw on."

"I'll admit I didn't agree with your emphasis on poetry and memory when I first came," Marie, the third-grade teacher, said, "and to a degree you convinced me, but things are changing. We don't have the mandate to teach the way we did. We don't have the authority to make our judgments accepted automatically."

"Rote learning is"—Darren, the fifth-grade teacher, was being careful—"out of fashion now. People think it stunts mental growth. Parents say it isn't creative."

Clara felt an emotion that had become annoyingly familiar in the last years. It was an impatience and frustration that emerged as sorrow, not anger. There had been a time when she had waded into the familiar argument, proving, defending. But then the teachers themselves had all memorized the preamble to the Constitution, the Pledge of Allegiance, the words to "America, the Beautiful," all four verses, and whatever poems and speeches their own teachers favored. The new generation's teachers had never been taught to memorize anything, and they had never heard a defense of memorization in their schools. "Teach them how to think," everyone said, as though memory had no bearing on thought.

Sharla said, "Some fourth-graders like the poetry contests. They like the mastery of big poems and long words."

"Then it's in the fifth and sixth grades that you are encountering criticism?"

"Yes," Darren said. "All of the new people ask about what college will accept a Gold Flume education. From the early grades on, they are aiming their kids at eastern or western colleges and scared stiff that Gold Flume won't measure up."

"Recitation day, spelling and poetry contests, sound as passé to them as McGuffey's," Darren continued, "and they're competitive. Parents think competition is okay in sports. They're in a sweat to start a Little League. They'll make their kids drill for hours catching baseballs or sinking baskets, but pull a drill in history or spelling and they're on you like glue. I could make the memory work stick because I'm a male teacher, but parents don't really want it. We've stopped being experts and have begun to be servants or, at best, baby-sitters, offering a product that parents vote on." He looked levelly at Clara. "And I've heard complaints about The Jail."

Clara had never called it The Jail. Years ago she had marked off a space in her slowly shrinking office, where children sat who had been sent there for misbehavior. It was the children themselves who called it The Jail and ascribed great importance to it.

"Parents complain that the kids are being publicly shamed," Darren said. "Everyone who walks by can see who's sitting there—"

"I don't know how we can fix that," Clara protested. "I often have to leave the office and I don't want youngsters poking around in my desk. The public gaze keeps them honest."

"I know the kids like to brag about their dramatic brushes with authority, and they do weave stories about The Jail. It's the same as the haunted house."

"What haunted house?"

"You know, the place down by the tracks where the old lady eats children."

"The *Tavistock* house?"

"Yeah. There's almost a body of myth grown up around it. I hear all kinds of stories, seasonal ones, some poetic and mystical, some funny, all terrifying, though. Old lady, big house—it's made to order. Rattling chains, ghostly screams."

Chessie French, still on summer break, was helping Andy with his new computer. Clara stopped in one morning. "Did you ever hear stories about Mrs. Tavistock—that her house was haunted?"

Chessie grinned. "We started hearing those stories after Mr. Tavistock retired. There were lots of them. What's funny is that those stories are the same ones I hear at college. Kids who have never set foot in Gold Flume tell about strange goings-on in other places, and the stories are the same. One is about children being captured and dressed to replace the dead children of the family, then killed themselves, of dead bodies embalmed and put around a dinner table." She laughed. "It's funny now, but when I was growing up, it was nightmare country. The first misunderstanding of words I can remember had to do with those stories. The kids heard the term *serial killer* and thought Old Lady Tavistock gave stray children drugged oatmeal."

24

*C*hessie went back to school and Andy began looking for full-time help. Although there were other surveyors in town now, Andy got most of the work because of his knowledge of the area. In November he went to a convention in Denver, partly to study the agreements of partnered men he met there. He called Clara the first night and talked about how surprised he was at the reactions of eagerness to his inquiries. Only a few years ago the suggestion of a partnership in Gold Flume would have drawn no interest. Now he was all but besieged with candidates. "I feel like a Hollywood director casting a movie. Where will it end?"

She laughed. "Have a good time down there and don't cast any leading ladies. Winter's come up here. The pipes at school froze and made a mess. Here the furnace man had to replace the widget-sprocket. I checked your office and you've got another leak in the roof. The management company promised to see to it. This conversation would drive anyone into the arms of a convention groupie."

"Two days away and all this? And Helene Singleton thinks small-town life is dull!"

"I miss you. They've lengthened all the days since you left."

"Give my love to Sammy Horner."

Buster French's cousin Sammy had been the school bus driver since he was eighteen. He was fifty now, driving the route every day and not drinking on the job. When Clara went out to talk to him at the school parking lot, she was still smiling inwardly at Andy's call. She told Sammy that the school administration was splitting the district. There would be three drivers. He asked if his two nephews Elvis and Johnny Ray could get the jobs. Clara wrote to Chessie, who said the two were all right. On Clara's recommendation both were hired. They got along with Sammy and did well with the children. They knew the routes and seemed to like the challenge of driving the winter roads. Clara was pleased.

The running of the school and administrative details took up so much of her day that the controversy about poetry projects, curriculum, and The Jail faded for a while. The halls were still lined with the biographies she asked each grade to write and post at waist level for the younger ones to read. But Clara was now and then aware of changes in the vocabulary and expression of the children, and of a tone at once more worldly and less knowledgeable. She still enjoyed sitting in on the classes for as long as she could, observing a discussion or feeling a mood in the room. Yet what was it flavoring the days? She had a persistent unease at what was there and gone, so subtly, at the edge of words. There was a certain incivility, a breach in some important element in the social contract. Or was there? Cruelty had always been there, surely. Had there always been this guardedness, this jaded quality, this passivity?

The Frenches were gone, all at the new school in Bluebank. The Gulch children had disappeared and an entire class of the starving poor had dwindled away. Everyone now had heat and water inside the house and a flush toilet. No one ate stolen horse fodder in winter or came to school with the welts of chilblains or fainted with the illnesses that hunger exacerbated, but . . .

But there was something smooth, passive, and arrogant in the manner of many of the children. They now said to teachers, "You have no right to touch me." "This lesson is too hard—my father said I didn't have to learn it." Their postures and faces said, "I will do nothing I don't agree to. The adult world is my adversary." Their manners said, "No one defines anything for me."

They were less judgmental of physical deformities in one another. They didn't blind cats or tie cans to dogs' tails to make them run in panic, but the thirst for learning Clara thought would bloom naturally in them when they were all adequately fed and clothed had not appeared.

Fewer parents came to school nights or other town events. The engineers' wives had jobs and worked at the new college extension in Aureole, and now it was difficult to find parents to set up and run the school trips. The six or seven programs Clara usually brought in during the year had no parental help. Yet the houses glowed blue with TV until midnight.

The snows came one after the other and the Christmas holidays were a record in the town. Every hotel and motel was filled, and the townspeople made money renting out their spare rooms to skiers. Nini put on three new workers and hired an office manager. Andy said that Hugh Singleton was awed by his wife. "He thought she would have a hobby designing, something to do

208

in the afternoons, which, if she was lucky, would pay for itself, and for the fabric she bought, and even for the hair salon and cosmetics bill, which is close to a small country's GNP. Instead, here she is, making double what he is, and pretty soon she'll be paying more income tax than he earns."

"Can he take that?"

"He's getting ready to."

"Could you?"

"I did, you remember, starting out. It was five years before I came close to the salary you got as teacher-principal of a one-room school."

"But you had every expectation of overtaking me—did it bother you?"

"I'll have to admit, it did. There was a time, about three years into the thing, when I wasn't getting on as fast as I thought I should—you'd gotten a raise, I remember, and we were paying John Steadman and you were pregnant with Joseph. It wasn't suffering—but I did feel a pang now and then. Hugh's situation is different. He'll never make a tenth of what she does if she keeps on going. Right now, she could buy him out and go to Paris if she wanted to. Although this will turn out to have been a good move for her—launching a career with skiwear—in five years, she'll be gone."

"I'll be retired by then, and I'll be able to go across the street and see her off. A bouquet of mountain flowers would be nice, don't you think? Devil's paintbrush?"

"Clara Percival . . . shame!"

The February thaw came early that year. The snow on the mountains went gritty for a week or two and the town snow turned gray with decaying mounds of half ice that froze and thawed in the daily rises and drops of temperature. Black ice gave at the edges but it was still iron-hard in all the low places, and the morning's cold wind rattled the teeth like loose windows.

Sammy had the south bus run. The north-of-town runs were given to Johnny Ray. Clara knew he was annoyed by children being tardy and keeping him waiting, and she had written notes home to some of the Flume Heights parents because of it. The day's classes had already begun when the school secretary, Alvia Dener, put her head in at the principal's office. "Carl Singleton's out here—"

"What's up?"

"You'd better come out and see."

Helene's son Carl was now in the third grade, a shy dreamer of a boy, still front-tooth-less from the second grade when all smiles were gapped like losing prizefighters'. He was given to long silences from which explosions of words burst out in rapid speech, drying up to nothing at the first request for explanation. He stood wide-eyed and pale with the fear children have at being singled out. Clara's eye passed down the plaid flannel shirt and corduroy pants. "Carl—where are your shoes and socks?" His eyes went brimming. "Didn't you come to school with them?" A shake of the head. "Didn't Mr. French notice you had no shoes?" Another shake. "Alvia," Clara said, "call Helene Singleton and ask her to come over here with some shoes and socks for Carl." She got up and went to the lost-and-found box and got two mittens and put them on Carl's feet. Alvia called the Singletons' home. There was no answer. "Call the factory," Clara said.

The woman came billowing into the school, her eyes wide with fear, looking past them, exactly like her son. "Where's Carl? What's happened?"

"Didn't Mrs. Dener tell you over the phone?"

"Where's my son?" She was walking swiftly as she asked the questions, and they came into the outer office where Carl was sitting next to Alvia's desk. "Carl—" She didn't notice the mittens on his feet.

"Helene," Clara began, "didn't you get Alvia's message?"

210

"I was at the atelier. One of the workers answered the phone. She said it was about Carl and I came right over." Helene was staring at the little boy, who was now weeping with anxiety and shame. "What is it? What's the matter?" Her voice was strident in the silence of the room.

"He didn't wear his shoes and socks to school," Clara said.

Helene exploded. "How could you have been so stupid! I thought he had been hurt. I rushed up here thinking God knows what. You could have told me over the phone."

"We tried, Mrs. Dener tried."

"When I came in—"

"We thought you knew—"

"Why didn't you call the housekeeper?"

"There was no answer," Alvia said, beginning to lose her timidity in annoyance.

"She might have been in the basement, or busy. Why didn't you wait and call again?" Helene demanded. Clara could see the darkening in Alvia's face. "Stupid," Helene muttered, "just stupid. Now I'll have to call her myself and get her to come over here—"

Alvia opened her mouth to say something. Clara said quickly, "I'm sure you're relieved that Carl is all right. Things like this happen all the time. Youngsters hurry to school and coats, lunches, books get left behind—"

Helene was dialing the phone. She spoke briefly and hung up. "The housekeeper is coming over with the necessary clothing," she said frostily, and left.

Behind her, Clara heard Alvia mutter, "You're very welcome, I'm sure."

"It's only her embarrassment. Don't take her seriously."

"I'm not going to be spoken to like that," Alvia said. "That woman is going to apologize."

"Let it go, Alvia—she's so embarrassed she wants to disappear in a hole."

"That," Alvia said, "might be arranged."

When Clara got home that evening Andy was already there. "The deed has been done," he said, "and tonight Mr. and Mrs. John Isabella are coming up for celebratory drinks. Break out the beluga and the beakers of champagne. I have an associate."

They were nice people, the Isabellas, but had no children, which was why Clara hadn't met them.

The evening got merry. Clara made a party dinner and everyone ate well. The Isabellas had brought champagne and after dinner they all sat back and found themselves swapping town legends. The Isabellas knew some of the French stories, even though the French compound was gone. By now the tales had a mythic quality and were told with a certain flair. When the sheriff's office opened its substation, the officers were called French chauffeurs. Buster French got drunk and fell off the railroad trestle into its stagnant pond—French dip. "Not Buster, Kester," Clara said, and then she laughed, but both she and Andy had the awareness that these tales weren't invested for the new tellers with a knowledge of the Frenches as real people.

Clara told about Mrs. Kenner, who, if she liked you, would knit you a pancake hat like the one Erasmus wore, or socks with knots in the toes that could cripple you; about Evelyn Matske, whose stroke made her aphasic except when singing and swearing, which she kept up until her death. "Did you hear the one about Andy Percival, who was running for the fire truck on a false alarm, tore his coat on the closing door, fell, and sprained his ankle?"

Denise Isabella unfolded the lurid tale about the old recluse in the haunted house. "Of course I've never seen her."

"She's real enough," Clara said, "but I think she'd be horrified by the stories because they make her sound low class—common, and she couldn't stand that. The truth is that she's stuck in that house missing people I miss also."

"Were there children?"

"There was a son and a daughter. The daughter is a successful sculptor in Taos, but never visits Gold Flume. The son died as an afterthought to the Korean War."

"I hate coming in in the middle of the story," Denise said.

"When the Tavistock house was built," Clara was enjoying her tale, "Gold Flume, Callan, Bluebank and Granite and Aureole were all big towns. This valley had a population of three hundred and fifty thousand, and almost as many millionaires as Central City. When the Tavistocks came, we all thought the mining would start everything up again. When I came, Gold Flume had about fifty people living in it, most of them old. Now it's a tourist town—"

"—and land prices are out of sight," John Isabella said. "We can't afford anything near town, but we just got five acres near Callan and we're going to put a house trailer on it until we can build. It's halfway up Wildcat Mountain—"

"Near the Boda place?"

"Cyril Boda sold us the land—"

"It was funny," Denise said. "He didn't say two words to us. His wife did all the talking."

"Cyril's not much for talk," Clara said, and began to tell stories about him. His brother, Sulo, had died in 1966 under a tractor he'd been fixing, and at the funeral she had gone over and drawn Cyril's attention to the grave of Peter Tavistock, Cyril's only school friend. It was on the other side of the graveyard but visible from where they stood. "I had once put a wild rosebush there and it had been torn up. The grave had gone untended for years, except for its big stone, but then someone had come and put three large wild rosebushes in the waste space behind the grave. The bushes had grown up, protected by the stone, and they made a kind of bower all around the untended grave. I told Cyril I thought I knew who had done that. He looked at me with that stare of his and said, 'I saw how things was when I came to bury my dad. Peter was my friend,' and that was all."

"You'll have to visit when we get the house built, then," Denise said.

"Nice people," Andy declared when they had gone. "New friends, maybe."

As Clara lay in bed that night, her mind drifted back to Carl Singleton standing in the office without his shoes and socks, to Helene's anger, to Alvia's set face. Alvia Dener was now dealing with a lot of parental resentment. She had been a school secretary for ten years, a position of sensitivity and great respect in a town like Gold Flume. Many of the new people treated her like a low-paid clerk or office underling. Alvia sometimes expressed the feeling that she and Clara stood against these new people and their demands. Look at that lawsuit—it was true that the McLeans hadn't carried it out, but who can expect that children won't fall, get sick, lose things, fight during a day?

And Alvia knew even more about students' private and home affairs than Clara or their teachers did. She had had to learn complete discretion, but now she was angry and felt embattled, at fault because she hadn't headed off the unreasonable mother. Should she laugh with Sammy at the bus stop or complain at the altar guild or in the robing room at choir before church, the town would have the story in an hour wafted all along its older streets. The thing would take air then and blow full like washline sheets in the wind. It would get funnier, wilder, the frazzled mother being made to seem loony and bizarre, and when it got funny enough, it could cross the barriers between the old Gold Flume and the new. Helene Singleton would hear it and assume Clara had spread it. "I've got to tell Johnny Ray and Elvis to check the children for clothing, and to send them back home if they don't have coats on or shoes and socks. I've got to tell Alvia not to mention—not to say—" And then Clara was asleep.

214

25

The new development south of town was now so large that its residents petitioned the highway department to build another exit off the interstate. During its construction, the engineers were forced to divert all the adventitious creeks and runnels of the Ute back into the mother river, and the oldest of these, Selevan Creek, had been rediverted just down from the southern edge of the old French encampment.

Alvia came into the office early and stood before Clara at her desk. "Do you know what's going on at Selevan Creek?" She was still in her coat and hat.

"No," Clara said, "but there's something I need to discuss with you."

"They're going to try to keep it out of the paper," Alvia said, having launched herself, "because there's going to be more. They're going to dig down to bedrock right there and down creek all the way to the old fishing rock."

Clara knew when she was beaten. "What's this all about?"

In the diversion of the creek, Alvia said, the skeletons of three tiny bodies had been revealed. Two of them had been fetuses, one had been fully formed, and the doctor said it might have weighed as much as nine pounds. The little bone baskets hung on rocks in the creek bed, sketchy as scrimshaw.

"Frenches," Clara murmured.

"No," Alvia persisted, "the Frenches *had* all their babies, but didn't you know three of the older ones in that family were granny women? They must have taken the fetuses they got out of the girls and women and thrown them into that creek. The sheriff's going to Frenches' to question them today, but they'll get out of it. They'll claim ignorance, and how can anyone prove anything? Half the town's at the creek now, digging down to see what else there is. . . ."

Clara hadn't known that the French women did abortions. No wonder Frances was bitter and thought the Town people were hypocrites. During the day, the digging revealed six more skeletons, some of them almost full-term babies. Over the following weeks two camps of opinion formed. One said the bodies were from the Frenches, another said that they had come from far upstream where they might have been buried and that the bones were from some old family graveyard and had washed down to that stagnant bend below the compound.

The Town people could bear pain, sorrow, poverty, even tragedy, Clara thought, but not the ugly banality of what they did in secret. Theories ranged from a cult of devil worshipers to a prostitution ring up in the next county. And wasn't there something mystical, symbolic, about the disposition of those lacy little bones? people asked. Hadn't Clara seen how the bones were lying when they were found and how they lay in relation to the ones that had been unearthed earlier?

"Don't you tell me small-town people are lacking in imagination!" Andy mused as they compared stories at dinner. "There's more deep fiction coming out of that firehouse than out of TV in a week." He put on what he fancied was a Gulch accent. "I tell you it makes me proud to have raised up chirren in sich a rich envirement."

"Not funny," Clara said. "Gold Flume's *chirren* will be dreaming about this, having nightmares. Those little bones are closer to their size than ours. A kindergarten child or first-grader can easily picture his own little corpse down there in the water."

Two days later a heavy snow fell, and when it stopped, an unseasonable, bone-shattering cold followed it. Pipes froze and burst all over town. Power was off, car batteries defeated. Clara closed the school and for three days everyone was sent backward into Gold Flume's past, the wood-burning past, kerosene and candles and thunder mugs and water settled out from melting snow. Clara heard the stories: God's anger, the atom bomb, the Russians seeding snow clouds with sodium iodide. She thought of the barren prescription, "Teach them how to think," and muttered, "If I teach them how to think, I'll be alienating them from their parents." God, Russians, and atomic power relented, and the town thawed sufficiently for school to begin again. Soon the skiers were back decorating the slopes and filling the saloons.

"We have to steal a march on reality," Clara said. "We've had Selevan Creek and we've had the cold snap. Next week there's an eclipse, and we teach it before someone ties all three of those things together and starts dancing naked in the street." She was eating lunch in the teachers' room. "Let's declare an Eclipse Day, study it, read Mark Twain's account in *A Connecticut Yankee*, and trace all the places the sun will eclipse—it would have to be on a line, wouldn't it?" She sensed unwillingness in their silence, heads down. "What's the matter?"

"These breaks in routine take more than they give," Sharla said, "and the children don't have an idea of the world yet, mine don't, so all the lines and talk wouldn't mean much. The parents wouldn't like it because I'd have to make up the day's lesson, somehow, and that would mean homework."

"And what if it does?"

"Only a quarter of the children *do* the assignment, any home assignment. Parents get angry, kids get resentful, and it just isn't worth it. I don't give them homework anymore."

Clara's eyes went from teacher to teacher. Two of them only shrugged.

"This is an eclipse, a total eclipse," she insisted. "We may never get one of those again in our lives."

"And what if it's overcast or cloudy?" Sharla said. "They'll feel it as a betrayal. Their ordinary lives are too shaky—with moves, divorces, custody problems. A quarter of my class isn't living in the same place with the same family it was three years ago, and I've just got Claude Sargent calmed down. He had three tantrums last week. Claude can't take changes and we're behind in the curriculum already."

"Claude's problems are hard on everyone, but this is an eclipse!" Clara said. She said it into their bored faces. The unapproachable moon had been reached, walked on, and was now passé. The teachers had already informed Clara there wasn't much interest in outer space, and the order sheet for the series of books she had wanted on space exploration lay on her desk. With such a response, she couldn't justify filling it in and she couldn't bear to throw it away.

The mountain spring, still half winter, lay its equivocating hand on the town. The snow drew away, revealing last November's lost sock, blown newspaper, and a dead bird or two the cats had missed. There would be snows through May, but now Clara yearned for soft winds wandering like tourists through the town, bearing the ferny, mulchy smell of soil swelling with spring beauty and wild chive. If only the winter's end would come without the wet, heavy snows and the mud!

The teachers had begun to talk about the spring sales. "Everything in Gold Flume is overpriced," Marie said. "I'm waiting until school's out to get the discounted winter stuff, whatever's left."

"Nini's got a sale."

"Too rich for me," Betty said.

Clara looked over at the second-grade teacher. "I didn't know you skied."

"I do, a little, but Nini has more than skiwear now. It's not a full line, but there are blouses and things. There are hats, too—it made me think maybe I'd look better in a hat. . . ."

After school, Clara walked down into town feeling excited and slightly wicked. For a year or so there had been time only for quick errands. Today she looked in windows and went up and down streets, random as a tourist. Two blocks off Main Street a big new deli and bakery had gone up, and a florist shop and beauty parlor were now in the old ski area building. She went down by the depot, now a fancy restaurant, and across the bridge.

She had imagined something like a row of shops in the cleared space of the Frenches' compound. What she saw was a new street, parking, shops, a background of foliage, but nothing remaining of the terrain that had been there. Low places had been banked up, higher ones cut away to make the street level. A new, terraced earthworks had been built up and the shopping street lay entirely separated from the Tavistock house, banked off by a hill.

Clara went slowly down the street, shop by shop. There was a travel agency, a gift store, a boutique selling underwear and lingerie, a children's store, and then the place that featured Nini.

Helene's things were only part of its window display, but there was no mistaking them. The front had two windows. In the first were the ordinary blouses, skirts, and dresses. In the second stood a mannequin posed in full ski outfit, of bright royal blue on its top, then shading through the blues: electric, cerulean, French, powder, lighter and lighter to a baby blue so light that it was almost white. The figure of the skier seemed to float, and there was a special emphasis on the lines of the lower back and behind. The look was of speed and lightness but was irrepressibly feminine. No wonder they can't keep these in stock, Clara thought, and went into the store.

A few weeks before, Andy had surprised Clara as she was looking dubiously into the mirror. "Do you like what you see?" he asked.

"No. I've gotten thick and wrinkled."

"Why not go downtown and get yourself something with bows and polka dots? We've had a good year. We own the house and the car. If you see something that will set my pulses racing and drive me mad with desire, mortgage the house and buy it."

"Buy it and never count the cost?" Clara had laughed and forgotten.

But now, she stared at the price tag—seven hundred and fifty dollars. And the sportswear—blouses and tops mostly—had price tags that made Clara wonder if she were reading them correctly. Still, she thought, she might buy one blouse, one special blouse—that light green one. She went over to where the blouses hung, took the light green one down, and walked over to the mirror. Its color brought out a delicate tone in her face and harmonized with her hair, the gray looking whiter. Her eyes now had a pure green color instead of being nondescript. She took in her breath.

But the style—it was all sleeve and front fall. This blouse, these clothes, had been made for other lives than hers, younger ones, and with no children's reaching hands, no fussy cookstoves or dishes of spaghetti or need to wash out chalk dust. Still, if that color ever showed up again, that delicate green . . . where would she ever find such a color in such a fabric? Buy *this* blouse? To wear with what? To wear *to* what? She hung it back on its hook.

Then she wandered slowly through the display, idling a little, sad but relieved of the burden of choice. There was a little L-turn, and behind it she heard women's voices. Clara went around the L and saw four of the ski area mothers standing together: Rosalie Treece, Mrs. Keller, Mrs. Deaton, and Molly Sargent, Claude Sargent's mother. It had taken some time to learn their names, except for Mrs. Sargent, whose son's problems had made her a regular at school. She stood a moment, getting them right.

There was something familiar about the group—she had seen it before, just the way these four had placed themselves. She moved out around the displays and came toward the women, and except for Mrs. Sargent, they greeted her without recognition. She was, out of her context of school, simply a local, a Flumer. The working jacket covering her dress didn't help any. There was a pause in their talk and then laughter. They had finally placed her. So this was how the Frenches felt in town. No wonder they stayed away and sent the kids for what they needed, and why they never ambled the streets or looked in the store windows.

Clara walked back up the street and was comforted to see familiar faces. The ordinary daily sounds came and went, greetings and small talk, and it seemed to Clara that she hadn't heard it in this way before, as a defense against the loneliness of a separated life. In her absentmindedness, she turned the wrong way and started to go up the bank building's stairs to Andy's office, but the office hadn't been there for years and she stopped with a feeling of being caught out at something.

As she continued up the street to where the office now was, Clara remembered where she had seen the group of women standing in the same way. It had been at a parents' group social moment. As she looked at the group in her mind's eye, something was obvious that had not been so before. Town and Ranch people and ski area people had always been separate socially. What was new was that the groups were standing far apart from each other, two separate bodies. A newcomer would have to choose, would be made to choose one group or the other.

She hadn't realized how rigid that separation had been. When had people stopped talking across the groups, finding middle ground, making compromises? Clara had a feeling of helplessness and that reminded her of her age. She was an old, forgetful woman, who had lost something she cherished without knowing how or when it had gone.

Andy was out of the office and John Isabella was busy. Clara walked the two miles home, trying to banish a gnawing anxiety and a sorrow that made her shiver.

"It isn't me they hate, but Gold Flume!" she protested to Andy that night. "It makes them want more than any school can give."

"I'm surprised the teachers voted you down on Eclipse Day," Andy said, "but that reminds me. I stopped in at Doc's office and got that bunch of old X rays you wanted. At least the kids will have something to look through if the sun does its job. The sun in splendor and Mrs. Jurnigan's kidney."

"In the old days we would have said just that," Clara said, and then shut her mouth on the words. She had sworn to stop sifting the tailings of the past for its forgotten treasure. The level of the children's chosen poetry had gone down. The length had halved because no one praised the activity or took for granted that a child could learn all of a Keats ode or Gray's "Elegy." Every time she witnessed the falling-off, she found herself beginning, "We used to—" and had to amputate the words. "Eclipse Day has been called," Clara said, "but Raptor Day will come. It's going to be the Wednesday after next. Can you come?"

222

"What is it?"

"I'm inviting the town, anyone who wants to come. This has been in the works for two years."

"What's the attraction?"

"Talks about raptor birds, yes. Pictures of raptor birds, yes. This time we will *see* the birds themselves: eagles will be there, and falcons, owls, hawks, trained and wild, right before us, close up." Clara's eyes were shining. "They didn't want to come all this way, the raptor people. I had to make it worth their while—to get the other valley schools involved and to get the raptor people invited to two nights' lodging and food. Still, it has happened. I will look into that eagle's swiveling eye and hear its wingfeathers snap like a fan."

Andy was looking at Clara. She was almost an old woman, but sometimes he saw her pull out a sudden radiant beauty from somewhere and put it on, and it fit smooth as her own flesh and it lay there as naturally on her old woman's face as though it had always been there and always would be.

Through the next week Clara paid particular attention to the weather. March was a heavy snow month, but weeks might go by as mild as May. If a snow closed the passes and roads, the raptor people wouldn't be able to get through, and they wouldn't travel in bad weather.

"When you invite folks," Alvia said as Clara peered at the clouds coming and going over Gold Flume Mountain, "you suddenly become responsible for their trips—the odd storm, the food along the way, and the dead battery in their car."

"I will stand at the door and I will say: 'Welcome to Gold Flume School, Mr. Falcon, Miss Hawk, Señor Gavilan, Señora Zopilote, Madame la Chouette. Fly right this way. . . .' "

"Bird-crazy!" Alvia snorted. "This job has driven her cuckoo."

"It's rapture of the raptor. They're coming—can't you hear their wings applauding?"

26

*T*he weather held, an ideal bright, cold weather, dry in the valley but with two or three inches of soft snow falling by night on the high slopes. The awe that comes with great good luck silenced all but the rowdiest skiers, and they moved in that silence, almost tiptoe in the streets of Gold Flume. Such was the new snow at the end of March, so light it could be sent back into air with a whisper.

Raptor Day came, and Clara stood at the school door and waited for the blue van the raptor people would be driving. Two boys were sent to the office for fighting. "Not today," she said. "I have no time for stupidity today." They went back to their rooms pride-wounded. Nine-thirty came and passed. Ten. Perhaps the van had met with an accident coming over the pass. Clara saw the cages on the road smashed, the birds crushed, and an aimless drift of feathers awakened in the wind of passing cars. Then at ten-thirty she saw it moving out of the traffic of ski buses and cars and coming toward the school up the road. "They're here!" she cried to Alvia behind her. "Don't call the children out yet—there may be some elaborate procedure of unloading—"

"Good Lord!" Alvia cried. "I've never seen you as fussed as this."

"I never have been. I've seen big birds up close twice in my life—one great horned owl and one falcon, and I never forgot it."

The van came to the school entrance and stopped. A young woman climbed down, looking very official in a khaki uniform. Clara went to her and they talked about unloading the birds. The woman was defensive about their lateness. She had also mistaken the Callan and Bluebank exits for Gold Flume's, but she couldn't resist Clara's utter joy and was soon lost in it. "Wait till you see what we have—I was lucky to get our largest birds—"

She and her partner were soon unloading and setting up the cages and displays in the gym. "This is going to run into lunchtime," Alvia said with a little irritation.

"We'll have it after lunch, then."

"What if it runs past three?"

"Then everyone will be late."

"I've had calls, four calls."

"Good," Clara said, refusing to be drawn. "Tell whoever calls that we plan to start in an hour or so."

By the time the raptor people were ready, it was lunchtime. Then Clara called the children to come, class by class, to the gym, where the sixth grade had prepared things earlier that morning. Every time there's a program, parents complained, the children have to waste school time putting up the chairs and taking them down.

"We're teaching them that effort has to be taken," Clara had said. "They lie in their seats like beds."

But the time had come and the first-grade children moved through the hall to the gym, and then the second grade, moving past Clara, who was standing at the school office door. The third grade passed. She was about to say something like "You're going to enjoy this program," and she had begun to say it when, on the neck of a small boy passing, she saw a little dot. She stopped the children and said to their teacher, "Go on, Mrs. Cannon, I just need this boy for a moment."

It was Carl Singleton. She looked at the dot again. A tick. It was a little brown tick. She had always been amazed at how, even with fading vision and from many feet away, she could tell that the small, brown, motionless dot wasn't dirt or a freckle. "You've got a tick on your neck," she said to Carl, "and I'm going to get it off. Then we can go to the program." He looked up at her, confused about why she had taken him out of the group.

She turned to the secretary. "Alvia, why don't you go on into the program?" Alvia hesitated, looked at the tick, then nodded and left.

Using turpentine and tweezers, Clara took the tick off, pulling against the slight resistance of the gripping head. She looked down his back, pulling Carl's collar away from his neck. There were more.

Clara knew the rule. Teachers were forbidden to undress students, but Clara had bathed filthy bodies and sponged scrapes and pulled wet clothes off freezing children for thirty-five years. Ticks were carriers of disease, but she hated them with a visceral loathing that exceeded their danger. Pulling ticks was a truer local spring ritual than rolling Easter eggs or gathering flowers.

There were four ticks on Carl's skinny body, three on his back and one on his chest, and Clara's distaste of the insects must have shown in her face because his lip began to tremble. She calmed him with the explanation of what she was doing. "I think you may have more ticks. Take down your pants and let me see."

He opened his pants and let them fall. No underpants. He must have dressed himself, Clara thought, or the housekeeper might not be all Helene would have wished for.

There was a tick on his buttock, at the end of his spine, and that tick was fat and full of blood. There was a tick on his testicle, but it had just settled and she got it off easily. Carl pulled up his pants and two tears rolled down his cheeks. The turpentine might be stinging, Clara thought. She wrote a note and pinned it to his shirt, telling him to take it to his mother. The note alerted Helene to Carl's susceptibility to ticks and said he should be inspected for them every day from the first of March through the season. They hurried to the program.

Everyone was impatient but Clara got order and the raptor woman came forward with a hawk perched on her arm. Its presence drew a sound of amazement no one was aware of making. The two experts showed the owls and told stories about owls' skills at hunting. They introduced hawks, falcons, eagles, and the smallest and largest of each species to the wide-eyed children. The silence and attention were all Clara could have wished for, and when the birds were taken into the audience to be touched and seen up close, some of the children wept with awe.

She was glad the program had been held over. The children would have been fit for little else after that, and now they would be able to talk about it on the buses, all of them reminding one another how the piercing eyes of the owls looked and of the sudden shudder of a stretch the bald eagle had given, two yardsticks wide, and its sudden collapse into its tight, compact perching stance. As she walked to the buses, Clara saw the children miming the birds, becoming the birds, wishing themselves into that purposive, complete, and graceful power.

The days were now obviously lengthening. Another spring was opening outward. Snows fell, but they fell blue and the sky above them was so blue as to be almost purple. At sunrise, white haze blew virga into diamonds through the air, and on some mornings, fog roiled in all the low places so that the rising sun underlit the fog and made of the whole valley a smithy of angels.

Clara and everyone else in town was tired of snow. It made April the low time of the year. They were tired of driving in it, walking in it, clearing their walks of it, and unpacking school-children from winter clothes, of its melting into mud and ugly slush. In the school, new children had come and one or two of the new parents had shown interest in chaperoning the yearly museum trip to Denver that Clara now had so much trouble putting on. She hoped the parents would be as good as their intentions. April limped into May.

The state had mandated new tests, and Clara and the teach-ers had their hands full scheduling them. The state-mandated curricula hadn't accounted for the days of snow closures and Clara's extra programs. She was also trying to find an expert who would provide guidance for her as she struggled with Claude Sargent's behavior. He was a child of sudden, uncontrollable rages. During these, his violence seemed to know no separation between people and things, himself and others. Sometimes he would sink into a dreamlike, walking blindness, going in and out of the classrooms, touching himself and other people on the face or body. Usually, he sat staring, empty-faced.

Clara had told Claude's parents about his behavior. They had denied it. She had called and written to the administration for psychologists, but without the parents' cooperation, no help was available and the new laws said she had no power to remove a child from school. The county had a home-teaching program, but the Sargents wouldn't consent to it.

In the middle of May the valley got a deep, gummy fall of snow, wet and very heavy. Katy called from Aureole. Oliver was working too hard, she said. "I hate it when he's up all night. He should have retired three years ago, but when he started in the system you didn't have to show a birth certificate and he gave his age as younger than it was."

Clara knew from Tom's years with the county that the spring snow removal was the worst part of the job. Oliver had been at it around the clock for days, grabbing only an hour or two of sleep, pulled off on the roadside. The new people weren't content to stay snowbound for a day or two until the plow could get to them. He had a county low-band at home and a CB radio, so he wasn't isolated on the gulch roads or between the towns.

Oliver was checking in every few hours, Katy said. Then, when all the roads were open and Clara's anxieties were calmed, Katy called breathless with weeping. "He came straight off work yesterday. He drove the plow home instead of leaving it at the shops. He was so tired he could barely take off his clothes." Katy described Oliver's heavy sleep, his sweating and pallor. She had called the doctor, and then the whole world had fallen in on them. Oliver had been so exhausted that even now they couldn't tell how much damage his stricken heart had sustained.

Flowers bloomed, the school trip came and passed, the year moved toward summer recess, and Clara went through the days only peripherally conscious of the work she did. Oliver and Katy's kids came back to help on weekends. Clara and Andy visited and helped with shopping and visits to the hospital. At first the doctors thought it had been a light attack, then that it had been a serious one. Oliver was in ICU, then out, then in again. One of the medications had had a reverse effect and for a while there was a worry that it might have caused permanent damage. Clara came and went only half-attentive to school problems and meetings. Her attention was concentrated on the daily rise and fall of Oliver's condition.

A group of parents presented complaints at the spring meeting. Why were there no individual computers at school? Why were the sports programs not more competitive? Why was there no soccer in the grade schools? Clara reminded the parents that all these were matters mandated by the county and should be discussed with the superintendent of schools. The parents seemed aggrieved by this answer, and one said, "If you had fought for more—"

"I won't fight for more because I don't believe in too much dependence on computers for children at this age." She was being impolitic and she knew it. There were ways of making personal wishes seem the hostage of forces outside of one's power to change them, but she was now too tired to dissemble. She told them the children needed more direct experience, not less; more field trips, and not fewer; less either/or reasoning, not more. "That's what I believe. The administration has decided to give computer training and the children have the program. It takes up four class hours a week for every class. The fourth grade can't sing the national anthem or point out where Europe is."

They stared at her. She had expected to see Helene Singleton among the parents, and was relieved that Helene wasn't there. A newly arrived father said, "You're still making them memorize poems."

"True."

"They don't like it."

"I know, but once they do the work, they're proud of themselves and we hold poem duels and the winners are admired. They still gape at the power, the lift, of sonorous words. That gift grows."

"Why do you give them those mottoes?" the man persisted. "Don't you know the old answers don't hold anymore—even the children know that."

"The old questions are still the same," Clara said, and felt her age. "Shouldn't we dress them beautifully?"

Oliver began to recover, but as he took strength through May, they saw him as he now was, not as the brother and brother-in-law they had seen years ago and preserved in their eyes from habit. This was a pinched, drained, and querulous old man. They came home from a visit and saw themselves in the instant's mirror-glance newly old and puckered, as though they hadn't seen the wrinkles deepening for a decade, the grayness for a score of years.

The summer vacation came closer and the children began to see it over the rims of the mountains and in the cloud-billow that caught the westering sun and sifted it into roads of light down which daydream horsemen rode. The happy children pulled and heaved against the discipline of the waning days; the unhappy ones kept their heads down and sighed at the draining away of their season of order, continuity, and hours of safety.

The first June meeting of the school board was held just before the summer vacation, and its affairs were traditionally the details of the closing fiscal year. The new budget would be presented at the Aureole meeting later in the month. With the growth of the county, meetings had been scheduled twice a month, Thursday nights, one at a local school, one at Aureole's county office. Teachers and parents usually attended only the first one.

This meeting was held in the new Callan Junior High, and the main subject, Clara knew, would be the location of four new schools projected for the next five years. She wasn't surprised at the large turnout. Pictures of the proposed schools were displayed on a stand set up outside the gym and people had already begun to argue over where the schools should be situated.

Orval Bordereau, her onetime student, grown up, grown middle-aged and prosperous by building houses in the Valley towns, was head of the board, and he brought the meeting to order with practiced ease. New business included the conflicting claims of one or another of the towns wanting the schools. Clara knew the arguments were mostly wind and window dressing. The board had been working for a full year with statisticians and accountants and the decisions had been carefully made. The only thing remaining was to let people see how many competing interests were involved in the placement of the schools.

She was sitting near the front of the room, and after the arguments had been stated and restated, she began to drift away into daydream.

Someone at the back of the room had begun to speak, and there was a change as people murmured and shifted in their chairs. Clara turned also and saw Helene Singleton, standing, reading, and next to her were the Sargents and the Treeces and some of the parents who had protested the poetry days and the scarcity of computers, and there, big as a Buddha and gone gray, as though she was dusty, Dorothy Tavistock was sitting. Clara came wide awake.

". . . to lodge a petition of complaint against Principal Clara Percival that she be removed from her position at Gold Flume School on the grounds of gross incompetence, cruelty, child abuse, and assault. We are preparing a criminal prosecution for sexual abuse against a child."

Clara's mind had stopped and then it had begun to run as though to escape, and then it had hit something loose and her thoughts were in fall, her mind vague and sick. What's happening to me? She was dizzy with the fall, ice-cold in the cool June night. The spinning stopped. She found herself standing up as the accusers were standing. The room was dead still. Someone had asked for a repetition of the words for the secretary, and Helene came down the aisle and passed Clara without looking at her, to give the petition to the board member who reached for it. Clara noted that it was not Orval. She thought stupidly, Is there another Clara Percival in the system, someone I'll have to meet?

27

When the meeting broke up, people came to Clara to reassure her. There were only seven names on the petition, after all. Dorothy Tavistock was a signer, but she hadn't had a child in school in thirty years and so her complaint had little standing. Everyone knew she was mad as a moth. The Treeces were ghosts of the Singletons, the Sargents were a question, Carly Deaton was a hysteric, and Helene Singleton couldn't even get her husband to sign along with her. All but Mrs. Tavistock were new people, ski people who had come out from the Reiber ruin to work in Gold Flume.

Clara sat mute in the indignation of her supporters, barely hearing Orval's encouragement. "I don't know what's behind this, Miz Percival, but I'm going to find out. I'll get the board together and we can see how to approach this—" He saw her out as though afraid she would faint. "Are you okay to drive home?"

"Yes, Orval, I need the time alone."

"Now listen"—as she slid into her car—"I was a student in your school, though you may have forgotten it."

"I haven't forgotten."

"I know you; I know what you done for every child in the three towns in them days and since. I seen the statistics that come out of your school."

Part of Clara fought the urge to correct Orval's grammar. Does it help for the defender to say "She done a fine job teachin'"?

But for the Sargents, for whom she felt an irritated sympathy, the names on the list evoked no feeling until Clara was almost home, and it was with the Sargents that she wrangled through a sleepless night.

"They're the ones with the weird kid, aren't they?" Andy had asked when she told him the names.

"Troubled kid," Clara said, "lost kid, but they're the ones pressing the child abuse. What I can't get over is the word *criminal!*"

"What did they say the abuse was?" he asked. "Was there any?"

"In a sense there was, and is, but the abuse is ignorance, not evil, and it's not mine. Their little boy, Claude, *is* disturbed, severely so, and there's nothing we can do for him. You know how hard I've tried. His parents say he can be calmed by holding him. That may take thirty minutes at a time. What teacher has that time available with thirty-five other students waiting?"

"Why do they blame you?"

"Sharla, the fourth-grade teacher, can't cope with him. She sends him to the office. We can't cope with him there, either.

234

The tragedy is that there's no place for him in the school, no one who can deal with him."

"This family wants to charge you with something?"

"I told them Claude was emotionally disturbed. They think I'm calling him insane and that designation will further alienate him."

"Isn't he alienated already?"

"Of course he is. The other children mock him in spite of all we do to stop it, but they are troubled by him, frightened, really, of his behavior. I've pleaded for help from the county and the state, a psychologist, someone to come and provide guidance for all of us, but the county says there's nothing and the state won't act without parental approval. Here comes the strange part. Remember the raptor program? In the presence of those birds he wasn't awed the way the other children were. He was—for the first time—still, utterly still, utterly himself. I watched him. There's something in that, something important. I wanted to talk to the father. Mrs. Sargent is so defensive she would think I was suggesting that Claude has an animal's mind."

"What are we going to do about the petition?"

"I don't know. The Sargents are the only parents who have a case, and the case isn't against me, really. The Treeces are scared their girls won't get into Stanford University. Dorothy Tavistock has no standing. Helene Singleton hates me because her picture of herself doesn't include neglecting a son so badly that he comes to school barefoot and with ticks on his body that even a cursory look would have noticed. She hates Gold Flume, too, damn her. She's the one organizing this."

"What's your plan?"

"I guess it's to wait for Orval to call and tell me what the board says I should do."

Days passed and there was no outward change in Clara's life. She came and went under Jackass Mountain and thought, The top of this peak shines in the sun and goes purple in shadow.

Days warm, nights cool, and new snows fall. On the surface nothing lets the witness know that at a shout or a step, the mountain is ready to disrobe itself in avalanche. Where do I step? How loud can I speak? Her nights were full of raging defenses and justifications and the statistics of her successes past and present, thrown up against the overwhelming words: *cruelty, gross incompetence, child abuse.* All night she wrestled the words and all day she watched under the mountain.

Orval called. "I don't know why they done this. I been hearing one thing and another, and it's all moonwinkle, road glimmer. Every principal and teacher in this valley has things said, and you less than most. School's too lenient or else too hard, or some mama thinks teacher's taken against her child. Here, last year there was Tom Weedy up at Callan, shaking and pulling the kids. There was bruises, proof, and the kids spoke out, too. With you there's nothing but some talk about poetry contests and The Jail. I talked to some people about Sargents' kid and they say he's a loony. Ask anyone what happened to him or her personally and it all goes away."

"How can I fight this?"

"I talked to the other board members last night. We have to take up the petition and investigate, but they'll have to bring proof. I don't think 'old-fashioned' is a reason for dismissal, and you send kids to the junior high better prepared than either the Bluebank or Callan kids are."

"Orval, I did not abuse—"

"Good God, woman, would anyone think you did?"

"If I called them—talked to them individually—"

"I wouldn't do that if I was you. It would seem like you was begging or arguing."

Andy agreed. At first he had been incredulous, laughing at the charges. "This will blow over." But then he had gone still, and she was trying to spare him as much as she could of the night-wrangling defenses, the useless justifications sent again and again to the mind-shadow judges. "Don't let this get to you," he said, and then said no more until she asked him.

"What if I talked to them, reasoned with them one by one?"

"Don't even think of doing that. Let the board do its job and present its report. Then you can heal the breach because the power will be on your side."

Clara resisted as long as she could. When she couldn't resist any longer she picked up the phone and thought, The mouse has to run and the owl has to follow. Its wings clap open like a pistol shot. The sound shatters the surface of the snow a single millimeter deep and half a mile wide and then the snow shrugs its clothing off the shoulders of the mountain, and there's an avalanche. It's inevitable.

Rosalie Treece said, "I've already told you my objections: The Jail and all that memorizing."

"The *children* call it The Jail."

"It doesn't matter. You're not providing them with the proper role model."

Clara had heard the phrase recently. People parroted it as a profound truth but her anger was so sharp and sudden, it took her by surprise. "Role model? Is that any reason for dismissal, for ruining a career, for child abuse charges?"

Rosalie hung up.

She called the Sargents. "You abused our child," Molly Sargent said. "You called Claude mentally unbalanced."

"I told *you*, not him."

"The children all laugh at him."

"He is desperately in need. As he is now, no school could teach him."

"You should have stopped the children from teasing him. He comes home with his clothing torn."

"It's a tragedy, not any abuse. . . ."

Molly Sargent hung up.

Clara called Helene. Helene hung up as soon as she identified Clara's voice. She called Dorothy Tavistock. "How long has it been since Peter's funeral? Isn't it time to bury our feud?"

"You alienated my children. Peter is in his grave because of you. All those wars and battles . . . he could have been deferred, but you influenced him, and when he was over there it was *you* he wrote to, *you* he confided in, while I starved for word of him. Lucinda left home because of you and your advice. She's in New Mexico and she never visits or writes, but she writes to you, doesn't she? She tells you all the news and what she thinks and what she feels?"

"No, Dorothy, I haven't heard from Lucinda in years. She has Peter's letters, not I. We're both old, now. Let's be old together in peace. Call Lucinda and get the letters and read them—"

"They were written to *you!*" Dorothy screamed, and hung up.

Carly Deaton said, "They call you Old Lady Percival and The Witch. Dana has nightmares about you."

"Work with the nightmares, don't destroy *me*."

"All the parents say you're destructive."

"Helene says I'm destructive. The Sargents say I'm destructive. There are hundreds, maybe thousands of parents over thirty-five years—"

"Dana is frightened of you—"

"After the accusations, not before. . . . I know Dana—" Carly hung up.

Clara sat and cried. The avalanche had passed, inevitable. She had thought there would be relief, but structures that had stood in the path of snow were no longer there. She had thought that the accusers were sitting in comfort judging her. Now she knew that although the accusations were false, the pain behind them was real. That knowledge sapped her resolve and drained it away.

"Orval . . ."

"We're still getting statements and information. Rima Bishop's term is over, and so is mine. New members are getting ready to run. It makes sense to keep putting things off, examining the charges until the parents move out of the elementary school, but if we do that, we may pass them over to new board members who don't know you. There's no evidence, of course, but there's been a charge that will have to be investigated. There ain't no proof, so the truth will come out."

"Orval, this accusation is as serious as an accusation of rape or murder. My name is tied to it. Is there any way to stop it?"

There was a long pause, and Orval's quiet, "Aside from quitting, no."

"They said I abused, sexually abused a child. How? When? Can't we make them prove what times, what occasions, before they blast the words all over town?"

There was another pause and then Orval said, "I talked to Rima about this and she said that the new people is used to male principals with master's degrees and a certain professional chat— the words that let people know you've been to the university."

"I've been to the university. I've taken summer courses every other year on everything from sex education to computers. Why don't they ask to see my certificates?"

"You don't talk like what they're used to."

"If I did, most of the parents wouldn't know what I was saying."

In the silence over the phone, Clara intuited Orval's shrug. She had been asking rhetorical questions. The avalanche had thrown her down, and in her head-over-heels, airless, breathless, directionless state, she was reaching out foolishly, in the panic of need. She listened to Orval's silence and blushed and then tears came and she said good-bye quickly and hung up.

The *Ute River Voice*'s article was short and factual. It was the fourth article on the first page: PRINCIPAL ACCUSED. The article said there had been a petition presented calling for the removal of Clara Percival, principal of Gold Flume School, on charges of incompetence, cruelty, and child abuse. Clara had opened the paper idly, had been caught, shocked to stare numbly at the lines. It occurred to her that she should keep the paper, save it as part of a collection of all the relevant materials of the case. She got up and got the scissors, but as she did, she forgot why she had them in her hand, so she put them away and went back to the kitchen table where the paper was. She had gone through half of it when she saw the continuation of the article on the sixth page—PRINCIPAL ACCUSED—and went back to the beginning and remembered why she had gone for the scissors. All over Gold Flume, Callan, Bluebank, Granite, and Aureole, people were coming home as she had, opening their *Ute River Voices* for the first quick look. Was there a horse for sale? A farm auction? Had the accident they had passed on the highway been serious? Was their school principal accused of horrors? Oh, yes. Oh, yes. Clara got up again and began to walk around the room, straightening, with her left hand, the yellow curtain that hung on the kitchen window. Then she remembered a newsreel picture she had seen when there were still newsreels at the Aureole movie house, when there were still movies in Aureole. A hurricane had destroyed a woman's house and she was poking in the wreckage, picking things up and dropping them again, and as the camera passed her, she reached down and straightened the clothes of a headless doll.

28

$\mathcal{A}$ reporter called from the *Denver Post.* Clara spoke with conviction. The charges were absurd. She had been principal of Gold Flume School since 1947 and had been awarded honors by the school and the county. The reporter asked her if she knew from what the charges had sprung. Clara answered that she thought they concerned a troubled boy. She wanted to say, "It's Claude Sargent. Call the mother and listen to the hysteria and defensiveness I've had to deal with," but she couldn't. "The board is investigating," she said. The reporter began to read the names on the petition and Clara found herself defending, in spite of herself, indefensible realities. "Dorothy Tavistock and I have been in a long feud, years of it. Her children are grown and one died in the Korean War. His sister in New Mexico has letters that no abused child would send to his abuser."

"Love letters?"

"No, not love letters—we were friends and his mother resented it."

"I see," the reporter said. Then, "Let's go on. Carly Deaton—"

"Her daughter heads a clique and cliques, as you must know, cause a lot of pain and social dissension in schools. I backed the teacher who separated the Deaton girl from her followers and made the children sit alphabetically. The mother complained to me and I agreed with the teacher."

"Sargent—"

"A troubled boy," Clara said.

"Treece?"

"She's overwhelmed and follows the originator of this petition. Helene Singleton has a boy, Carl—"

Clara saw Carl Singleton as she had seen him in March, with the tick at the base of his spine, his pants around his ankles. She said, "Let me just get at this—" And there it was, there was the source of the sexual abuse accusation, and it was so simple and innocent a confusion that Clara burst out in a laugh, light-headed with relief. "It was the ticks, that was it!"

"What?"

"In March this happened. Carl Singleton had ticks on him, seven or eight of them. I took them off, that was all. Everyone was at a program, but the bathroom door was open all the time. If I had been abusing that little third-grader, would the door have been open for anyone passing by to look in and see us? He's a sleepwalker of a little boy, and I sent a note home with him, but the housekeeper might not have delivered it. There had been an incident before that and Mrs. Singleton was defensive, thinking

I was critical of her—it's the trust, you see, the trust that's missing because we're Gold Flume people."

Her explanation seemed limp and false. The word *trust* must have sounded to the reporter as though it was trust of Clara as a principal. She tried to describe how nervous and anxious the Reiber people were, how lacking in trust for the competence of a rural school system, but she had spoken the word, *trust*, herself, declared that trust was missing, and when the reporter hung up, Clara realized she hadn't made anything clear, hadn't conveyed what had happened, hadn't mentioned Alvia being there, and had forgotten to ask the reporter's name. Through confusion and incompetence, she had lost a possibly strong ally. All through the day, Clara indulged in fantasies of headlines she would read in a month or two.

PERCIVAL CLEARED: SERIES OF MISUNDER-
STANDINGS UNFOLDS
ROSALIE TREECE CANNOT GROW ROSES,
DECLARES MOUNTAINS HER ENEMIES
SHOELESS, TICK-INFESTED CHILD MAKES
MOTHER DEFENSIVE

"I got a call from the *Denver Post* today," Clara said when Andy came home. Her daydreaming had made supper late.

The phone rang and Andy went to answer. He came back looking grim, shaking back the hair that was now thin. "It was just a hate call. I'm worried that if we get too many of these, we'll miss the ones we want—Oliver and Katy's calls, for instance." He began to outline a telephone code, a system of rings and redialing so they would know who was calling. Had he foreseen this from the beginning and planned a response to it? Clara began to ask him, but he waved the words away. There was bitterness and impatience in his gesture.

"I didn't bring this on us," she said. "I didn't cause it."

"I know, I know," but he didn't look at her.

They went to Aureole that Saturday to get away from the phone and its obscenities. They had turned the ring low on Friday and Andy planned to get an answering machine to screen the calls. "Are you getting these at work, too?"

"Yes. John Isabella's very patient, but it's a strain."

"I'm sorry."

He nodded.

There was a time when a visit to Oliver and Katy's might have brought some of the comfort they needed. Before Oliver's illness Katy would have been the first one to know of any trouble—after Alice. The men used to do repairs on each other's cars, they painted each other's houses. Katy and Clara gathered berries and sewed together, and there were always picnics—first with children and later, when the children were gone, long afternoons in backyards. They had come to be natural and easy in one another's presence, and when Clara lost Julia and then Alice Bogard, she had gone to Katy and cried in her arms without shyness or reticence. But Oliver's heart attack had turned him so old that he had stopped caring about anything beyond the range of his room. He had become temperamental and querulous, bitter that he alone of all the world walked hesitantly, afraid of the clutch of his angina. Katy, pulled from wife to servant, had gone gaunt with running in his service up and down stairs, putting right what never could be put right to his satisfaction. She heard Clara's troubles with sympathy but had no energy to give to them. The visit was strained. They ate lunch, heard a wrangle between Oliver and Katy, and left. Oliver napped between one and three.

"What do you want to do?" Andy asked Clara outside in the warm afternoon.

"I want to go to the library," she said, "and talk with George Eliot, or maybe with Tolstoy. I don't want to read anything new just now, but I need a visit with Kitty and Levin or a look in at Mr. Casaubon."

"All right, but what about a walk through town?"

"Lots of people here know me. I don't want to wonder about the people we pass, if they have read the papers, if they are or are not thinking of me as someone doing horrors to little boys."

"What about a hike, then, or at least a walk up Pickaxe a little way—"

"I'd feel I was being sent into exile."

"If only . . ." Andy began.

"If only?"

"Nothing." His hand had come up, fanning his word away as he shook his head. It was a gesture as quick and unconscious as the slap at a mosquito. Clara hoped it meant that her innocence was so obvious and clear that the hand he raised was himself saying to himself, Ridiculous.

They went to read at the library for an hour, but Andy sat with his chair pulled into the shadows at the back of the room, and when they went to buy the answering machine at the mall, he waited until the store was nearly empty before he ventured in.

Tom called from Denver. "What's happening? I've been trying to get through. . . ."

"It's fame."

"I had no idea. Are people calling you that much?"

"Oh, yes. We get phone calls and hate mail. Every troubled, angry, or guilty person in the United States needs to register his disapproval. I've become a symbol."

"What can you do?"

"I'll tell you what I can't do. Did you ever read Maupassant's 'A Piece of String' or Porter's 'Noon Wine'? I can't do what those people did—I can't go here and there, house to house, day by day, pleading my innocence, telling everyone my version, how it was, how it is."

"Tell *me*," he said.

She told him, and as she did, there was a momentary freeing of spirit. It was as though the words lit the truth and brought its shape out of the darkness: This was the way it happened. Here's where I stood and this is what they said. When she finished, the picture was complete. He asked a few questions, she supplied the details that were missing. He was angry for her and that was gratifying, too, for a moment.

"Will you get a lawyer?" Thomas asked.

"When there's a hearing—"

"I think you should get one now."

"The school has a lawyer," Clara suggested.

"You need your own."

"We've been thinking about it."

They said good-bye and for a moment or so a light flickered over her words and then it began to fade, a long, slow fading through the evening, and the roiling darkness returned and took its accustomed place. Joseph called from his job interview in California and left a message they got between two hate calls. He sounded hurt that he had been answered by a machine. When she called him back, Clara had to apologize and remind him to use the code. They were getting calls from all over Colorado and from every state in the country. There was mail coming, too, but the voices were the most frightening because the most intimate—hate spewed in cultured tones and in ungrammatical voices, inchoate, veiled threats and overt ones. Now and then Clara picked up the phone and tried to explain, but the callers didn't want to hear her; they wanted only the chance to excoriate, to free some vileness in themselves.

Among the letters of outrage—most assumed Clara had confessed or had been found guilty—there were jittery condolences. The writers of those had been accused or were the wives or sisters of the accused. "My heart goes out to you. By the time it's all over, you'll wonder how you ever thought human beings were decent." "My brother took his life five years ago, and I got calls saying it was a good thing." One wanted her to join a group called the Brotherhood of the Media-Crucified.

These letters were worse for Clara than common hate mail. They told her that she might be turned into such a writer, her wounds forever open and moving with the maggots of injustice year after year. Some of the events the writers described were a decade in the past.

They debated going to church on Sunday. "I think I'll stay home," Andy said. "I go to work and that's enough. I go to the firehouse and out on calls, where people are glad to see me because something's on fire or someone's hurt badly and needs my help."

"We have to go, don't you see? This isn't Aureole, it's Gold Flume, where people know us well. I need to pray surrounded by familiar faces. The guilty hide and are ashamed. Innocent people do what they've always done. They have . . . equanimity, and no one can drive them away."

"Where did you read that one?"

"I made it up. It's what I want to happen."

It was a sweet day, warming. The ski area had closed for the year and the streets were empty of cars and noise. A spring wind pulled at their clothes and over the church parking lot the sky hung delicate blue; "fool-you blue," Clara had called it. On such Sunday afternoons people planted things one month too early. Andy got out of the car and looked around. He seemed glad she had talked him into coming. Pastor Cantrell was no Pastor Frailey, whose retirement everyone regretted, but people had wanted to give Cantrell a chance, and by now, a year later, he was habit. Congregants getting out of their cars nodded and smiled at the Percivals, but there was something strained about the greetings, Clara thought, and then censured herself. The phone calls and newspaper articles had made her raw and supersensitive. As they walked together toward the church, Andy whispered in her ear, "This feels wrong—let's go home."

"Let them get used to us," Clara said and began to go up. The white painted steps were steep and Andy struggled.

As the service began, unfolded in its accustomed order, they sang the hymns and spoke the familiar prayers, and were comforted. When Andy sang "World Without End" in the doxology, he sang "Okay" instead of "Amen," looking at Clara amusedly, then puffing out his cheeks. They were old townspeople, long in this church, patrons of the town library, pioneers, in a sense. Around them were many of Clara's students, grown up and some with children, and one or two with grandchildren she now knew. None of the ski people came to this church. Andy had told Clara that Hugh Singleton wanted to come here. Helene had turned the idea down cold. This church was for Town, and Town people went to it. Pastor Cantrell began his sermon.

At first his subject seemed to waver—there were bits from Leviticus, Acts, Epistles. "They in power who misuse authority . . ." ". . . the corrupt judge . . . and sometimes we wonder where it will all end, when those in high places, our officials, our sages and leaders, those in our schools stand accused of corruption, vileness, abominable acts . . ."

The air in the church went vibrant with interest. People changed positions in their seats, Clara looked at Andy, who had made a move as though to get up. Then he let himself back into his place, his face unreadable.

The sermon was what Andy would have called a handwringer. It didn't propose anything or explain anything but circled their sins over their heads. "Is this what we've come to?" It was asked rhetorically, but people's glances were gliding toward Clara and Andy, sidelong or directly, moving in and veering off, called back like hunting dogs. The looks had sympathy, alarm, hate, above all, a vast and profound curiosity. "I speak no one's name," Cantrell said. He didn't need to. Clara and Andy sat through the remainder of the sermon and the prayers that followed, got up, left the church, got in the car, and drove home in silence. They didn't speak of the incident then or ever.

That afternoon, Orval called. Because of the news articles and publicity, he said, the board, reluctantly, was forced—it was a shame, a damn shame—to put her on leave, *with pay,* until the thing could be investigated, until people could be given a chance to bring out whatever they thought they had against her. There was about a month of school left before the summer. During the summer the charges would be investigated and the decision made and she would be back in September as before. "And you'll be back, no did-she/didn't-she."

"But if I'm not *in* school, people will think the charges are true, or that the board believes they are."

"There's not a board member who thinks them charges is true, but the publicity has forced this—"

"It's not fair, Orval."

"It's *with pay.* You can tell folks that. We wouldn't do that if we thought there was anything in it."

His voice was high with urgency and Clara suddenly remembered the boy he had been, had a clear, vivid memory of him fearfully watching Sulo Boda in the school playground long since swallowed up and now lying under the school gym and the south parking lot. She could smell the dust and see the faded clothes they wore, Orval, tiny for his age, and big Sulo, moving in bully's menace toward him. Sun; blue, blue sky; floury dust. She had come quickly between them and said, "Sulo, would you come with me for a minute; I need help with the water buckets—"

"We've got a man coming to be acting principal for the month," Orval said.

"What?" She was still half in the sun-glare of that distant afternoon.

She had used to make patronizing remarks about old Mrs. Kenner, who had complained, "The long past looks so bright to me and the memory is so clear—how can I remember what I ate for lunch when all the food tastes the same?" Mrs. Kenner had died during the winter. There would be no more knitted hats or torture-chamber socks. Clara hoped her own lapses were simple old age and not the awful pain that kept pulling her into the past. She asked after Orval's wife, the kids and grandkids, said good-bye, and hung up. Then she cried.

29

So the next day, a Monday, Clara found herself at home painting window sashes. On Tuesday she relined all her cupboards. On Wednesday she scrubbed the walls of the guest room they still called Julia's. On Thursday she did the boys' old room, working the way some people drink. Friday and Saturday there was the kitchen. The work was harder than it had ever been; the house had gathered its grime for years. The TV was on loud enough to drown out the constant telephone and keep her mind occupied. The work had no joy in it and made Clara feel even older than she was. She got up every morning stiff and sore.

It was necessary to make three trips to school. A Mr. Leeper had come as acting principal. Since he had less than a month to serve before the summer vacation, her things remained where they were, even to a forgotten jacket, left since February on the coatrack.

At the school Alvia's greeting was manic. She wanted to show support and had no other way but dithering and talking too much and waving her hands like papers in a wind, but she seemed frightened also and dared not touch Clara. It was plague, the virus of accusation. This virus might go epidemic or dwindle, ordinary as shingles, but no one could predict which. Like the fetal skeletons in Selevan Creek, Clara now represented more than herself.

The accusing voices on the phone and the words in the letters were frightening. They accused Clara of satanic worship, sinful lust, and every kind of depravity. The only defense against this assault was a rigid order. She wrote out a schedule dictating hours of hard work sprucing up the house and grounds. She allotted one hour only to the work on her vindication, gathering the papers and letters that testified to her competence and praised her skill. She recognized the danger in dwelling on defense and justification. She vowed to herself that she would not be swallowed up in them.

Her inability to read frightened her as well. It was a deep disappointment to sit down at leisure, at long last, and pick up the eagerly awaited book, only to find concentration holding for no more than three or four minutes before it yielded to fantasies of defense, revenge, rage, self-pity, whining, and the exhausted lumbering up and down the mazed alleys of proof and disproof. Or she would drift off in a doze, only to take up the self-torturer's games at midnight, wide awake and blind in the dark beside Andy, who lay in the sufficiency of sleep.

In the allotted hour, she went through her school collections: evaluations of all the years from superintendents, letters of students and parents, year after year. For the first time she studied those names, signatures at which she hadn't even glanced before. Listing them, she wondered if the sometimes glowing words would help her now. "Innovative." "Creative." "Friendly atmosphere in school." Could there be a friendly atmosphere when the principal was misusing a jail and abusing the children? "Note: I was told by a tiny girl to wipe my feet when I came into the building. 'This is our school,' she said. The admonition speaks to the spirit and unity at Gold Flume School." "Dear Mrs. Percival: This is just to tell you how pleased we are . . ." "We are leaving town as Don's job is moved to Texas, but wanted to tell you how good it is here for all our kids due to you and what you done . . ." ". . . wouldn't have believed how he likes to read the poems." "When I started college I was scared. None of my family had gone past sixth grade. Then, I thought about the things you had us learn at Gold Flume School and the speech on self-reliance you made us memorize . . ."

On another day Clara called or wrote to all the former school secretaries and asked them to write depositions, to testify regarding the charges that were being brought against her. Had there been, to their knowledge, any abuse of The Jail or of children? One of the women was retired but lived in Granite, one had died, one had moved to Kansas. Alvia had been at Gold Flume School for ten years. Didn't the fact that there had been so few secretaries speak in her defense? Would a secretary stay, having witnessed a principal's abuse or cruelty? "Secretaries see principals at work every day," one replied. "The principal's office is open to the school office. Secretaries know when you come and go. They see you with the children throughout the day. There was never a hint of impropriety, cruelty, or abuse. The charges cannot be true."

Andy was in the middle of his own tide of work, a relief to Clara. Most of the people who needed survey work were new and didn't know about trouble at the grade school. He was coming home later and later in the evenings and avoiding people on weekends. After the Sunday of Pastor Cantrell's sermon, they didn't go back to church, and on June 1, Andy took his pager, fire coat and pants, uniform, badge, and helmet down to the firehouse along with his letter of resignation. "Andy . . ."

"I'm too old anyway. I was sixty-five last year, and yes, I remember Old Man Adamson and Jeff Williams and all the old guys who stayed on, but most of them were more trouble than they were worth, and I don't want to be like that."

"You don't eat at Payson's anymore, do you?"

"No, and that's all right, too. I can get more work done if I take a lunch and eat at the office."

"Andy—"

"Leave it alone," he said. "You can't change anything, and what happened isn't your fault."

"Can't you let up a little on the work?"

"We're land-poor now and I don't want to be one of those old people who went along with all the growth here in town and thought they were in the catbird seat, thinking land taxes would stay the same, and who are now without savings." He showed her how they would have to work to keep even until retirement, when they would sell some of the now very valuable twelve acres. "We might even want to sell out altogether and move." He had never hinted at such a thing before. She tried a joke: She had kept up correspondence with the youngsters in San Pablo, who were now parents and some of them grandparents. Maybe they would move down there, or down to Mexico, the child abuser and her mate. "Just think—no more mail, no more phone calls—" He had murmured something and then turned away.

School board elections were held in June, but the new board didn't begin to serve until September; the July and August meetings were used as a kind of training. Orval's term was over and he was to be replaced by a lawyer named Eubanks. The other new board member was Hugh Singleton. The main work of the June meeting would be the introduction of the new members.

On the night of the meeting, Clara took the two ream-size typing paper boxes that held the relevant papers and some of the more recent letters and let Alvia drive her to the meeting in Aureole. Andy was on Hungry Woman Mountain on a job, and Clara was pleased when Alvia offered to drive her. It was a kind of evidence, she thought, to have the school secretary come in and sit with her.

They talked on the way. "How's the new principal?"

"Leeper? Terrified. He's not strong. He goes by the book, right down to not letting teachers have a minute's discretionary time. The school is like a Halloween spook house. We're all waiting for a parent to jump out and yell 'Boo.' "

The school parking lot was full and Clara's heart began to pound even though she knew that some of the crowd was there to see the installation of the new board members. She set her face and got out of the car. Orval was there at the door. "Miz Percival," he said, "would you let me carry those boxes for you?"

Clara and Alvia chose seats near the front of the room, but they were surrounded by an unfamiliar stillness. As Clara looked around she saw a woman in a flowered dress and a man's torn sweater. She half rose—"Frances?"—thinking it was Frances French, but the woman turned and it wasn't Frances, but a stranger.

Orval called the meeting to order, thanked Rima for her service, and introduced Hugh Singleton and the lawyer, Eubanks, new members. "Let's get on with it," he said, "there's lots of business." First item: minutes, report from treasurer, old business. Item: repairs on two new schools. Item: school insurance; the rates were up. Perhaps they might look around for a new carrier. Item: the Percival matter.

At the back of the room, Helene Singleton was speaking. Clara looked at Hugh, who was sitting at the board's table facing the audience. His face was blank, but she thought she saw a tightening of his mouth and jaw as though he might bite his wife's words the way a seamstress bites the thread to end the sewing. Many people praised Mrs. Percival, Helene was reading from a paper she held, and indeed, before there had been standards in the county, she had filled a necessary place, but the old days were full of cruelty, of teachers whipping students and using humiliation to force discipline. Mrs. Percival had been cruel in at least one case, had practiced sexual abuse on a child of eight, her son, Carl. Her methods featured the rote memory of long and obscure poems. She had a jail in her office. Children forced to be there were humiliated before the entire school and whoever came in. And there was more. Clara sat immobile, staring ahead. Mrs. Percival had come to the school, Helene continued, under false pretenses. Her life before Gold Flume had been full of lies and evasions. During her schooling in a now defunct teachers college, she had lived in unacceptable lodgings, which, when the school found out, it forbade her to use and to which she returned secretly. Her father was a professional criminal and she had aided and abetted his violations. During World War II she had lied to the government, impersonating another worker to get a soft defense plant sinecure with paid vacations while others worked night and day in the nation's war effort. A liar, impersonator, and perpetrator of psychological and sexual abuse was in complete charge of a school full of defenseless children. Helene sat down to absolute silence.

The silence went on, building an awful tension. Clara faced front. Then, at the back of the room, someone cleared his throat. She knew it was time to get up and give a defense, but how could such a defense be begun? She had made a terrible tactical blunder, not to have guessed that Helene and Dorothy Tavistock would spread their accusations as wide as they could. She had ignored Thomas's advice to have a lawyer.

"Excuse me . . ." It was the soft, tenuous voice of Mrs. Bordereau, old Mrs. Bordereau, Orval's mother. "The convict wasn't Mrs. Percival's father, but her *father-in-law*. Town's known that for years. I don't believe that other business, and heaven knows where they got it. A war cheat, well, we were all war cheats one way or another. I know some high-and-mighty people who registered their cars as farm equipment so they could get C-stickers and more gas ration points. They kept cows and animals they didn't register and traded milk and butter for sugar and coffee the city people couldn't get. That's what *she's* dragging up—garbage like that!"

More silence. Clara turned on her chair to see who had been standing but wouldn't speak, the one who had cleared his throat. It was Cyril Boda. "I just listened to this here complaint." His voice was too loud at first. He stopped, and went on more softly. "There was four things in it. First was about doing wickedness on a child, and we didn't hear no evidence. Second was about some mess she was supposed to have did in the years 1941 to 1945, which is before that lady over there was born. The third was about cruelty which I didn't see or know from Miz Percival one minute, nor my sisters nor brothers neither, nor none of my kids, which I asked them about and which, counted up, covers fifteen or sixteen years. The fourth was about poetry. The poetry I learned seen me through hard times. I make my own kids to keep up their poetry, too. They recite it to me every year, and by now it's almost a bookful, theirs and mine together. It's wisdom, and thinking on it is good for anybody. Thank you," and he sat down.

There was applause and here and there a few whistles. Clara was moved. It had taken all Cyril had to make him speak out that way, but as she looked at him, she saw what the new people must be seeing—a heavy-bellied country man, his hair slicked down with water, his Town clothes years out of date, his grammar faulty. She looked over at the new people sitting behind her. Their faces had the polite, removed amusement seen on the faces of grown-ups at performances of children. It gave her the anger she needed.

She stood up and began to tell them, point by point. She tried to make everything clear, precise, and thoughtful. She had been speaking for a minute or two when the realization came that such a defense was damaging in itself, and no one should have to defend an entire life. Cyril had been right; the accusations had been allowed to spread like burning magnesium that runs away, carrying the fire.

And this wasn't a law court—no formal charges had been made, and yet here she stood, defending, and it dawned on her also that defense was a kind of admission. In responding to accusations so wild and unfocused, she was granting them validity. A wartime shift had been blown into treason, and Arlo's parole violations hovered in a gray area from which the law itself shied away.

She began to answer the statements of the petition. She described finding the ticks on Carl Singleton's body. Here and there parents smiled and nodded. "I know I should have left them there and sent him home with a note, but would any of *you?*"

A murmur went up, very low, and here and there, "Well, if it was *ticks* . . ." "Cruelty? Was *that* the cruelty?"

Then at once, exhaustion came. She took another breath and said, "Here are some letters and my evaluations. None of them talks about a jail in my office. Whipping? I never did that, although years ago I slapped hands and I got rid of *that* as soon as I could. No one says that my discipline shrouded my message. *Ask the children.* Ask them."

Orval acknowledged the boxes and said the board would study everything she had submitted. "Talk to the children," Clara said again, and sat down beside Alvia, who patted her hand annoyingly.

The realization came that the board hadn't wanted to deal with the Percival matter, and that in demanding exoneration, she had sacrificed the option of evading and playing for time and had

258

imprisoned the board in an action that gave equal strength to both sides of the question. The knowledge pulled at her like a wind, sudden as a draft blowing shut a door when one is alone in the house.

Sitting bolt upright beside Alvia, she felt it necessary to hold the rigid posture, eyes front. The meeting went on to other matters, and gradually she let her glance drift. A neighbor caught her eye, another smiled. Others looked away.

Someone was standing behind the right side of the swinging gym door; there was the movement of plaid fabric changing as the person shifted his weight. The door was being held ajar for ventilation and the space made by the hinge was wide enough to see—

It was Andy. He had shifted again, and she caught a glimpse of cheek and eye and hair in the two-inch-wide crack. How long had he been there? Was he thinking about shame, and his position in town after all these years? Or had it been his way of helping her? He had known that courage was necessary here and not courage-draining sympathy. Clara knew she needed the dry, matter-of-fact detachment she had learned at nine, walking up the gulch to where Mama lay dying and Father sat trying to impose his blistered picture of the world on her. The dear man had wanted to see how things were going in case he was needed but without defeating her, and so he had chosen to stand hidden and follow things unseen. She breathed in the strength he had willed her and, calmer now, turned back to listen.

They were discussing school lunches, then the sports program. It occurred to Clara that Orval had done what he could to lessen the impact of her case, by putting it dead center on the agenda, one item only in a list of items for consideration. It had been cleverly done. When this is over, she thought, I'll have to take some time to think about all of it. There are bits of wisdom to pull from this—wisdom I don't yet have. Now I want it all to be over and me home again.

She looked back at the space behind the door. It was empty. He had gone, back to Hungry Woman Mountain and his work.

The meeting adjourned at last. Clara ached to get out into the covering night. She wished she hadn't come with Alvia but could get into her own car and be able to be still, not to have to hold her face in a pleasant, equivocal expression, but to shout if she wished, curse if she wished, or be mute as the need took her. Instead, it was necessary to stay and say good night to Orval and Mrs. Bordereau, to thank Cyril, to be seen as calm and serene, acknowledging her supporters in the face of her accusers. She had her purse and nothing else. For the first time in memory she carried no papers or reports; now that the boxes had been delivered, a hand was free.

Finally they were able to go gratefully into the darkness to Alvia's car. Andy had remarked to her that even in the matter of automobiles the new ski people were different. Flume people drove big cars, American cars, that they kept for years, repairing and repainting, or they drove battered trucks. The new ski people drove foreign cars, small and underpowered but with four-wheel drive for the snow. Some people on the lot waved to her and some passed her and touched her, murmuring words of support. Clara was conscious of the need for Alvia's symbolic support in the shared ride. Now she mustn't be seen going into the night alone and would be watched for meanings beyond the ordinary acts of a day. It might be months before she could move normally again, without feeling she had to present herself. That feeling reminded her of long ago when, at thirteen and fourteen, she walked the gulch to the Prillers', her back straight, eyes front, past the few houses of their little settlement and against their neighbors' stares—Gulch child—filthy people up there—hair's probably full of nits. There had been other times, too, like the early times in San Pablo when she had to wear a clean white blouse every day so as to look prosperous and cared for even as poverty made her clutch with panic over a stain or tear on one of the two skirts she owned.

She was silent. Alvia wanted to talk. Had Clara paid attention to the new board members? Had she seen the look Hugh had shot his wife? And the lawyer, Eubanks—what had Clara made of him?

But Clara was thinking of Miss Willa Optegard all those years ago and how it must have been for her, walking behind that little swell of belly day by day, in town. She must have limped home with the touch and smell of Kester French on her. She must have washed and washed, and when her periods stopped and her breasts swelled and went tender, she must have walked with the face Clara would hereafter be wearing: proud but not vain, serious but not sad, gentle but not weak, and careful, infinitely careful of every look and every word.

Alvia had to bring Clara out of reverie two or three times during the drive back to Gold Flume and had to be thanked earnestly when Clara got out. The house was dark. Alvia hinted about coming in for coffee, but Clara pretended not to hear the hint. She pleaded exhaustion and went inside.

But once Alvia's car was out of sight, Clara opened the door cautiously and went out again to watch the sliver-honed moon catch its sickle in the trees to the west of the house. The night was still and sweet, with only a touch of cold borne down off the pass. She heard a coyote laugh and dogs here and there answer, like grouchy sleepers in a dormitory when someone's snores half wake them. Here she was with all the other dwellers in the valley, dogs, people, friends, enemies, skiers, ranchers, teachers, children, river and rocks, all. She got a comfort from this she hadn't thought to find and, alone in the mellow night, allowed herself to smile.

30

School was out and the summer tourists began to idle in the streets of Gold Flume. At this time the children were usually invited up to see the Bible herbs and Shakespeare flowers in the garden, but Clara's walks in town soon told her that such a plan would cause more pain than it was worth. Lines had been drawn by need, conviction, fear, habit, alliance, and necessity. The Bordereaus and their relatives greeted Clara in a friendly way. So did the Matskes. The ski parents shunned her, although Mary Anne Van Dyke looked sad. All the professional people became formal and a bit chilly, giving clipped greetings but not outright cuts. The Percivals' doctor and dentist maintained genial relations, but their wives cooled. Other new people, merchants and motel people, tried to take no side, but many of them got drawn in, depending on personal friendships. Those with children in the schools were credulous with fear. Any invitation Clara extended would be received along these predrawn lines. There had already been casual vandalism at the Percival place. On the street, children were pert to Clara and some were rude and weren't stopped from being rude by their parents. Her trips to Gold Flume began to seem like the patrols she imagined Peter Tavistock had walked in Korea and Junior Austin in Vietnam.

One of these trips was forced by bank business. Clara found herself standing behind Hugh Singleton on the teller's line. He didn't notice her until he was leaving and then he gave a nod of greeting. When she came outside, he was waiting. "Mrs. Percival—please stop a minute."

"What is it?"

"I . . . I wanted to tell you, or Andy—but Andy's not at the firehouse now—how much I don't want this. I never did." He looked tired and harried.

"We're talking on the street," Clara said.

"I know. I want us to be seen talking on the street. Let the whole town see. I'm not part of my wife's . . . crusade. I don't believe you hurt Carl in any way. The housekeeper never looked after the kids, and Helene was guilty and ashamed."

"Why did she accuse me?"

"Guilt. The woman never bathed him or taught him to bathe himself, and she never even checked him. We've been through two or three housekeepers since. It's hard enough to get them out here. And Helene would never accept a local person."

"That I know," Clara said.

Hugh began to talk about his wife. They had met in college. "Helene was always ambitious," he said, but her parents thought of her designing as a hobby, a decorative flair. He had Clara's arm. Helene had wanted to go to F.I.T. in New York, he told her, but her father forbade it; a technical school, a dangerous, polyglot city. She had gone instead to one of the women's colleges in Maryland, where design was one class in a home economics major. She had patched a program together from drama (costume design), fashion, sewing, history (costume arts), and whatever else she could find, to get what she thought of as a second-rate education.

Hugh Singleton was well built and conventionally handsome. Clara could see how Helene would be attracted to him, but hadn't they ever talked about how they wanted to live? Perhaps they had. Maybe Hugh himself didn't know there was a home waiting for him in an unnamed valley between unimaginable mountains, half a continent away. It took coming to Gold Flume to tell him. Perhaps Helene didn't know that not everyone wishes for an elegant life.

As he talked with increasing eagerness and animation, standing close, people were passing, looking, some staring at the two of them, involved in what was obviously a deep but friendly conversation. Word would go out. If Clara had committed sexual abuse on the body of little Carl Singleton, would the boy's father stand as close as a friend, hands shaping the eager words?

But as Hugh went on, Clara realized that his purpose was to move her to a forgiveness for which she wasn't ready. "Are you trying to tell me to forget this, not to fight it?" she asked. "If so, what am I supposed to do, let her accuse me of a crime as bad as rape and not answer it?"

"You're close to retirement," he said, "and I want to stay here. But the town is divided—we get hate calls. The fight is splitting the whole valley apart—"

"Oh, do people call you? Do they call you from all over the country, accusing you of atrocities you can barely tolerate hearing about? How many calls have you gotten? One? Ten? Fifty? Would you change your situation for ours?"

"At least," he said, "don't see us as a couple. I think Helene will get an offer, if not now, a year from now. She'll go to New York or L.A. or Paris, and the kids and I will stay in Gold Flume."

"So she'll ruin me and then leave," Clara said, and heard the words in her ears full of the self-pity she couldn't stop. Then she laughed. "It's Town, sure enough. Years ago, a man named Kester French raped the young schoolteacher who was my predecessor, and she had to pass him in the street and teach his children and relations every day until she was driven out, pregnant and shamed. I'm not going. She can go, or you, or all of you. My last years here may be bitter, but I'm not leaving. Town will swallow me the way it swallowed Kester French."

"Is that why you pulled up the hedge you planted?" His voice was softer.

"Vandals pulled it up," she said. "If they come to the place again, what should it be—buckshot, or tea and cookies? Justice or mercy?"

His face had gone white. "I didn't know," he said. "I'm sure Helene didn't know—"

He turned to go, but she followed him, talking in the same intense way he had done. "You said your piece—here's mine. I had a plan, once. I said: In two years I will retire and with the respect I have in the valley and my awards, there will be a place for me on the library board or the school board, and I'll do tutoring in Spanish and volunteer a poetry class or a book group with the children. I've been seeing that as my future for years now, watching it move toward me season by season. It was a worthy life I saw, a great happiness. It will never happen now, and your wife and probably the Treeces, too, will be gone—"

"Please—" he said.

"I just wanted you to know." She let him move away from her and up the street, hurrying.

Who had seen that, Singleton hurrying away from her? Was that another chance lost? Oh God, will I ever be done with this?

She looked around. Here was a long, fine day, the errands were done and the house clean, and up in the spring-eager creeks, torrents were now pouring snowmelt into the Ute. The wild strawberries would be ready and the first shaggy manes, wild mint, and watercress. She could leave this wrangle behind, go home and get her gathering baskets, and go mountain walking.

In an hour Clara was hitching a ride with a tourist up Jackass Pass. At the top, she struck off on an old mining road that lost itself and became a deer trail, up and up along the watercourse. The walk was so leisurely she felt little tiredness. Every few steps there was something to see, stop and marvel at, a cluster of shaggy manes to pick, pot greens and salad herbs to gather. She found her patch of strawberries in a squatter's woodlot, a cut-over place, abandoned now and grown over with lamb's-quarters and nettle. It was possible to lose Gold Flume and Gold Flume School in the need to study the ground and the slope, the sun and its shadows. Reciting the new poems of Colorado writers— Howell, Saner, Krysl—she neighbored herself against Helene Singleton, Leeper, Dorothy Tavistock, and all the spirit-killing of the last two months. Was that a flash of red under there, under those leaves? Were they cherry leaves? They were. Ground cherries were rare in this place. It was a pleasure to be here picking, reciting, and then walking on, up and over, following another old road to another abandoned mine and to its sluice-source, then down another trail, all the long, gracious afternoon.

By the time four hours had passed she had been forced to remember her age. The gathering baskets were full and she was tired. When had this gulch gotten so steep, this way so treacherous? Just as she reached the top of the pass road, the sun began to go. A truck came over the crest, unmistakable in the waning light: Buster French's wreck. She signaled him.

"You broke down somewheres?"

"I'm broken down, and my car's home."

He stared at her for a moment, then gave a short, cackling laugh.

"I've been mushrooming up the gulch and I've got dinner for us and for you and Frances, too. Cyril once told me you mushroomed all over these mountains, morels and all." Buster said nothing. "Did you ever teach that to the kids?"

"You're the teacher," he said shortly. "Ain't everyone all that jumpin' up eager to let the world in on everything."

"Right you are," Clara said.

Buster stank of booze and sweat and long-worn clothes, and the truck reeked of chicken feed, droppings, and rank humankind, but his presence was the first natural one Clara had encountered since the school meeting. He was the same he had always been, angry, secretive, and half-drunk. Himself. She relaxed with relief.

Buster drove with skill on a rutted mining road that paralleled the paved highway, wisely avoiding the main road where the state patrol would arrest him on the disrepair of the truck and the strength of his aroma. "I'll let you off here—" as they came to her turnoff. Then he looked at the portion of mushrooms and greens she had allotted him. "Never mind, I'll run you home. If you was to croak on the way, Frances and Chessie'd get blubberin' around."

"Thanks, Buster. It's been a long day and I'm played out. Is Chessie home for the summer, then?"

"Yeah," he growled. "That damn girl was always too good to touch our shadows. College girl. Big words." He spat out the window.

"Doesn't it make you proud, even a little?" she asked.

"What do you think she's gonna see when she comes home again or brings her some doctor or lawyer to visit the folks? *Scum.*" The word had edges. "I don't aim to be among those present."

"I had to do what I did." (*Careful*, went the warning in her mind.) Clara kept her voice level. "Chessie's too bright to . . . to end up working jobs she hates on the low end of things. If she could marry a doctor or a lawyer or be trained to be one, why should she settle for a harder life?"

He was silent, then said, "It's your job, ain't it, improving people? Okay, you done it, but it's pulled her away from her own. You see that."

"Yes, I see that."

They came to the house. The light was on; Andy was home. "Thanks, Buster," and she gathered up her baskets. "It's what *she* wants, you know."

"Just don't expect no nip-ups from me." His voice was bitter. He reached over and wrestled the stuck door open.

The truck's sound had gone before it, and there was Andy, coming out at a run, panic on his face.

"Wild supper," Clara said, showing the baskets.

"I think it's time for a visit to Ross Clayton," Andy declared. "Let's stop fooling ourselves. This isn't going away and the board isn't going to end the accusations with any careful study."

"We haven't gone to Ross since he worked out our wills. . . ."

"It's time," Andy said.

Ross Clayton expressed no surprise, but Clara assumed he must have known about the accusations or had at least heard the rumors. "I've never had a case of this kind, not in thirty years of practice."

Clara was glad she and Andy had dressed so carefully. The formality of their appearance made the event less personal. She spoke objectively, giving only the facts as she knew them: complaints from parents, her response, Claude Sargent, Helene Singleton, Carl's shoes, Carl's ticks, the old battle with Dorothy

Tavistock. She had resisted visiting the lawyer, she realized, despairing of her ability to tell the whole thing to anybody. The story went well, though, without digressions or embellishments. This formal setting and Ross's judicious questions here and there helped her work past forests of detail. When she came to the part where the accusations were read at the board meeting, Ross scowled. When she said the board would investigate, he scowled again.

"Of course," Clara said, "the principal is supposed to be an example to the community. . . ."

Ross breathed in. It wasn't a gasp, but Clara was aware she had said something that troubled the lawyer. "*Principal*," he said. "I'd forgotten you weren't simply a teacher."

"I never was simply a teacher. When I started at Gold Flume, it was a one-room school, so I was both principal and teacher, and my position has always been a little different from principals in schools who started with clear lines of demarcation."

Ross began to study a book and then a three-ring notebook. "I thought I would get a handle on this before you came, but I didn't listen when you said *principal*." He closed the books and looked straight at them. Andy shifted uncomfortably. "You see," Ross said, "if you were a teacher, there would be a whole catalog of defenses and procedures we could use, a grievance procedure that went point by point and would keep most of those charges from being raised at all. As a principal, that's not available to you. Is Gold Flume an administrative district?"

"It was when I came, but they might have transferred the authority to the county when the new school was built."

"Do you have a letter of authorization?"

"Yes, do you need to see it?" It was in one of the boxes she had given to Orval.

"No," he said, "but to whom do you report officially?"

"The county superintendent—his name is Miner."

"Do you know him well?"

"No, he's a new man—I've met him two or three times." It occurred to Clara that all the administration was new compared to her. Terence Miner had been superintendent for about three years, but she had barely seen him except for the standard meetings and exchange of reports. "Gold Flume is at the end of the valley," Clara explained. "It's a small school, as the new schools go, so it's almost off the map of influence."

Listening to the echo of her own words, Clara realized how true the description was. What loomed so large to her, what was so dear and vital, so heavy with intricate detail and philosophy, meaning and reason, was for everyone else hardly to be noticed. Even for Mr. Miner, her problems would be a bother, no more: keep this old lady or replace her. The philosophy, the ideas, had no more meaning than quilt scraps blowing out of a sewing basket, color, color, color, blown here and there without pattern or form, a moment's look and gone.

Ross was saying, "If you were to sue for redress, it could only be on the grounds that you are still a teacher. Principals are retained or not at the will of the superintendent. They have no more power than that. I don't think you have a case." Beside her, Clara heard Andy sigh.

They left in silence. Andy looked pinched, pained. He hadn't spoken since Ross had put the first question to them, and it made Clara wish she had gone to the lawyer alone. But the exclusion would have been an insult to Andy. "As long as we're here," she said, trying to sound cheerful, "let's do the mall and grocery shopping. I'll spring for the smoked oysters."

It was an old joke. Joseph and Thomas had once given them a Christmas present of gourmet treats. The boys had spent all kinds of time and money for the gift which, as Andy confided to Clara over the long months of their using it, had forever gratified his curiosity about the taste of snails, caviar, and smoked oysters. "Okay," he said, trying, hard.

They drove over to the busy mall, and went into the bewildering plenty of the food store. Aisle Four: fruit juices. "Let's get passion fruit. Until last year we didn't know there was such a thing." She was trying hard herself.

"Let's not. We've had all the passion we need right now."

"I'm fighting back," she said, "and I'm going to get two new foods every week. It will be something to look forward to, a surprise, and who knows, maybe we'll discover some glorious new flavor."

He shook his head and gave her the half laugh of his incredulous affection. "Carry on."

They went aisle to aisle, cooled by air-conditioning and lulled by the routine. "Look—" At the end of that aisle, carts together like companionable rowboats, the mothers of two of Tom's best friends were standing, talking. They were in the middle of the cross-aisle, and when Clara saw them, her face lit up and she began to walk toward them, Andy behind her with their cart. She had the words ready, about Tom's new job, Gudrun's grant approved, their plans to start a family. She saw the women look up, recognize her, and then she saw their faces freeze. She watched their bodies in slow motion as in the seconds before an auto wreck, breathe in, turn, lean into their carts like rowers pulling for shore, and move away, leaving her with the greeting caught in her mouth. Clara turned to look back at Andy, hoping he hadn't seen. He was white, standing still. She became conscious of the buzzing of the fluorescent lights over their heads.

31

A letter was waiting in the crammed mailbox. Terence Miner, superintendent of county schools, wanted to meet with Clara at the administration office in Aureole. She handed Andy the letter and said, "We get punished for our sins, you know. If we had stopped at Oliver and Katy's after seeing Ross, we would have missed the bad moments at the supermarket. This time I'll go to Aureole by myself, see Miner, visit Oliver and Katy, and do what I'm supposed to do." Andy nodded but didn't add anything.

The next day she called and made the appointment. Then she went to Gold Flume School. There were relevant papers among the records in the principal's office, school evaluations and statistics for the years she had been there. "Hi, Alvia, is the Man available?"

"You mean the *Acting?*" She grinned and motioned with her head.

Leeper met Clara with a little rictus of distaste on his face. She noticed that his office door had been closed. "I'm meeting with Superintendent Miner on Thursday," Clara began, "and I want to show him copies of the school evaluations. I can run down to the bank and copy them and have the originals back to you in half an hour."

"Any records the superintendent wants, he can send for," Leeper said. "We can't let these records leave the building."

"All right, I'll copy what I need by hand, right here."

"I have no authorization to allow that." Leeper's tone was tight, supercilious. "You are not a parent. You are not involved in a legal proceeding. You no longer work here."

"That material is public property."

"Not strictly speaking. The public record is on file at the courthouse. Go there."

"Be decent about this."

"I don't have to be," he said. "You are *out.*"

Alvia intercepted her, whispering gleefully, "He's furious. Yesterday he found out he won't be coming on as principal here. Because of his charm and other attainments they're going to use him as acting everywhere."

"Who will Gold Flume have?"

"First-timers from now on, or discipline cases—people being punished. Because of what happened to you and what *he's* told them up in Aureole, this school now has a reputation."

"What's that?"

"Impossible. Rednecks and bluebloods. At one another's throats, everyone yelling, 'My way!' Word will get to the candidates for this job: Take a whip and chair!"

The administrator's outer office was dominated by an aerial map of the county, and Clara spent the half hour she waited marveling at this view of the towns and the river, the mountains and gulches. Perhaps the waiting visitor was meant to realize that the particular school in which he was interested was only a small part of the whole. Clara was amazed at how peopled the Ute Valley had become. Gold Flume at the far end of the wall had houses clustered and growing up all its gulches. The town reached halfway to Callan, and at the other end of the map was Aureole, almost to Granite. Schools were designated by green, blue, and red dots.

Terence Miner came out of his office and stood by her. "Impressive, isn't it?" he said. "But a job, let me tell you. Except for the Denver–Boulder–Colorado Springs axis, the fastest-growing area in the state." He put his hand on Clara's shoulder, a gesture meant to be chummy but that raised her hackles. "Come on in, Clara," he said, and moved her toward his office.

Clara stiffened; he was unaware of it. She thought, I'm old enough to be his mother, and wanted to say, "Okay, Terence." He gestured her to a chair, sat down at his desk, and steepled his fingers over his blue-suited little belly. "I want you to know," Clara said before he could begin to speak, "that I am not a child abuser. When I started at Gold Flume, I slapped hands and used the duncecap because teachers who didn't were considered remiss. I stopped *that* as soon as I could. I never struck or abused, or sexually—"

"Of course you didn't," he said, his voice gluey with placation. "I've talked to the teachers, the secretary. . . ."

"As for my alleged incompetence, you have only to look at the school achievement tests, year after year. My books are balanced, my school has passed or exceeded every requirement—health, safety—"

"I know that, too."

"Yet you're going to let me go."

His eyes went wide with surprise. "I haven't said that. . . ."

"I know it all the same. It's mother-wit." Actually it had been the hand on the shoulder and the "Clara."

He sat the chair up straight. She noticed, and was glad that he had stopped thinking of her as senile. "It's nothing you've done," he said. "It's about power. The school is being pulled apart by dissent. You are vulnerable, being a woman and without an advanced degree. Things have been said about you—" He raised his hand to silence her defense. "Fairly or unfairly, you are a controversial person."

"Let me have my last two years," Clara said. "Let me retire. That will silence the rumors and leave me something of a reputation."

"We can't. It's gone too far."

"The town will think the accusations are true."

"We'll make a statement of support for what you've done in your very long and dedicated career."

"Something like the honor they gave the dull old peasant in *Madame Bovary?*" Clara asked.

He stared blankly at her, then said, "There has been too much criticism of your methods—your denial of a modern curriculum which has been tailored to developmental needs."

She saw that no proof would do. Her beliefs, for all their proof, were out of date. Cyril Boda might save his poetry, but Cyril couldn't help her. Peter Tavistock was dead. The zoologists, mathematicians, and artists who had had their beginnings in Gold Flume School would thank their universities, not their elementary education. The truckers, refinery people, construction workers, and housewives would congratulate themselves. Who remembers how he learned to count or read?

She got up, being sure to take her purse and the small folder she had brought, and said, "It wasn't ever to be defended, was it?

'No reck'ning made, but sent to my account with all my imperfections on my head.' "

"What?" Miner looked puzzled again.

Why shouldn't he be? He had been raised with the education he advocated. Perhaps he had heard of *Hamlet.* He hadn't read *Madame Bovary* or *Don Quixote.* What *did* these people read? "Since I can't retire as principal, what will I get?"

"Well—" He began swiveling again, as though he hadn't decided long ago. Then, realizing that being on her feet gave the woman a kind of advantage, he got up, as well. "You're not at the level of the other principals in the county."

"I've taken and passed all the coursework. I have certification to that effect. Your predecessor said I was up to par."

"Your retirement will be based on your highest average salary, like any other separating principal." He said this as though it were a victory he had won for her.

Clara nodded, then decided for a last question. "What was it that made you decide not to fight for me? Was it a difference in philosophy, or simply my age or my gender?" He stood. "Have I been ruined for a cause or am I just an embarrassment?" He didn't answer. "Is this a bang or a whimper?" She waited again. "All right, whom do you see in front of you," she said, louder, "Joan of Arc or Minnie Mouse?"

He allowed himself a little meanness in his look. "It wasn't any of the things you mention. Gold Flume is a school in transition. Schools in transition are pressure cookers. You couldn't keep the lid on."

Clara left the office.

She had reconciled herself to a visit with Oliver and Katy, and she walked the four blocks muttering. I don't want to be here. I want to be up at Alice Bogard's. I want to be sitting on Alice's back porch with my mending and the afternoon ahead of us, talking and sewing. I want her voice in my ear, I want to hear her questions and her laughter. I want to see hawks, riding up over Fern Hill, soaring up and circling down—such a glory that we forget they're only hunting lunch. "Oh, Alice!" she said aloud, and put her head down and forced her steps to Oliver and Katy's house. "I got fired," she would say at the door. But she didn't.

Oliver had a list of new symptoms, and new bitterness. It might be a relief listening to someone else's rage, Clara thought. Katy went to the kitchen while Oliver sat and gave Clara a long diatribe against doctors, prescriptions and side effects, Katy's incompetence, Clara and Andy's uncaring. In the middle of a reprise of this, Clara shouted back at him, "You're alive, Oliver, still alive, so sit up and shut up!" Then she watched him go from shock and anger to a teary self-pity, so she went and found Katy in the kitchen. "I blew."

"I heard."

"How do you stand it?"

"I don't listen that much anymore, and he's not usually this bad. You're a fresh audience. He *is* getting better. Think of all the energy that rage draws on."

In Alice Bogard's honor, Clara said, "Let's go out on the back porch and sit for a while."

The next day Clara saw Buster French on the road and asked him if she could rent his truck and his services some afternoon. "I got nothin' to do now," Buster said, so she took him back to the house and they loaded all the yard ornaments into the truck—the windmills and the iron deer, the leprechauns and Snow White, the birdbaths, and all the years of figurines the parents had brought, and they took them down to Gold Flume School and set them in front of Mr. Leeper's window. When Andy came home that evening, Clara was lying on a lounge chair in what had been the middle of the display.

"Where'd it all go?" he asked, staring at the cleared place.

She grinned at him. "School property should be at school. I'm not pending anymore, I've been sacked. In the words of the esteemed Buster French, who is now thirty-five dollars richer, 'What ground grew *this?*'"

"Why did you do it?" Andy had hated the display so much—why was his tone pettish?

"I'm no longer the principal, and the way things are, I won't be able to teach anyone *anything* ever again, but neither will I have to supply anyone with delight. The circus has left town."

"Where did you take them?"

She told him. He stared at her a long moment, then burst out, "Don't you see you're provoking the whole town—advertising the disgrace, rubbing their noses in it?"

"I won't beg the children to come up here. I won't beg the town. Leeper deserves to look at the circus for as long as he's here, and the next man will need it as a guide to his constituency. Next week I plan to move the washline back to its old spot. The new place is inconvenient. If Helene Singleton and Rosalie Treece want aesthetics, let them move to Monaco."

"Don't you see—you're advertising the dismissal."

"You think not enough people know already? Is there one person in town who doesn't know? Remember, those figures don't belong to us. We can't store them or burn them. I'm angry, yes, and I'm going to get something out of this dismissal, at least our east acreage. I'll replant the hedge because it's not nice to be a bad neighbor, but if anyone pulls it up again, I'll go over to the sweet old development and tell them the hedge stays or they get Grandpa's long johns flapping in the wind."

She looked at him and saw that he had none of the anger she had but all of the pain. Anger sweeps the cobwebs out. Its wind blows the stink of loss and shame through the windows vandals have broken. He hadn't come to anger, yet. Perhaps if he had, he would have exploded with it. In an orphanage, anger gets you a whipping. In a foster home, it gets you reminded of your father's criminality. He looked defeated and old, standing still and looking at the part of the yard he had always loathed and avoided. Now it was cleared. "You always yearned for this," she said.

He looked down at her miserably. "Be careful what you yearn for."

After a time he seemed to shake off the mood. "Well, I have to go and pack."

"*Now?*" She had forgotten the trip. The plain south of Gold Flume was going to be developed and there were plans to control the river with a dam or series of levees. There was to be a meeting in Denver with state authorities and the developers, and Andy, who had surveyed most of that land and noted the river's changes over the years, would be giving a presentation.

At first he had wanted to cancel. "We're still getting hate calls—I can't leave you like this. We've had vandalism; there might be more."

Clara had argued, "You should be there. The presentation is important. Isn't it bad enough that *I'm* stopped? It's worse when you are, too."

"But—"

"But my firing has changed things. It gives me something to tell the hate people and make them feel vindicated. The shotgun is by the door, and it's loaded. If something happens I'll call you, and there are still friends in town—" She had said that without fully believing it, but Andy had accepted the arguments. Now he went to pack his clothes, and they both pretended his going was no more than one of his occasional trips.

He left before dawn, kissing her good-bye, in her roll-over half sleep. Something in her let down when she heard the closing of the front door and she slept for five more hours. He would be away for four days, and for four days Clara would wear her face normally and not have to be cheerful, stage-managing herself for him. She could sag, weep, walk at night if she wished. Andy's pain had caused her more suffering than her own, and she thought about that briefly as she turned one more time before the last, luxurious doze.

He called from Denver the next day. "I'm fine," she said, "but I feel guilty driving around in your new truck while you have to go all the way to Denver in my sick old car."

"I understand her ailments better than you and I've put her in the shop while I'm here."

She asked about the meeting, and he said there had been a dogfight between the developers and the land use people. "Tooth and claw. I was one of the bite-ees."

"Why? I thought your report was objective."

" 'Objective' means hated by both sides equally." He seemed to be talking to her from a great distance, pausing for long moments between thoughts, the words meaning less than the silences. When she asked him if he was all right, he said, "There's a lot I need to think about, to feel and get over feel-ing. . . ." His voice trailed off, and when they said good-bye, she had a picture of him still holding the phone, wanting to say more.

His letter came two days later, a day before he was to return.

Do you remember when I broke my arm and walked off Vic-tory Mountain with it? Doc Pratt said I was a stand-up guy, but it was really desperation. When he set it, I wouldn't take the mor-phine, not because of heroism but fear of addiction.

I didn't take our troubles with Julia well; I blamed you, and nearly ran as I am running now. I love you and the life we have together, but I can't take the shame—I'm not man enough. People in Gold Flume pass me in the street, people I've known for years, and they look at me in a way I remember from Arlo. We worked so hard to build the respect we deserve. I wanted to stand by you, to support you, but I couldn't even tell you this over the phone. I can't

280

come back right now. I have to get up the nerve. I don't want to give up the life we have, to run away, but I can't help it.

In the meantime, think about a move. Our land is valuable now. We could live in Mexico, as you once joked, in the mountains—we wouldn't have to give that up. I'll tell you where I'll be as soon as I know. Forgive me.

Clara read the letter, shocked. For a long time she sat with it in her hands like a document in a strange language, whose contents it was life and death to understand. She read it again, still shocked, but no longer surprised. She found herself saying, "I knew all this—"

Andy had been hanging in misery, fighting it every day and pretending he suffered no pain. Clara tried out the feelings she had—sorrow, disappointment, and loss. But there was also relief, with clear eyes and a wry and knowing look, viewing itself. There was a freedom in this awful loss. She had her pain but not the additional load of his. During the day she could pursue her own strategy, go to town, be seen as part of every normal day, do all behavior he considered provocative, and she could lie on the rack of night, free to indulge in tears and curses and defend herself to her four walls without apology or the need to hide her pain from him.

As it was, full-night sleeps were rare at her age anyway. At two or three the familiar deadening of a hand or an arm would come, the sudden urgency of leg cramps or the summons of a full bladder. Afterward the night winders of the rack would readjust its ratchets and she would lie back, sleepless, to pull reasons, stretch and reach in the memory: event, event, event, until she shattered into justification and tears again, again.

She got another letter, this time from Colorado Springs. "I have run out on you, I have *not* deserted you. I will call when I can stand to hear your voice without breaking down."

During the days there was work enough. The house was clean and silent, but it had a pleasing order in it, dead as that was. She continued her bookkeeping and got two more clients, and with Social Security and retirement and the pickup work, she could get by for a while, even years. "Forever, if I have to," she said to the equivocating dawn outside the window.

August came and it was still difficult to do the reading she wanted, and although the numbers in her clients' ledgers were clear to her, it took all her energy to concentrate on them. Andy wrote from wherever he stopped. They were simple notes about where he was (westering, to Durango, then Cortez) and what he was doing (being a tourist). Joseph and Thomas called every week, and Clara told them she was fine. She didn't mention Andy's leaving. Neither of the boys had known about their father having seen his own father in shackles in a line of convicts or thrown on the ground and handcuffed. They had known a few facts: orphanage, foster home, but nothing Clara could say would give them an understanding of his reasons for leaving.

Julia called on her way to Mexico. "I'm making important changes in my life. Liberty needs friends who aren't racists and exploiters, who aren't materialistic or chauvinistic."

Clara decided not to tell Julia about her trouble. "Did I tell you—both Gudrun and Barbara are pregnant. I thought I would never hold a grandchild—everyone waited so long!"

"You have Liberty."

"Only two pictures."

There was a pause, then, "Yes, I guess that's true."

"Oh, and the yard toys you raged at for so long are gone. Now our yard looks like everyone else's."

"I never raged about the yard toys," Julia said. "I kept that embarrassment to myself."

When Clara hung up she said to the August hawk, spread-winged on her calendar: "Autobiography is fiction practiced by amateurs."

A minute later the phone rang again. It would be Julia calling back with something she'd forgotten. Without thinking, Clara picked up the phone. A young voice, cool and soft, said, "You deserve to die."

"Maybe so," Clara said, "but not to be fired."

"Whore! Bitch!"

"Sleep well," Clara said.

Andy called. He had been offered a job for the winter as watchman in a mine complex kept working for summer tourists. It was near Cripple Creek. "Are you going to take it?"

"I have to."

"What about the office?"

"John Isabella can run it for the season. Clar—I love you and I miss you more than you'll ever know, but I can't go back there, not yet. When I was in Gold Flume I had nightmares, terrible ones. I was reliving all the shame and sinking under it."

"And I was so preoccupied I didn't see. You want to leave, to move, but I still love this town, and most of the people. Why should a few DP's who will soon be gone drive us out of our only real home?"

"Those people at the supermarket—they were friends, once. They turned away—"

"That'll die down."

"Don't be so easy and forgiving. Repeat after me: Andy, you cowardly sonofabitch, you emotional cripple—you've run out on me. Whatever happens I'll know that, forever."

"Okay, but when you say *sonofabitch*, I have nothing against your mother. Realize that I don't know anything forever—I don't know what will happen next week, so I think I had better just sit tight and not call people names. Anyway, who's the coward, the one who ran away or the one who can't start over?"

There was a long silence and then he laughed the dear, warming laugh she loved. Then he said, "Here's my number and address. Will you come sometime? I'm alone and it's lonely as hell."

The September school board meeting came on an evening portending snow. Clouds banked the northwest and the wind tore the smoke out of people's chimneys. Lower Gold Flume stank of creosote. Clara had been driving Andy's pickup around town as a sign he hadn't abandoned her, and when Alvia offered to take her to the meeting, Clara refused politely. "I'm washing the truck for the occasion." Then she thought about leaving the meeting early, driving to Aureole and spending the night there, or going up over Victory Pass to turn and see the valley, all the long spread of it with outpost lights at the first two towns, and the rest lost in distance-mist. If it snowed . . .

She packed a suitcase, feeling adventurous. There was no requirement to attend the meeting, but there was a rightness in standing up. Clara was learning that. The dark blue wool suit would do. It was years old and worn into compromise with her aging figure. It would be nice to have some kind of emblem to remove—the star the sheriff in *High Noon* held in his hand, a baldric with a disk for each year of service, and the removal—a slow rolling up before its placement on the table, making the act of leaving voluntary. She remembered with what grave ceremony Willa Optegard had taken the notebook with the students' names; Thomas, then Andy, folding their firemen's coats for the last time. "This should have music," she muttered. "I should come in with Brahms's Fourth on a cassette player. Full volume." All of a sudden she felt better.

The truck was ready, warmed and loaded and with the heater on so the windows could be open for the smell of the snow.

There were quite a few cars at the school lot. "Their sound has gone out unto all lands." She was wavering. "Do I give this a pass, go and see Andy, and disappear with him down the mine? No? Then I'll go in here and get patronized or shamed, or both."

The room was full. Alvia was there, and Clara sat beside her. Arly Bogard, Alice's second, came over and told them she was moving back to town. Clara saw Helene and Rosalie Treece with the ski people who had made their places on the left side of the room.

Clara amused herself by looking around at the people in the room, one after another. *Your* life has been hard—one illness after another. *You're* one of the fortunate ones; I wonder if you realize it. *You* drink and everyone knows, even though you think you're hiding it. *You* drink and don't hide it. *Your* husband hits you. *Your* wife cheats on you. When *you* were a boy, you stole and stole. Do you remember? When *you* were a girl, you lied and lied. Do you remember? I remember, generations deep. Memory goes like the chambered nautilus Holmes wrote about and I've never seen.

The meeting began. The minutes mentioned a complaint lodged against the Principal of Gold Flume School. It was one sentence only, the fact stripped of all emotion. She saw the box of relevant papers on the table and knew then, fully, that her cause had been lost way back in April when the petition had been circulated and when the *Ute River Voice* had printed the first article. The simple accusation, unverified, unproved, had made everything else irrelevant. No defense, however valid, vigorous, or persuasive, no lawyer, no boxes of evidence, or witnesses, had any more effect than a sneeze in an avalanche. There had never been a moment when the course of the avalanche could have been altered. Instead of incurring despair, this understanding brought an unexpected sense of relief. She would be able to stop cursing herself for ineptness or mistakes in a defense that had been hopeless from the start.

They were finishing the financial report. Then came old business. At the end of old business were the hail-and-farewells. Four new teachers had been hired for the Bluebank and Aureole schools. They stood shyly. All were young and two were very pretty. These teachers would be, in a way, servants to the parents whose children they would teach. They wouldn't pull a tick or tip-toe the class outside when wild turkeys strutted by on the hill behind the school, and they would join with the parents in the belief that children's memories were too fragile to weight with the world's great words.

32

*A*nd here came the eulogy. Mr. Leeper was reading it from a paper: one-room school, a career encompassing two generations of students ("Three, if they were Frenches," Clara murmured)... many of the people sitting here would always remember Mrs. Percival's million-dots poster and the handmade arithmetic blocks, the poetry duels, the battles of the books... but old ways give place to new.... Clara allowed herself a visible sigh. Had he ever *read* anything, he could have done better than that tired bit. "And so, Mrs. Percival..." With that, he motioned her up and she stood. Alvia and three or four people in the room stood with her applauding, the pitiful sound of their scattered clapping hands swallowed by the bulk of the bodies around them.

From somewhere there was a hissed "Child abuser!" Mr. Leeper's face registered amazement, then fear. Clara's glance had gone from him to Helene Singleton, cool and stunning among the ski people. The Treeces were sitting next to her. Hugh, of course, was at the board table. When Clara faced him there, she was surprised to see that he was looking directly at her. He smiled slightly, gave her an almost imperceptible nod, got up and began, very slowly and clumsily, to applaud. Since the first applause had ended, his sound was alone, persisting for perhaps ten seconds as he continued to look at her, clapping.

The new board chairman took over. Clara had to fight the urge to leave the meeting and go outside, to the merciful night. How nice it would be to walk out into the stillness that smelled of snow. *Nunc dimittis . . .*

Through the months, Alvia had kept telling Clara that she could be vindicated. "When the student scores go down, people will see—" But Clara had always known that any loss would be ascribed to TV or modern life. There would be no vindication at the end and no music in the background.

When it was over, Clara said good night to a saddened Alvia and went up to the table to retrieve her letters. Helene was standing near Orval, talking to two other board members. When she saw Clara she began to turn away, but the thought of something stopped her and she turned back to face Clara. The board members' faces tightened with anxiety.

Clara would have liked to say something brilliant and cutting, but nothing came. Her knowledge of the foregone nature of things had deadened the rage that sometimes engenders brilliance. She had been destroyed back in the pre-spring, and all the rest had been the running and scrabbling that lower animals do when their heads are off and their legs not yet aware of it. Did

Helene know what a child-abuse charge does to a family's life? Even if half the town doubted the accusation, the stench of it would hang like the fume of a dead body and would draw all kinds of vultures down. "Don't worry, Mrs. Percival," Helene said after a moment's silence. "You'll soon find some Bible tag for this: 'When in disgrace with fortune and men's eyes . . .' "

"That's not the Bible," Clara said. "It's Shakespeare."

"Touché. Does anyone else know that, or care?" And Helene turned back to her friends.

Outside, the sudden spill of cold air from the mountains smelled of their primal snow. Clara set out for Aureole. In the truck locker there were a bedroll and blankets for camping and changes of clothes. She was free.

The long plain between Callan and Bluebank, Bluebank and Granite, could be traveled by moonlight. She played the slow jazz tapes that Thomas loved. She drove without lights, pulling the knob only when she saw the approaching beams of another car, visible for miles on the long floor of the valley. The heater purred, the music rose and fell. Sufficient and content, she let the road pull her to Aureole.

South of town was the new all-night restaurant the *Voice* had written up. It was full of tourists and teenagers, and, ballasted with a cheeseburger, Clara decided to go over the pass. She changed clothes in the ladies' room, to jeans, her warm boots, and Andy's old sheepskin-lined denim jacket with his good, familiar smell. The thermos was filled with hot coffee and she got back in the truck feeling awake and excited. Which tape would be best to listen to on the way over? Should it be something romantic, Grieg's piano concerto, or some of the sweet math of Scarlatti?

"The old-fashioned teacher has a tape deck," Clara muttered to herself. Could anyone have imagined, growing up in this isolated place, the luxury of the world's finest music so plentiful and cheap? Tapes had introduced her to classical music. She had made plans to bring it to the school. It wouldn't happen now. Well. "This evening," she said aloud, "Scarlatti." The music rose with her as the road turned up Victory Pass.

At Avalanche Turn, three-quarters of the way over, the headlights met snow, great white petals of it. The road was white but not slippery, and visibility was good, so she went on, the muffling snow making a contained, intimate feeling inside the truck. In the old days, a driver had long periods when his would be the only headlights seeking through the shredding curtains. Now every five or ten minutes a truck or car would come, neighboring for a moment and then pulling ahead or passing, as it went toward Aureole.

On the other side of the pass the snow stopped and Clara pulled over on to a logging road, got out the blankets and bedroll, and went to sleep in the truck bed. She woke in full day, and only then unfolded her map to find out how she could get to Cripple Creek, where Andy was.

Peace was breathing in. Maybe Andy was right and they should cut themselves free, stop wanting place, relinquish location and preference, habit and association. Perhaps they should see the land as design with no other meaning, a thing to please them, a scene to be put past them when they were finished appreciating it, replaced by another.

At a small mountain town that kept alive for hunters as Gold Flume did for skiers, Clara stopped to eat under the glass gaze of a dusty, morose moose. The road turned sunward, windward, south and east, and then she was in another canyon, with mountains on both sides and the water that had created the canyon spilling with a vigor unusual in September. The coiling, sliding, accommodating water could work its will on granite. It had sacrificed nothing, seeking only what was downhill and easy, what was permitted to it, a lazy worker with forever to work. The result was a canyon a mile deep and twelve miles long.

Clara pulled over onto a service road, stopped, got out, and stretched. The day was warm, bird-loud, and there was a deer trail beckoning upward on the hill. She started up, reading their tracks, and a rabbit crossing, and then a trailing fox. There were no houses here. It was foolish to hike alone—hadn't she told Julia, Joe, and Tom innumerable times? Hadn't she told all the hundreds of schoolchildren? "I've been wise long enough, and prudent long enough," she said, interrupting a bird eating a beetle on the path.

Fir dominated here and the duff of its centuries covered the gray bones of the mountain, so walking was difficult. In a quarter of a mile of steep upward climb, Clara was exhausted. "I keep forgetting I'm old and that wind and legs don't work for any length of time." The words came between pulls for breath. "The mirror isn't lying. Why am I amazed when my body betrays me?"

The way was getting rockier and steeper and at the rate she could travel it might be impossible to reach the top. "If I die here in a fall or just get lost and die of cold, everyone will think I committed suicide. Andy will think so, too. *Damn old age!*" she shouted between wheezes: "Damn doddering and incompetence. Damn child abuse."

At the side of a rock-face there was a brush pile and at its bottom last spring's birthing bed for a deer. One of those branches was long and straight, and Clara wrestled it from the pile, then hit it against a tree until it was the right length for a walking stick; snedding it, she found it help enough. A second stick was nearby and with two, the walking was easier. Now there was breath to curse. She used her carrying voice, her school voice. It didn't echo but reverberated off the knees and elbows of the mountain. " 'When in disgrace with fortune . . .' She thought that was in the Bible. Ignorance buys its books and designs its clothes and spews poison in its own bed and stays ignorant still! Damn you, Helene. Damn all of you who can't grow roses in the Rockies, whose children don't succeed according to your plans, who make no allowance for your children's madness!" Then she stood back and leaned against her sticks and howled. "I'm old, witch-old, crone-old, old as cursing. Be rich, Helene, and friendless. Follow your model, your Dorothy Tavistock, into wealth and withering, hate your children's friends, envy their teachers, live out your beginnings!"

The reverberation sang in her ears then died away. She had her breath back and the feeling, evanescent she knew, that she might walk the rest of her life, light-footed and easy as a child.

The birds had been shouted down and now they reasserted themselves, louder, it seemed, than before. "Right you are! Here comes a senile old human from miles away to spew futility on your landscape and who, because of bad eyes and spiritual dyspepsia, can't look upward. . . ."

But then she did. Crowning a spur of the mountain was an aspen grove, and as she moved upward to it slowly, it widened in her sight. Because of some unique miniclimate in that location, the grove had changed color early and through every yellow lens of its million leaves, light vibrated with the intensity of blazing fire. Then, in her turn around the knob of the hill, she saw the fire break wildly, fluttering and leaping against the deep blue of the sky.

Two crows exploded up the slope and hung above her and the wind scattered them, shredding their wings until they laughed and gathered themselves, stitched black seams in the sky back and forth, then pulled out the thread and disappeared. Clara talked Yeats to them, Frost, the Pearl poet and Sor Juana, then Crane's poem about the Brooklyn Bridge, which she was just learning. Then she sat down against a pine tree where she could look at the grove which was still above her.

She thought of the old Callan School, tall and dignified, of the old teachers, reading as she had liked to read to the classes, smooth-voiced, serene, in the smooth, serene afternoons of those long-past days. She had been taken by the words and the rhythm of them, flow, sound. Meaning came later, deep, deeper, and she had known instinctively that to partake of those words was to partake of the gentility and serenity of the teachers—how crisp their white blouses were, how smooth their voices. For years she hadn't known whether she loved the words, the ideas, or the gentility and order they created. When had she gone from memorizing to owning? The words trailed off and she thought that at some unnoticed time, what she had put into her head to transcend Placer Gulch now belonged to her. She saw with her own eyes and with the eyes of the writers she had read and the writing she had loved.

The sun was well past the place it should be for an easy walk down. Clara began to hurry, but at a resting spot she said, "Helene Singleton told me to be content with the rags of my calling, last year's poets and writers out of fashion." And back at the deer rock, she said, "She never saw it, but I had a royal mantle sewn with pearls." Before the steepest place, she said, "Don't dither at me, ladies and gents; your curator will watch her step."

The sun had pulled itself behind the mountain's western knob, and it was afterglow. The way soon lost its detail, night moving upward from the ground. Clara was on the deer trail and hurrying as fast as she could. "Two more minutes on this road and it won't be Shakespeare but the Our Father!" Just as fear was making her movements clumsy, she saw the road and the dark shape of the truck. She almost fell several times getting to the road and made it with no light to spare.

The feeling of grandeur persisted through an indifferent dinner at a crossroads beer joint. She had Salisbury steak and Boston cream pie, and knew that Boston and Salisbury would never get redress for the slander they were suffering.

In the whining motel bed she said to the thousand poets, "Rhyme me to sleep."

The next morning she woke aching as from a beating. At least it hadn't been the night thugs of remorse, but hiking and bad bedsprings, and she regretted that the high thoughts of high places flow downhill, and their ores flow away in creeks roiling with mud in which only glittering chips remain. After breakfast, Clara called the number Andy had given her and, after ten rings, heard his incredulous voice.

"Hello?"

"Hi, Andy."

"Clara!" She heard a gratitude so naked he had to cover it. "Is that you?"

"Get rid of the girls and the booze. I'll be there in an hour or so. I'm on Highway 24 and I'll soon turn on to 67. Tell me how I get to you."

He gave his always precise directions and she followed them, getting more eager as she came, making the proper turns, and at last there he was, standing at the entrance to the campground where a big chain closed off the road. She pulled up and got out. He made no move toward her—he must have felt he had lost the right. She went to him slowly and deliberately and saw his face and body relax. He said quietly, "The woman's wearing my coat. That's a good sign."

"It's a fine old coat," Clara said. "Warm. It just fits me, too. It could stand a little mending here and there . . . the lining needs work. . . ."

Andy picked at a grease spot on the sleeve with his ragged nail, and then they hugged for a long time.

Then he parked the truck and took her on a tour through the place, old mine buildings cleverly restored to their original purposes, miners' houses, manager's house, company store, the mine itself shored and made safe for the tourists. "They let them keep the ore they get. Most people like to take away a souvenir. It was crowded well past Labor Day. The tour guides talk about the old days, but your dad did his assays that way."

"How are you?"

"I ran away," he said. "I came here for sanctuary and ended up in exile." He looked around them. "I couldn't take a real present and ended up in a phony past."

"Let that be a lesson to you," she said smarmily. She giggled and they began to laugh. He took her to his room over the store. It was orderly and sterile. "I think your dad did time in rooms like this," she said, looking around.

"God, lady, I miss you. I miss our house and the life we used to have, and I found out I was gutless, too. When you got rid of those toys I hated, I yelled at you."

"Yes, you did, but there are some things no one should have to go through twice. There are ghosts we can face and ghosts we can't. I haven't faced mine, yet."

"What more do you have to face?" he asked, touching her cheek.

She looked away from him. "Maybe that my day is over before I want it to be, maybe that rock and roll comforts them more than poetry."

"The shame doesn't bother you as much as that?"

"Shame fades, like glory. The next scandal will come, and ours will sink away and be as sketchy as the skeletons at Selevan Creek. In ten years no one will remember."

"In ten years *we* won't remember, if we have ten years."

"Let's walk a little."

"I like it here," she said that evening. "Why don't I stay for a few days? I can come back in between snows and visit you."

"I don't deserve you," he said. "I ran out and left you alone to take Miner and that board meeting."

"I thought that your half appearance behind the door of the school gym was your delicacy and tact."

"Not tact, cowardice. I couldn't face their pity, their fascination. It was the same look I saw in the gawkers' eyes when Arlo was lying in the street. It was the same look I saw in courtrooms and jails. 'That's his kid.' I couldn't hear them say, 'That's her husband.' I failed you. How could you forgive that?"

"We can both get past it. Did I tell you—Joseph and Thomas and their families are coming for Thanksgiving? If you're not snowed in, why not have Thanksgiving here?"

"Could we do that?"

"Why not? You'll have to wash all the dishes."

"You wouldn't want to go to Mexico, then."

"We can't, now. Julia's there and she'd accuse us of crowding her."

"How did you get so strong?"

"Poets, living and dead. It's a velvet mantle with matching earmuffs and mittens. When you get home in the spring, don't be surprised to find the yard full again. Everyone who's ever taught me something will be there. Life-size. Plastic maybe, or Styrofoam tastefully painted and accurately costumed, all my friends."

"Can I talk you out of it?"

"Sure. What's for dinner?"

"Pork and beans."

"Good. Cervantes was a jailbird, you know, and Plato, and Thoreau."

"Thoreau? One lousy night?"

"Wilde, then."

"Some friends!"